I0699755

Littlethumb Sneezed

Littlethumb Sneezed

a novel

Truant D. Memphis

I thank Bob for his many blessings. To my family and friends, I love you. Thank you for your unceasing support and for enduring my obsession. You know who you are and you are the very best. Roscoe, thanks for all of the patience and advice. You are a great friend, mentor, and doggie. Special thanks to Gusthoff Gusthoffsen. You know what you've done. Special thanks to Natewood for your legal expertise. Last but not least, a very special thank you to long showers, Quack's big-ass leather recliner, and humanity for being so wonderfully absurd. Peace.

Once when he was a boy,
Littlethumb sneezed and the whole world froze.

Part I

I

The recently present, told in the slightly past tense. I remember an unusually temperate Fourth of July weekend. Global warming jokes flew about as busily as the endless supply of summer mosquitoes. The jokes could sting as well, and depending on the social circles in which they were let loose would open the door for more serious conversations about the state of the world's environment, politics, and of course, what we would do with all the old folks once Florida finally sunk.

A young girl, probably eight, nine, or ten years old, walked along the boardwalk of Coney Island. She was eight. That's right. Eight years old, named Isabel, and enjoying the lively boardwalk crowd with her nanny. Isabel was a plump little spirit in a red and white polka dot dress, accented by red shoes and a little white hat with a single red rose pinned to the side.

She wasn't fat, mind you. I said plump. The roly-poly roundness of a child who will stretch out on her own with time. Isabel's head was covered in strawberry blond hair and her face with freckles, and to be honest, she already put off a bit of a bitchy vibe. This wasn't her fault. Everyone knows a redhead is the product of an angry conception.

I kid. Please beware of wandering non-sequiturs. In truth, the child was a little darling. A little darling who started the day wearing a pair of white gloves but quickly realized they impeded her ability to navigate the touchscreen of her stupid "smart" device. She held her phone out in front of her face, thumbing away at the controls with impressive speed and accuracy.

Isabel's governess was named Maria. Maria was tall, darkly tanned with even darker long hair, and despite no specific ethnicity I was aware of, she emitted the allure of foreign culture. You would expect her to speak with an accent and your mind would naturally assume every word from her mouth to be sensual in its delivery. Not in some cheap, unimaginative sexual way. She was stunning. Lovely. Dare I say, angelic?

The child and her nanny held a special bond with one another. In an earlier era, they most likely would have held hands, swinging their arms back and forth together as their heels gently tapped along the boardwalk. That day, they were connected at the wrist with Velcro straps and a stretchy cable to ensure they couldn't be separated. Children on leashes. Not such a bad idea but still seemed odd to me, though I'm glad all those old phone-cord manufacturers found a way to rebrand their product after communication went wireless.

Maria had a mobile phone in her hand as well. She read as Isabel sent her text message after text message. The child's thumbs were much faster than Maria's, so the conversation was fairly one-sided. Besides, Isabel was not a child who asked a lot of questions. Most of her conversations were one-sided. Maria either nodded in agreement, smiled, or shook her head "no" to keep up her end of the tête-à-tête. Isabel had learned to communicate with Maria in a manner that almost always made one of those three responses the one she was looking for.

As they made their way, enjoying the sights and sounds of the boardwalk on a holiday weekend, they happened across one of the last bastions of artistic dissidence: a caricature artist. Isabel had made a beeline for cotton candy. She wove her way through the crowd, cutting a path through the main flow of human traffic, pulling Maria behind her. Once they popped out on the other side of all the people in their way, Maria and Isabel discovered the caricature artist set up next to the cotton candy stand.

The cotton candy purveyor was yammering to the artist while the man with the brush in his hand quietly put paint to paper. His little easel was turned at the necessary angle so no one could see what he was working on, unless they were able to sneak up on him from behind, which would have been difficult as his back was to a fence running along the elevated boardwalk, separating the thoroughfare from the beach and ocean below.

The artist had an empty chair for his customers to sit in, a little wooden folding TV dinner table to hold his paints and brushes, and the short easel. A stack of about twenty thin canvas boards of various sizes leaned next to the table's leg. If you looked closely, you would notice the paint brushes all looked like they were made by hand. The bristles were secured to the handles with hot glue and duct tape, and the handles were made of decoratively carved wood.

The artist looked up to see Isabel staring at him. He smiled hello and studied her from head to toe. The leash coming from Isabel's wrist caught his eye. He followed the cord over to Maria's wrist and traced the path of her arm upwards, taking in the rest of her figure.

Maria was staring off at some unknown thing. Her head was turned sideways, hair blowing in the breeze, producing one of those quintessential "beautiful woman" moments often captured on film. The artist dropped his paintbrush. He scrambled to retrieve the brush, over-correcting his body and bumping into the table of paints.

All of the canvases fell over and the man was barely able to keep his table of paints from following suit, though he managed to save the paints and a touch of his dignity. He restacked his canvases against the railing behind him and straightened himself in his chair, aiming a tight-lipped smile of humility at the younger lady.

Graceful as she was, Maria did not let on she noticed the artist's brief discombobulation. She had though, and the man, despite his vagabondian ("My name is Bond, Vaga Bond") appearance, was attractive enough and exuded such a comfortable energy she took his cupid-inspired buffoonery as a genuine compliment. After allowing him to regain his composure, she turned to face him and smiled warmly. Not too much though. She didn't want him to be too encouraged. Just enough to put the artist at ease. She had been putting men at ease with this particular smile since she discovered its capabilities in the eleventh grade.

The artist vacantly stared at Maria. Who knows the portrait he was painting of her in his mind's eye? Whatever his vision was, he finally moved his mouth, which had fallen slightly open, into a welcoming smile. He turned his easel around so Isabel and Maria could see the canvas. Surprisingly, though the artist seemed to paint with broad strokes only moments before, all that appeared on the canvas were the words, "Portraits, Ten Dollars." Isabel didn't have to text Maria for permission. All it took was a smile and a pair of raised eyebrows. Maria nodded her head yes.

Isabel took a seat as Maria handed the artist a ten-dollar bill. The man waved the cotton candy dude over, who complied, bringing a cardboard cone of his finest spun sugar with him. The artist gave a dollar to his friend in exchange for the cotton candy, then handed the wispy pink goodness over to Isabel.

"Do I have to wait to eat it?"

The artist shook his head with a smile. Maria took note he smiled with his mouth closed. She thought she might have seen a hole where a tooth should have been in the brief moment he'd stared at her with his mouth hanging open. Along with the smile on his face, the artist wore a plain white T-shirt and khaki cargo shorts. There was a pair of empty sneakers next to his chair, not far from his bare feet. The sneaks were low-top Converse Chuck Taylors, old-fashioned white. Part of a lanyard circled his neck before disappearing under his shirt. He wore a flimsy, navy blue beach hat with enough brim to shadow the top of his tanned face while he worked. Maria noticed the extremely dark hair sneaking out from under his hat. Okay. Despite the potential of missing teeth, she admitted to herself this vagabond was very attractive.

The portrait took longer than necessary. The artist worked slowly, basking in Maria's angelic presence, peeking up at her from his work as often as possible. The cotton candy had been a stroke of genius, as it kept Isabel quiet and enjoying her role as a model for longer than the average child her age could typically sit, even when they're being immortalized on canvas.

Eventually, the artist came to terms with reality. He could not keep Maria there forever. He finished his portrait of Isabel, then turned the easel around for Isabel and Maria to observe his work. What they saw was no goofy, over-sized headed cartoon of a young girl sitting with cotton candy. In fact, he hadn't included the cotton candy in the portrait at all.

Although in my mind a laudable life station, this man was no simple caricature artist. No, it was immediately clear to Maria this man had a gift. Isabel wouldn't quite understand the significance of what she saw until years later, with a little more life under her belt.

The portrait illustrated Isabel as the child she was this day, turning her head to see the woman she would become, with shadows of the physical and mental transitions that would take her from child to adult, pulling the two versions of Isabel together. Smith's painting somehow portrayed the good and evil inside Isabel, and the hope her goodness would guide her through life. The representation was more honest than a photograph.

Isabel was giddy, especially with the artist's portrayal of her as an adult. The child's face was ablaze. Fire burned in her eyes as she bit her bottom lip while studying who she might be someday. Without looking up she held the picture out for Maria to take. When she felt its weight leave her hand she stepped forward and hugged the artist around his neck.

"Thank you," she said. "What's your name?"

The artist reached into his shirt and pulled the rest of the lanyard into view. A plastic sleeve hung on the end with a white piece of paper inside. One word was written on the paper. Isabel reached forward and held the lanyard up, reading the word aloud.

"Smith. That's your name?"

Smith nodded.

"You don't talk much, do you?"

Smith shook his head.

"Neither does she." Isabel tossed a thumb in Maria's direction. "Her name's Maria. She can't talk. Can you?"

Smith nodded his head again.

"You're funny," Isabel said. She stepped back and turned to Maria, holding her hand out. Maria returned the picture and Isabel soaked it in again with a fierce smile on her face. "Thank you, Smith. I love it."

The artist smiled and tipped his hat to the little girl, then looked up at the woman who watched the exchange with obvious joy. Maria smiled warmly at Smith, this time a little differently than before. This smile coyly stated, "maybe in another time, in another place, just maybe."

Smith held his hand up in an obvious request for Maria not to leave. He took up another small canvas and a brush and quickly went to work. Within a few moments the new painting was finished. In an act of shyness, Smith handed the canvas to Maria face-down. She promptly flipped the canvas over to reveal a drawing of two stick figures. A man and woman holding hands. Maria knew the couple was a man and woman because the woman had long hair and ample round bosoms, as only a boy could perfectly draw on a stick figure lady. The male stick figure in the picture wore a large smile. Exercising good taste, Smith had not painted a representation of any other specific anatomy on the man.

2

Past. It feels like yesterday. It isn't. Littlethumb woke up in his own bed for the first time in what felt like forever. Part of him wanted to get up immediately and run around the house, checking to see if his world had returned to order. Another part of him, in this instance the stronger part, decided to stay in bed and see if a sign the Occurrence was over would reveal itself. Also, maybe he would snooze awhile. The long journey home had exhausted Littlethumb, both mentally and physically. Falling asleep in his own bed had felt luxurious.

He propped his head with his pillows and pulled his covers up tightly under his chin. His eyes wandered his room looking for anything in motion. Everything remained still, as a room full of inanimate objects should have, and still the early tinges of fear crept to the front of his mind. Before his fear could plant roots, Littlethumb thought he heard a noise. Fear transitioned to hope. Was that a noise?

There it was again. This time he recognized the sound as the slight knock the building's furnace made before coming to life. He could hear the sound traveling through the air ducts and a smile opened up across his face. What time was it?

He rose from the covers and went to his bedroom door. He put his ear against it to check for sound outside, hearing nothing. He opened the door, a tiny gap between door and frame, and held his ear to the crack. The sound of light-footed movement echoed through the hallway. Those were his mom's footsteps.

Littlethumb's mind brightened with thoughts of his mother's tenderness. Waiting to give her a giant hug would be painful. He wanted to run to her but none of his family knew anything had happened. If he made a commotion he would have to explain himself, and he wasn't ready to discuss his journey yet. He wasn't sure if he would ever be interested in talking about what happened to him.

If Littlethumb had been born with a mind for science, he might have tried to figure out how the Occurrence . . . occurred. How had he sneezed with his eyes open? Wasn't that impossible? And his eyes were just fine. They had definitely not popped out of their sockets. Also, he was in the bathroom when the Occurrence began. How come the whole ordeal came to an end with him asleep in his bed? Perhaps he may understand someday. He figured it was more likely he would not, as Littlethumb had not been born with a mind for science. Littlethumb was born with art in his blood.

The bathroom was a quick sneak across the hall. Once inside he positioned himself exactly as he stood before the fateful sneeze. He turned the sink's hot water handle and joyfully watched the water run into the basin. With back-to-normal verification step one accomplished, he left the bathroom and retraced his steps from a morning that felt so long ago, although it was, in fact, this very same morning, the exact same day as this day.

His brother and sister were found in the same places he'd seen them before, seemingly in their exact instant of motion as before the Occurrence. Only, they weren't frozen. Their movement continued as they dealt with their morning business. His sister Heather's morning business was followed by a soundtrack of bad pop music coming from her room. She was still a new teenager, fourteen years old, and a pretty consistent example of what you might expect from a fourteen-year-old girl of her generation. She liked bright colors, desperately pined over the current teen heartthrobs whose posters adorned her bedroom walls, and absolutely needed to do anything and everything her friends were doing. Littlethumb did not care for her taste in music.

His brother Freddy's morning routine consisted of a lot of standing, staring, head-scratching, butt scratching, crotch scratching, and the releasing of noxious gasses. Freddy was a bit of a knucklehead. Super moody as well. He was highly intelligent and athletic, yet somehow managed to make bad grades and refused to participate in sports or almost any other group-oriented activities. Freddy liked to stare at birds and build birdhouses. Their building's roof was littered with them.

Despite feeling like a complete loner, as many boys his age do, Freddy had a small, close-knit circle of friends who each felt just as isolated as he did. Before the Occurrence, Littlethumb had worried he might wind up like Freddy when the hair started to show under his own armpits.

Anyway, Littlethumb loved his siblings with a boundless enthusiasm. Of course they did not always get along, but he sure was glad to have them back. By the way, time displacement aside, Littlethumb was a brand new ten years old, having celebrated a birthday shortly before the Occurrence. Heather had turned fourteen a few months back and Freddy would turn thirteen in about five months.

After checking on his brother and sister, Littlethumb continued retracing his steps, leading him to his parents' bedroom. He peeked in the doorway and saw his father in front of the mirror, putting together his necktie. Littlethumb's father was a fastidious man. His hands moved sharply, creating the knot in his tie and tightening it around his neck.

Walter Brooks was by most accounts living the American dream. He was a successful and respected financial consultant with a home on the Upper East Side of Manhattan, New York. Granted, their building was on the cusp of being too far north to be considered fashionable or safe by the standards of certain snooty jerks, but he did have three kids. Walter and Elisabeth thought each of the children having their own bedroom was important for the development of their identities as individuals. Four-bedroom apartments in Manhattan were not cheap, so the apartment was a little too far north to be considered chic. This did not affect the straightness of Walter Brooks' spine. Walter's wife was beautiful. His children were handsome and adored him. Even the family cats paid him his due respect. Walter was also a full-blooded Wampanoag Indian.

We will get back to the family heritage in a moment. First, let's go meet Littlethumb's mother. He found her in the kitchen, as he knew she would be, floating about the room while simultaneously preparing breakfasts and lunches for her brood. If being alive was an art form in and of itself, Elisabeth Brooks was a virtuoso. This nature was gifted to her youngest son as well, and dominated Littlethumb's personality.

Besides being a wonderful mother, Elisabeth was also a music teacher. Like Walter, she was a full-blooded Wampanoag. Despite the direct lineage to ancestral bloodlines, this generation of the Brooks family was what I would describe as fully assimilated to the progressive, industrialized, free-marketed, capitalistic, technologically driven culture of the modern United States of America. Which is not to say they were shallow people, rather they weren't living some sort of antiquated, Hollywoodized notion of a traditional Native American's life. To be fair, I have no idea what any modern Native American's notion of what life is supposed to be is either.

When the Americas were discovered, the Wampanoag people were a Native American tribe mostly located in what would become Massachusetts. Walter Brooks' lineage traced back to the Wampanoag tribe of the Island of Nantucket. Walter's ancestors, along with several other Wampanoag families, decided to leave the island for a different way of life.

Apparently, Walter's forefather had been a bit of a charismatic rebel. He wanted to see what city life was all about. Everyone in the tribe thought he was super cool, so a number of the members decided to tag along. As the story goes, the small group of about twenty Wampanoag took boats from Nantucket to Montauk and migrated the rest of the way into Manhattan.

Despite this small clan's progressive mentality, many of the families continued to marry among themselves, maintaining a pure Wampanoag bloodline. I admit I find the dichotomy of these progressively minded folk simultaneously spurning the old ways of their people while attempting to maintain a pure lineage personally interesting. The ideas seem conflicting, which I suppose made the group about as "modern American" as can be. Perhaps ahead of their time.

Littlethumb's father and mother met while in college. Walter Brooks had no intentions, cares, or concerns for marrying within Wampanoag genealogy. He was, however, an avid historian, having minored in history in college while working towards his finance degree. He met the beautiful Elisabeth in a Native American history class. Although taking a Wampanoag bride had never concerned him before, he considered it kismet when he discovered she too was full-blooded Wampanoag from Chappaquiddick. Chemistry changes everything. Despite the fact neither of them thought they would wind up marrying within the tribe, they fell instantly in love.

The Occurrence and Littlethumb's subsequent return happened during a somber time in the Brooks household. Grandpa Kicking Rocks had recently passed away and a palpable emptiness loomed in the apartment. The funeral had been two days prior to Littlethumb's journey. The eldest Brooks had been living with his younger family for the past year or so. His death had left everyone grief-stricken, but perhaps none more so than Littlethumb.

Grandpa Kicking Rocks had given Littlethumb his tribal name. Everyone else in the family had one as well. The Brooks clan had chosen to maintain tribal names despite their move to the city. The eldest family members were responsible for providing these names to new members when they were born, but Littlethumb was the only one of his immediate family who chose to use his tribal name daily. His brother and sister would call him LT for short, as did his parents much of the time, though his mother would often ask where her "little thumb" was. To the rest of the world, if asked his name and he was in the mood to answer, the boy would reply, "Littlethumb."

Although he was extremely loving towards all members of his family, Littlethumb had been tagged by his clan as his granddaddy's boy. He was a naturally quiet child, instinctually choosing observation and movement over the spoken word, and his grandfather had always been the most enthusiastic member of the family for this behavior. Kicking Rocks would impart his wisdom of life to Littlethumb and teach him how to do things while the boy listened in silence. A decidedly suitable arrangement for an old man and his grandson.

Littlethumb quietly took a seat at the kitchen table to eat his breakfast. His mother took note of his entrance and offered him a warm smile. Next to Kicking Rocks, she was the most comfortable with the boy's quiet nature.

The rest of the family made their way to the table for breakfast. This was a different era. Although not too far in our past, we still weren't in quite as big of a hurry back then as we are nowadays. Family breakfast was still a common concept, though the custom was in transition. Both Freddy and Heather were consistently late to the table and often forced to stuff whatever they could into their mouths, book bags, or pockets on the way out the door. Walter's breakfast often found its way into his briefcase for the commute to work.

This day was a little different. The entire family quietly took seats at the table and a prayer was given. They ate mostly without speaking. Everyone was still heavy at heart with the loss of Grandpa. Everyone, that is, except Littlethumb. After the unbelievable adventure he'd been through, his heart was at peace where his grandfather was concerned. As he looked around at his family, despite their current sadness, his heart filled with joy. He was very happy to be home.

3

Littlethumb and his siblings attended a small liberal arts school in their neighborhood on the Upper East Side. Upper East Arts, or UEA, is a fictional school I created for the retelling of this story. The actual school Littlethumb attended had an ethical issue with allowing me to use their name for free. I was fairly confused by their attitude, but whatever.

Elisabeth Brooks didn't teach at the same school her children attended, as parents who are teachers often do. Elisabeth felt it was important for her children to develop their personalities without one of their parents in close proximity all the time. Littlethumb wished fairly often for his mother to teach at UEA. On the other hand, his siblings, suffering the travails of puberty, were in complete disagreement with him.

The school's curriculum was designed in the style of a liberal arts university. Students had a core set of required courses and could choose electives to fill their schedules. The classes were staggered throughout the week. Mondays, Tuesdays, and Thursdays were devoted to core classes, with electives on Wednesdays and Fridays. Research reflected a strong pattern of student success based on similar scheduling for preparatory schools in other countries. In a surprising twist for an American school, the administrators chose not to ignore the research. Anyway, I point this out because Littlethumb had art class on Wednesdays and Fridays.

The first two days of school after the Occurrence were exercises in tedium. As a matter of fact, Littlethumb learned the word *tedium* on Tuesday when he asked his English teacher to suggest another word for boredom. As her students quietly worked on a creative writing assignment, the teacher responded without looking up from the romance novel she herself was trying to write.

"Tedium," she said. The mild insult to her classroom environment had not registered with her. Or, perhaps she was feeling it too.

On Wednesday, Littlethumb was in high spirits as he and his siblings walked to school. Wednesday! Art class day, his favorite! Of course, art just *had* to be the last class of the day. Pain and suffering laid before him. Tribulations. Tedium.

But his spirits were high. Trudging through his other classes was a tiny hill to climb. Shoot, it was an anthill to easily step over. Suddenly he was a giant, slowly and laboriously lifting his giant leg over all the tiny obstacles of this day, planting his foot firmly onto the hallowed grounds of the UEA art room.

Freddy wondered aloud why Littlethumb was such a nerd. Heather told him to stop through clenched teeth because he was embarrassing her. Littlethumb realized he was walking like a big ol' giant in front of a bunch of other nearby people. Strangers headed to school and work and wherever else they might go in the morning. Blood flushed his cheeks with a child's half-hearted shame. Still, he had one more giant, mutant anthill to step over with his big ol' giant leg before he could stop.

One of the things Littlethumb had missed the most while he was away, besides his family, was art class. His reasons were twofold. First, he loved art. He loved staring at it. He loved making it. He loved when the paint or clay or whatever he was working with got on his skin. He loved the way his skin felt when they dried, and he loved cleaning the mess off. He loved staring at a blank canvas and having no idea what he was about to do with the empty space. He loved the instant gratification of making nothing into something. The simple act of adding a colored line to a blank canvas gave him great satisfaction. As a child he was smart enough to wonder why this affected him so, but also wise enough, especially after the Occurrence, not to waste much time on that wondering why.

The second reason he loved art class was his teacher. I know what you're thinking. Maybe? No. His teacher was not some lovely woman for whom the boy would have a romantic, artist's crush, affecting his life forever. His teacher was a young man.

Oops. No, though completely okay if he had, I did not mean to imply Littlethumb had a crush on his male art teacher. Okay, maybe I did if only to play with words and give you a quick giggle. The point is, his teacher was a young man named Sawyer Pettimore and Littlethumb thought he was the coolest motherfucker on the planet.

To be fair, Littlethumb edited "motherfucker" to "em-effer" in his own thought process, both out of fear of his parents and in response to their excellent programming abilities for their children's young minds. Littlethumb's childhood was during an era where even ten-year-olds were typically aware of these words and feeling them out for themselves, either in their minds or quietly out loud. You had to be extremely cautious to attempt a curse out loud. There could be no adults around. Or rats. As a child, you always had to be on the lookout for rats.

Now, who was this Sawyer Pettimore fellow? Sawyer was the type of person who usually did the right thing, but often against his own will. This meant he frequently did the right thing with a bad attitude. He was a little bitter. I won't sugarcoat that point, but in general, he was a decent person with a good heart. However, from my point of view, he could have dealt with a bit of an attitude adjustment. Just sayin'.

Littlethumb viewed Sawyer as a fantastic enigma, though he probably wasn't using the word enigma quite yet. He might have had a difficult time fully defining his enjoyment of Sawyer's presence. One thing Littlethumb appreciated was how Sawyer spoke to his students as if they were adults. Littlethumb respected adults who did this.

Truthfully, I'm not certain Sawyer was a fully formed adult yet. He was in his mid-twenties, twenty-six if I'm not mistaken, but he'd only recently earned his graduate degree in visual arts and entered the workplace. There is often a significant leap in maturity during this transition if the person hasn't already had one during their higher education. Of course, in many people this leap in maturity does not occur at all, but that's another topic altogether. I'm not certain which scenario applied to Sawyer.

Sawyer was a handsome enough fellow. Almost tall, a little impish, and thin enough to appear lanky from a distance. He came from an upper-middle-class family who frequently teetered on lower upper-class status. For Sawyer, this meant he was well versed in classism. His mother instilled this awareness in him, but I don't want to get into their relationship right now, if for no other reason than I don't want to seem chauvinistic. I might be chauvinistic, but I certainly don't want to seem chauvinistic.

Being a city kid of reasonably well-to-do means who was interested in art, Sawyer spent his educational years at the proper schools and within the necessary social circles, discussing art in highbrow fashion with other teenage sophisticates who were destined to become the future of the art illuminati in New York City. Secretly, Sawyer wished he could be the next depraved lunatic purist, like Jean-Michel Basquiat. When I say "purist," I'm not describing whatever style of artist Basquiat was labeled. I mean the purity of raw talent unscathed by formal training and preconceived notions.

Alas, though reasonably talented and tagged as a potential up-and-comer during his schooling, Sawyer did not possess the appropriate personality traits to delve into a world of his own design, abandoning our collective reality and living mentally in the place where true art is conceived. I believe there is almost always a level of detachment involved at those heights of creativity most folks would never be comfortable with. I say "almost" out of respect for the universe's love for chaos. None of this stuff mattered to Littlethumb. Littlethumb saw a kindred spirit in Sawyer.

Most of the other kids enjoyed art class. They would complete their assignments with smiles on their faces because the work was fun and easy and didn't require taking quizzes. None of them enjoyed art like Littlethumb. He understood this, and he also understood there was no point trying to figure out what was going on inside the kids who didn't like art class at all. They might as well be alien, which is funny because at least one of them was (another story for another day...).

Anyway, the Occurrence changed Littlethumb's understanding of the world. He'd come to terms with many aspects of the human condition. One in particular was people are often tremendously different from one another, purely due to the nature of existence. He could accept some people didn't care for art too much, but he didn't have to like their attitude. Nope. Nor did he have to waste his time trying to figure those people out.

His teacher got "it". Littlethumb was convinced when he talked to Mr. Pettimore, or more precisely when his teacher spoke to him, Mr. Pettimore knew Littlethumb also got it. The deep, instinctual, uncontrollable emotional reaction to art was clearly one of those things like-minded people sense in one another. Then you get excited and words blurt forth. "I love art!" "So do I!" "How do you feel about cheese?" "Fanfuckingtastic!" "Me too!" "Hey, aren't our mommas the same?" "They sure are!"

What Littlethumb could not yet see, because he was too young to pick up on the telltale signs, was the bitterness already eating away at Sawyer Pettimore's soul. If Littlethumb had painted Sawyer this would have shown through, but he never did. In Sawyer's mind, his social status and talent level had relegated him to the lowly role of teacher. Those who can't do . . .

The real issue was neither his talent nor his family's societal standing. What truly neutered Sawyer's art career was a personal attribute, and also the largest difference between him and Littlethumb. Courage. Or in Sawyer's case, a lack thereof. Sawyer never developed the stomach for putting himself out there for judgment. Littlethumb, on the other hand, was born with the ability. Courage was in his DNA at birth, then fostered by the way he was raised. What a blessing.

Littlethumb's return to art class on Wednesday was triumphant. Sawyer Pettimore noticed and commented on Littlethumb's exuberance. High compliment was paid to Littlethumb's still-life work. The class was presented with a lamp. Littlethumb drew a shadow the lamp might cast of itself once lit. Mr. Pettimore praised his creativity.

The best part of the class was they were given a homework assignment, due on Friday. The instructions excited Littlethumb. Homework was typically a chore to be labored through, but not art homework. Art was his ticket to another world where he was the boss. If getting to do the work wasn't awesome enough, the assignment was also another chance to earn the praise of his favorite teacher.

4

When Littlethumb was finally home for the day with his mother and siblings, he hurried off to his room with a grave expression on his face. His mother looked inquisitively at Heather and Freddy. Freddy shrugged his shoulders. Heather said her youngest brother had been muttering something to himself about art class. Elisabeth smiled after her little artist. Littlethumb would barely emerge from his room long enough to eat dinner.

Every night before dinner started Elisabeth called to her brood to let them know the meal was almost ready. When she alerted them this particular evening, Littlethumb poked his head out of the door and saw his mother standing with her hands on the back of the chair where Kicking Rocks was typically seated. She sighed and pulled the chair from the table. Littlethumb watched as she reorganized the spacing of the chairs for the rest of the family.

At the table that evening, the chatter was subdued, as there was still a somber air about the apartment. Littlethumb was his usual quiet self, listening and smiling while the rest of the family conversed. He shoveled his food quickly and requested to be dismissed at the earliest polite moment.

The next afternoon was almost exactly the same. Littlethumb adjourned to his room and shut the door as soon as he was home from school. When Walter got home from work and held his wife around the waist, as he was wont to do whenever he went from being without her presence to within her presence, he inquired about their youngest child's current mission.

"What do you think LT is doing in there?"

"I think he's working on an art project for school."

"You haven't asked to check it out?"

"I was enjoying the anticipation." Elisabeth playfully scrunched up her nose and gave Walter a certain kiss with which he was intensely familiar.

I know what that means, Walter Brooks thought. Suddenly, he was not quite as exhausted from work as he was moments earlier. You know how that goes.

Anyway, despite Elisabeth's alluring charm for patience in discovery, Walter wasn't as devoted to controlling his curiosity as his wife. Later, at dinner, he began his investigation. "I hear you've been working on an art project for school in your secret lair?"

Littlethumb nodded his head.

The family had grown accustomed to addressing Littlethumb in a manner which made head nods or head shakes a sufficient response. They didn't do this intentionally. The format developed as a result of all the times they would say something to him requiring a more wordy response and instead received only his stare. They eventually learned to break things down to yes-or-no propositions.

I know this might seem odd, but to this family, it was a natural progression. As I mentioned earlier, Littlethumb didn't refuse to speak. He just did so sparingly, and by all accounts was supremely thoughtful with his responses, to the point of achieving the utmost brevity and efficiency when he spoke. Over time, his family grew accustomed to speaking to him in ways that didn't take so damn long to elicit a response, which resulted in their current communication model. Early on, watching their facial expressions while awaiting a direct response from the boy was pretty damn humorous.

"Well, are you going to share it with the rest of us?" Walter asked Littlethumb.

Littlethumb shook his head with a sneaky smile.

"You little booger," Walter said.

Dinner went on as usual as the focus shifted around the table from child to child, and then eventually from parent to parent. Along the way, Littlethumb noticed something while the others were entrenched in conversation. The prevailing air of sadness that filled the empty space his grandpa used to occupy had slightly retreated. He could still feel the gloom for sure, but he could tell the family was a little better. Everything would be okay. He'd already known this, of course, but the healing was much nicer to actually *feel*.

After dinner, Littlethumb rushed back to his room and shut the door. Time to get back to work. Not only did he have to put the finishing touches on his homework, but he also had to devise a way to securely and discreetly transport his secret project to school the next day.

By the dreaded witching hour of bedtime, Littlethumb accomplished his mission. His art assignment rested on a child's washable finger-paint art easel he had outgrown, at least according to the easel's box. Littlethumb continued to make use of the easel by propping his matte boards against it and sitting on a low stool when working. Right before bedtime, he devised a way to cover his work with a pillowcase without the fabric touching the wet paint, allowing the painting to dry while keeping the work hidden.

His mother was the first to wish Littlethumb good night. He was the youngest, the first to go down for the night, and thus the first stop on her bedtime tour. His father would follow behind. Elisabeth oversaw Littlethumb's wardrobe change into pajamas and ushered him into bed. Walter safely tucked the child into his sheets and covers every night. If Littlethumb was already prepared for bed and out in the house somewhere when the clock struck goodnight, he gave hugs and kisses to mother and then his father would carry him to his bedroom.

This time of night, right before sleeping, was when Littlethumb often spoke most. He whispered questions quietly to his father about life, his day, and why things worked out the way they had. He listened to his father's reasoned explanations and reassurances. No one knew the content of these little talks between Littlethumb and his daddy but Elisabeth, and she wasn't privy to everything they discussed.

On this particular evening, once Littlethumb was asleep, Walter could not help himself. He looked underneath the pillowcase at what his son had accomplished. Walter knew this was a mild betrayal of trust, but come on, the kid was ten. Littlethumb would never know, and there was really no need to be so heavy about everything. This would not be the first time Walter Brooks or any other parent invaded their child's privacy. It was a parent's privilege, though from the child's point of view a pretty shitty one.

What Walter saw amazed him so much he immediately fetched his wife. Elisabeth admonished him for his sneakiness, but Walter's enthusiasm piqued her own curiosity. Within moments she had relented her playfully holier-than-thou position and done a little spying of her own. She was equally amazed.

The following morning, Littlethumb arrived at the breakfast table with his normal gear for school and his laundry bag. The child-size bag was printed with his favorite cartoon characters and had a drawstring at the top. Inside was the precious secret to which Littlethumb had devoted the last two evenings.

Walter and Elisabeth gave each other a knowing smile. They had decided in bed the night before they would say nothing to the boy about the painting until he chose to show it to them, though they wondered if he ever would. Once taken to school, there was a chance they might never see the work again. The child probably had no idea of its significance. Surely his teacher would, but what if Littlethumb's work wound up going unnoticed, landing in the garbage or among a stack of other paintings tucked into a closet somewhere?

They agreed those outcomes were highly unlikely, and they were willing to take the risk. Besides, this would not be his last endeavor. Both parents had gone to sleep realizing they may have created a child who was more than "every parent thinks their child is special" special. This kid might truly be gifted.

"Whatcha got in the bag there, kiddo?" Walter asked Littlethumb. His son responded with his sneaky little smile. Walter remembered the family's informal communication arrangement with Littlethumb and followed quickly with a more suitable question.

"Is that the mystery project you've been working on?"

Though within the rules of the game, Littlethumb did not respond to this question. He didn't need to. He knew his father knew what was going on. Instead, the boy laughed at his thinly veiled secret and kept eating his cereal. Freddy shook his head in mock disgust of his little brother.

"Such a weirdo," Freddy said with a smile, to which Littlethumb only laughed harder, mouth open and full of milk and cereal, inciting the rest of the family to join him.

Someday, Littlethumb would cling to this memory. He would cherish it until the end of his life. Even while in the midst of the laughter, he recognized the moment's significance. This was the first time since his grandfather died the family had broken down into a big, shared belly laugh not associated with a loving memory of Kicking Rocks, and therefore also associated with the sadness of his loss. Watching his family laugh together, Littlethumb's spirit was full of puppies and rainbows.

5

I won't regale you with the tale of Littlethumb's arduous, epic journey through the hours before his art class. Let's just say Littlethumb slayed several chalkboard-wielding gargoyles and numerous desk trolls. Teachers and fellow students alike were subject to his fantastical daydreams, cast in the roles of evil villains hell-bent on preventing him from reaching his destination: The mythical yet abundantly real utopia of art class. When the hour was upon him, Littlethumb stoically entered the room as if he were a member of an intense religious or military procession. One of those slowed-down walks they use on film to make everything seem more important.

Littlethumb's laundry bag was slung over his shoulder with his treasure inside. He dared not look at Mr. Pettimore lest the man see the desperation for approval dripping from his pores. Head down and eyes averted, he made his way to his seat to wait for the moment of judgment. Would he volunteer to show his work early to get said judgment over and done with, to feel the joy or despair and move on with life as soon as possible? Or, would he wait until a few others showed their work in the hopes their efforts might boost Littlethumb's confidence in his own?

The assignment was to find a famous painting and attempt a replication. "I didn't expect you to be able to replicate the works of history's most famous artists," Sawyer Pettimore said. "The idea was for you to see how it might have felt to paint such a thing. I wanted you to imagine what the brush strokes might have felt like to create a masterpiece. To imagine what might have gone through the mind of the original artist while they were painting. Did any of you wonder what it must have been like to be the person who originally made what you were trying to copy? Did any of you think about things like this while you were working on your assignment? Show of hands."

Sawyer was a little surprised not to see Littlethumb's hand in the air. He was the one kid Sawyer half-expected to understand.

"Good. I'm glad it worked for some of you. For those of you who didn't happen to have these thoughts, don't worry. This wasn't a test." He looked directly at Littlethumb. "This was an exercise, and all of our minds work differently. Oh, you guys can put your hands down now. We're good."

As those hands were lowered, one was raised.

"Yes, Josh?" Sawyer asked. Josh was a bit high-strung to achieve in the classroom at much too young an age. Behavior fostered by the boy's equally high-strung, overachieving parents. To be fair, the world needs obsessive people. A lot of our greatest accomplishments are the end result of obsessive behavior. The flipside of that coin is those people are very difficult to be around sometimes, that's all I'm saying. Anyway…

"Why didn't you tell us beforehand what we were doing, Mr. Pettimore, so we would know what we were supposed to be thinking?" Josh asked.

"That would have defeated the whole point of the exercise." Sawyer's answer confounded Josh, much to Sawyer's enjoyment. Sawyer knew he wasn't supposed to dislike the children, but Josh got on his nerves. His guess was Josh would grow into an equally annoying adult.

"Dude, chill the fuck out," Sawyer would have said if he could. "You don't have to be perfect at everything. And you can't be, so you might as well get over that shit right now. Otherwise, you're setting yourself up for a massive crash someday. Plus, it's annoying as hell."

That's what Sawyer might have said to Josh if the boy were his child, but Josh wasn't. You couldn't get away with such pragmatic bluntness when dealing with other people's children in the class-room. Especially children so young.

After the little "non-test" Littlethumb had apparently failed, his spirit dropped. He decided to wait to present his work until some of those desk trolls who had apparently "gotten it" showed their projects first. Of course, Littlethumb didn't realize those children had lied.

They were ten years old. None of them understood. Some of them lied immediately without remorse, hoping to please their teacher, and some lied half-heartedly when they witnessed classmates with whom they wanted to be associated raise their hands. Despite the Occurrence, group psychology was still a little advanced for Littlethumb's analysis.

By the by, I don't want to give the wrong impression of Littlethumb. He was neither hateful nor in a true state of emotional defensiveness toward his fellow students on a regular basis. He was simply fanciful, and since the theatrics were known only to him, everyone around him was an available actor for the role of a villain when his mind was playing those games.

Several students presented their work to Mr. Pettimore and the class. Littlethumb thought some of the projects weren't bad, especially Shelly Lechman's stick-figure portrayal of what you and I know to be *The Last Supper*. She had slightly stepped outside the assignment's boundaries, though, as the work was supposed to be an honest effort at duplication. Mr. Pettimore praised her creativity and interpretive vision anyway.

Despite some of the better works having been displayed, the presentations bolstered Littlethumb's confidence to the point he was certain he would receive the praise of his teacher. The next time the opening presented itself, he fervently requested to be the next presenter in the most common method known to a ten-year-old. He wildly waved his right hand while his left hand supported his right arm, which was stretched so far it was coming loose at the shoulder. Littlethumb desperately arched his back in an effort to keep his butt in his chair, knowing there was no way he would be chosen if he didn't come up out of his seat at least a little, at least to match the efforts of his classmates, who were equally as desperate to be chosen next.

"Littlethumb. Why don't you go next?"

Yes! Littlethumb walked to the front of the class with his laundry bag and placed his work on the easel. He loosened the bag's drawstring and tilted the painting forward, allowing the bag to fall. The unveiling was surprisingly effective. He leaned the portrait back against the easel and stared intently at Mr. Pettimore.

As he observed Littlethumb's work, Mr. Pettimore's facial expression shifted repeatedly until settling on confusion. This expression, in turn, confused Littlethumb. After several minutes of silence that felt like an eternity—seriously, Littlethumb had not known whether to go sit down or keep standing there—Mr. Pettimore gathered himself, stood up, cleared his throat, and told the class to take a bathroom and water fountain break. Everyone except Littlethumb. He was to remain behind for a moment and discuss his work with Mr. Pettimore.

Now, Littlethumb had imagined a similar scenario as this one, but had not expected this current situation. In Littlethumb's version, Mr. Pettimore was so exultant he dismissed the class out of pure celebration. In the real-life version Mr. Pettimore did not portray anything so positive. If Littlethumb had to choose a word for his teacher's vibe, the word would be "suspicious."

Mr. Pettimore walked over to Littlethumb and put a hand on the boy's shoulder. The hand gently suggested Littlethumb turn to look at his painting. Littlethumb turned.

"Let's talk about this," Mr. Pettimore said.

"This" was an exact replica of Leonardo da Vinci's *Mona Lisa*, its lovely subject quietly smiling at them from eternity.

6

You might think Sawyer Pettimore's immediate response would have been a phone call to Littlethumb's parents. If not his immediate response, at least his first phone call. Not the case.

When the initial shock had settled, wild speculation flooded his mind regarding the origins of the *Mona Lisa* replica. That shit had to be reined in before he could share what he was seeing with anyone else. Answers were needed. He wasn't sure what all of the questions were, but answers were needed. At least the first question was obvious. Sawyer looked at Littlethumb.

"Are you certain you painted this?"

Littlethumb was no dummy. Despite the wording, he knew the real question being asked was if he was lying. Are you certain? He was disappointed in Mr. Pettimore. Littlethumb held his eyebrows high with mild, honest indignation and nodded his head. That had to convince his teacher.

It did not, but Sawyer didn't become accusatory. "Littlethumb, you know you're one of my favorite students, and I think you're a talented young artist. But, do you understand why it might be hard for me to believe you painted this?"

Littlethumb shook his head.

"Hmm. That makes this a little trickier."

The teacher looked down at his student and saw the boy tilt his head in an expression of curiosity. His instincts for dealing with the child took over, the same instincts which made Littlethumb revere him in the first place.

"Okay, buddy," Sawyer continued. "Let's be real about this. I'm standing here, staring at an exact replica of Leonardo da Vinci's *Mona Lisa*. For the time being, I will accept this is one hundred percent your work, and your work alone. Cool?"

Littlethumb again nodded his head. Of course it was cool. He painted the stupid thing.

"So, I am supposed to believe a ten-year-old kid has somehow duplicated one of the greatest portraits of all time, the work of one of history's greatest artists? A master! I'm supposed to believe that? I'm sorry I'm getting so excited, but don't you understand why this would be so hard to believe?"

Littlethumb had not considered the situation in those terms. He nodded his head. He supposed this made sense. To this point, Littlethumb's most successful piece of work, not counting his painting from Wednesday's art class, had been a clever depiction of his grandfather as a bear. Clever, but by no means a highly detailed or realistic interpretation.

"Wait," Sawyer said. "Are you saying I'm supposed to believe you did this on your own, or you understand why it's difficult for me to believe, or both?"

Littlethumb nodded with a smile.

"Darn it, Sawyer, one at a time. You did this on your own?"

Yes, the boy nodded.

"But you also understand why it's difficult for an adult to believe a young child did this?"

Yes, the boy nodded.

"I need to sit down."

The other students filtered back into the classroom. The unsuspected break had placed them in an excited state, and surprisingly enough, Mr. Pettimore let them go about their horseplay and chattering for the rest of the period. Only Littlethumb made any notice of this change. The rest of the class did what they wanted without contemplating why they were being allowed to do so. Littlethumb watched them in wonder.

What was going on here? Mr. Pettimore's reaction surprised him. Sure, Littlethumb was proud of the effort he put forth on his homework, and he was excited to earn his teacher's approval, but he had not foreseen this sort of reaction. He would have wondered what the big deal was, except Mr. Pettimore had made that quite clear.

Apparently, as a child, Littlethumb was not supposed to be capable of such things. Littlethumb had nodded in agreement with Mr. Pettimore. He pretended to understand why Mr. Pettimore had such a hard time believing he'd made the painting, but the truth was he did not. In theory, he understood the notion, but he created the painting with relative ease, so truly appreciating Mr. Pettimore's conundrum was difficult. What was the big deal?

While Littlethumb sat in an emotional stew of mild consternation and developing irritation, Sawyer Pettimore's mind sailed the seas of endless, sudden realizations, moving port to port from one island of comprehension to the next.

Let's assume the kid actually painted this damn thing, he thought. *That means he is some sort of freak of nature talent. And if that is the case, what do I do? How do I handle this?*

For the first ten minutes or so, his thoughts were nothing but a series of questions: Who had seen this? What should he do? What if the boy was really this talented? Who should he tell? Did his parents know? Could he make any money from this? Was the question of monetary gain a dishonorable thought to have?

Now, I hate to be a downer, but once the thought of financial gain entered the equation, the motivation was not going away. Yet I have already told you at the root of things, Sawyer Pettimore was a decent enough fellow. So in this man, the thought of his own financial gain was immediately followed by guilt for thinking in such terms, which was immediately followed by thoughts of his responsibility to protect the child.

Having settled on his noble cause, the idea of any associated financial reward became a stoic recognition of how the world works and was no longer a source of guilt. The world needed to see what this young man was capable of, and the young man needed to be shielded from what the world was capable of. Who better to do so than the teacher who had discovered and nurtured this talent, and held a true affinity for the boy?

Once his mental justification for everything about to happen was etched in stone, Sawyer considered the next step. He would have to discuss this with the boy's parents. Yes. A simple, unavoidable fact. The conversation would need to be planned. The boy's parents might not want to expose their child to the pop-culture meat grinder the United States of America had become, despite any supposed gifts the child might have. This was a completely reasonable reaction and Sawyer would have to be prepared to respond in the appropriate manner. The Brookses had to be on board. Still, was talking to Littlethumb's parents the first step?

No, no, no. What are you thinking, man? Come back to Earth. What if this was some isolated incident? A freak occurrence. Not likely, but possible. The boy needed to be tested. He might be a genius, but in the world of art, true genius could be overlooked when not packaged and sold properly. Everyone knew pop art was more about the right people thinking something was cool than about the quality of the work. For God's sake, who really wanted a fucking can of soup hanging on their wall?

So, the next step was testing the boy. Yes. Tests were needed. Essential. But how? Figure the methodology out later, but don't say a word to anyone until you're certain. The boy's parents? Again? Yes, they exist. Must be dealt with. Back to contacting them as your next step? Yes, they would have to be spoken with, sooner rather than later.

Besides, they had most likely already seen the painting. Littlethumb is a child. Of course they had seen what their child was doing, and unless they were morons, which Sawyer already knew them *not* to be, they had to recognize the significance of this. Hell, they could be feeling exactly like Sawyer, wondering what they should do next.

Only he knew. Sawyer knew. Yes. First things first, hide the damn *Mona Lisa* before anyone else sees.

Jesus. On further study, Sawyer was damned if the boy's version wasn't somehow better. He could not have begun to explain why, but somehow, Littlethumb's *Mona* was more appealing than Leonardo's original.

Sawyer barely heard the bell ring to announce the end of the class, day, and workweek. He scarcely remembered sending a note home with Littlethumb asking his parents for a conference the following week, or reassuring the child the meeting was nothing to worry about and in fact, something to be happy and excited about. Even hazier was the phone call he made before class was over.

I mentioned earlier Sawyer's first phone call after the discovery of the *Mona Lisa* was not to Littlethumb's parents. Nope. The first call was to an old friend. Once the path before him revealed itself, Sawyer stepped into the hallway and pulled the door to the classroom shut behind him.

Trying not to look directly, Littlethumb activated his side-vision. From the corner of his eye, he could see Mr. Pettimore standing behind the door to the classroom, talking on his cell phone, staring through the door's window directly at him. Was Mr. Pettimore calling his parents? Was he in trouble? What for? Geez! All he wanted was to impress his teacher.

Sawyer Pettimore listened to his phone ring while staring through the window of his classroom door. He knew he probably shouldn't be making this call yet. He knew, but he couldn't help himself.

There was no surprise when his old friend didn't answer. No, Sawyer had expected this, had already scripted in his mind what his message would be and had rehearsed a few times out loud in the hallway before dialing the number.

"Hello Richard. It's your old buddy Sawyer. Give me a call when you get a chance. I think I found the next Tommy Toxic."

He hung up the phone. Perfect.

7

Dirty Dick Mann was the gleefully trashy professional name for talent agent-slash-publicist-slash-record producer-slash promoter-slash-all-around entertainment industry bad boy Richard Feinmann. In case you were wondering, the extra "n" was for naughty. This was boldly stated on his business card and everywhere else he could think to stick his motto, including a ridiculous tattoo on his left ass cheek. Why the left? 'Cause that was his ass's good side, baby.

Feinmann wasn't a bad guy, at least not when drawing comparisons to the depths of moral turpitude to which human beings can plunge once they've achieved the highest ends of financial success. He was kind of a sweetheart. A hedonistic, morally bankrupt, would sell his own mother's soul for another platinum record while snorting cocaine off the devil's dick, sweetheart.

Okay, so he wasn't a murderer. At least, not yet anyway.

Seriously though, Dick was not an easy character to judge if you are a person of moderate thought. He was amoral for sure, truculent at times, and definitely out for number one first and foremost. But like many human beings, he was a complicated study as he was also highly charitable, forgiving, extremely loving toward those he cherished, and, in general, genuinely kind to others. He felt good at heart. If he was a bad guy, and I will let you be the judge, he certainly did not feel like one.

Dick sat at his desk in the office of DDM Enterprises, Inc. when he saw the call from Sawyer come through, which he did not answer. He and Sawyer's friendship had devolved, been devolving, for a while. Dick figured over two years had passed since the men had spoken directly to one another, either in person or on the phone. Both had discovered a knack for reaching out to the other at times when they knew it was unlikely the call would be answered.

Not only had they been purposefully avoiding one another, but the calls and e-mails to check in had grown less and less frequent. Dick could only assume Sawyer felt more and more disingenuous with every attempt, while Dick felt there was no need to rub Sawyer's nose in things. You see, the unfortunate reality according to Dick was his friend Sawyer had a jealous and bitter soul. Sadly, as I have mentioned before, there was some truth to this.

Dick knew Sawyer was angry he'd relegated himself to the life of the pauper educator. Sure, there was honor in the role. Dick saw this and Sawyer knew. The problem was Sawyer wanted more, which Dick could also see. Basically, Sawyer Pettimore wanted what Richard Feinmann had, but he didn't have the emotional construction to achieve or handle the type of success for which Dirty Dick Mann had been born.

Dick also knew in Sawyer's mind that Sawyer didn't have the family means, talent, or courage to go after the wealth, social status, and overall success both men had realized in their youth Dick was destined to achieve. Sawyer handled this admirably as they'd grown up. When the time arrived for their futures to become the present, he had not dealt with his own, self-perceived shortcomings so well. Oh, and in case you were wondering, Dick knew all of these things because he minored in psychology for his undergraduate degree program.

Having recognized this dynamic of their friendship, Dick tried to include Sawyer in his success, but Sawyer would not allow him. For whatever reason, despite Dick's best efforts and the fact Sawyer knew damn well Dick had taken handouts from others to help gain his success, Sawyer refused to allow Dick to help establish him in the same manner. What's with people and self-righteous indignation? Anyway, the point is, he would have helped Sawyer taste opulence if only his pal had let him, but he never would. This irritated Dick, so he quit trying and the relationship fell into its current funk.

Enough of the pseudo-psychology.

When the voice of classic punk rocker Van Damaged screamed "Suck that gun!" from Dick's phone, signaling Sawyer had left a voicemail, Dick hesitated to listen. But, he wasn't in the middle of anything important and several months had passed since either man had reached out to…intentionally miss the other. In the end, he picked up the phone and hit play.

Sawyer Pettimore thought he had found the next Tommy Toxic. What a kitschy way to let Dick know. Dick could imagine the smile on Sawyer's face when he left the message. Interesting. Interesting indeed.

"Who was that?" Tommy Toxic asked. Dick's prized talent sat in a chair on the other side of his desk. They had been in mid-debate about a few aspects of Tommy's upcoming tour when Dick asked Tommy to hang on for a sec while he checked his voicemail. Dick was growing tired of placating Tommy, so the voicemail had also been a welcome ploy to pause the conversation, or possibly end it altogether.

None of your fucking business you little shit, was Dick's first thought. Then he realized Tommy wasn't really paying attention. The little shit was playing on his damn phone, as always.

"An old friend."

"What did they want?" Tommy asked, as vacantly as before.

What is wrong with these kids today? Dick thought. He decided to get Tommy's attention. "He said he's found the next Tommy Toxic."

Tommy Toxic was a child star of outlandish proportion. With the teamwork of his parents and Dirty Dick Mann, a monster had been created the likes of which the world had not previously witnessed. Seriously, I know we have obsessed over some kids before, and I know there have been some grown-too-soon child stars living screwed-up lives, but Tommy Toxic took the cake. He took that cake, defecated on that cake, and then ate that cake. Yes, it's gross.

The whole deal was gross. Child exploitation and deification is gross in general, but the direction chosen for Tommy was extra filthy. First, let it be known his parents were both junkies. This is not an excuse for them. They were shitheads before they were junkies. They ran out of smack long enough to sober up one day and realized their kid had taught himself to play guitar, and with amazing skill. The rest, they say, was history.

They took Tommy to meet Dirty Dick Mann. Dick was waiting for Tommy. Not Tommy specifically, of course, but the right child to fill the right role, and Tommy was perfect. One of Dick's talents leading to his success at a young age, besides nepotism, was his ability to envision original concepts. Innovation, baby. Innovation was his thing.

Dick knew early in his career one of the characters he would create for the public to consume, once he found the correct talent. Said character, was a filthy child punk rocker. Tommy Toxic filled the role with an insatiable appetite for the entire dirty business.

His parents brought Tommy to Dick when he was ten years old. Seeing the state of Tommy's parents, and hearing Tommy's gift with a guitar, Dick turned on a Bloody Evil Stepsons album and asked Tommy if he liked the music. The child was already emotionally turbulent, dealing with his junkie parents. He was also eager to please someone, anyone, and this man had a big desk and a shiny office. Yes, he liked the music. He fucking loved the music. Thus, the die was cast. Dick turned Tommy into the filthiest punk rocker of all time. Not the kiddy version, mind you, but a full-on fucking punk whose behavior wasn't suited for anyone, not even a fully aware adult who was willingly selling their soul for money.

Dick and his production team burned the kid's brain with the masters. Tommy studied the music and raw footage of the greats, and I'm not only talking about commercially successful punks like Horatio Fright and The Candied Asses. Dick took Tommy into the bowels of the beast. He exposed the child to the likes of J. J. Crane and other exhibitionists of similar ilk. Idiots who blew each other on stage and sliced themselves up with razor blades, or hung themselves from meat hooks. Poop-slinging monkeys they were, or regrettably misguided, if you want to be absurdly forgiving of that sort of behavior.

To be fair, Dick Mann was exposed to this garbage at an early age as well, and he felt he had turned out okay, so he didn't realize what he was doing to the poor kid. Honestly, Dick loved Tommy. When the kid's parents finally killed themselves melting spoons and cramming needles in their arms, he legally adopted Tommy and insisted the kid spent time in therapy dealing with the loss of his parents.

Tommy had discovered his parents' corpses, and apparently, the child spent several days at home with their dead bodies before alerting anyone. There were rumors Tommy might have administered the fatal dosages of heroin. Even Dick Mann realized how messed up that was.

Now Tommy was in the throes of puberty. To be frank, he was transitioning from a cute kid who played a punk on stage into an actual loathsome little shit. Dick had recently admitted to himself he was beginning to dislike his protégé. Tommy's fifteen minutes of childhood fame were nearly over.

He was thirteen years old and had become pimply and unattractive. While you might think this would suit such a filthy caricature, America wanted their bad boys to be cute. The real problem, though, was his voice changing. The acne could be dealt with. Tommy's awkward, out of tune caterwauling was a serious concern. Dick wanted Tommy to lay low and allow his voice to fully change, but Tommy refused. The boy insisted on touring instead. They were discussing this tour when Sawyer called.

"What else did he say?" Tommy asked.

"Nothing," Dick replied. "He said he might have found the next Tommy Toxic and then hung up."

"Who is this fucking guy?"

"Just an old friend. A teacher. A nobody." Dick studied Tommy. The kid was still pretending to be obsessed with his phone and only half-heartedly engaged in the conversation, but Dick knew better. "Don't let his bullshit bother you. There will never be another Tommy Toxic."

"I know." Tommy raised his head from his phone, but his eyes danced around, refusing to make contact with Dick's. "Why would that bother me? I don't give a shit. What the fuck does some teacher know anyway? I want to talk about my goddamn tour."

"Alright. Okay, let's finish talking about the tour. Anything you want. I give in. We'll blow this bitch out." The young star had to be placated for the time being, but Dick couldn't get Sawyer's words out of his head. The message conjured forth instincts rooted in his bones. He knew his friend well. Sawyer Pettimore would not have called if he wasn't convinced he had something real. That was a fact. Dirty Dick Mann was certain. Remember baby, the extra "n" is for N-telligent.

8

Have you ever been in one of those frantic mental states where minutes, hours, days, potentially weeks, and quite possibly months can pass and you feel like your brain has never shut off? No mental rest, no sleep. Whether for positive or negative reasons, eventually you are deeply exhausted. That's what the days immediately following the discovery of Littlethumb's *Mona Lisa* were like for Sawyer.

The meeting with Littlethumb's parents went as well as Sawyer could have realistically hoped. First and foremost, the Brookses confirmed their son created the astounding replica of the Mona Lisa. The three adults' wonderment over the creation was equal and shared.

Although not without some trepidation, the boy's parents agreed to Sawyer's tutelage. Littlethumb was so enthusiastic about the idea, and they also found Sawyer's presence comfortable. In truth, Walter and Elisabeth both took a liking to the young art teacher rather quickly.

Littlethumb's parents established a few ground rules which Sawyer readily accepted. He had no choice in the matter, but if he had, he wouldn't have argued against any of the rules. The first rule was, if at any time Littlethumb stopped enjoying himself, the mentorship ended.

"He's too young to be burdened by his talent," Elisabeth said. "We want him to enjoy and explore his gift, but this will not turn into a source of stress for a ten-year-old."

The learning environment would maintain the appropriate levels of creative tension for a child his age. Walter and Elisabeth didn't want Littlethumb pushed too hard, even if he appeared to respond well to the prodding. Sawyer had to control himself, no matter how excited he became with Littlethumb's capabilities.

Rule number two, Littlethumb's schoolwork could not be affected. Sawyer would do his part to ensure Littlethumb maintained focus on his studies. On the days he worked with Sawyer, Littlethumb's homework was to be completed first, and Littlethumb would receive no art homework from their sessions.

Next, Littlethumb's creative work must always be encouraged and never considered incorrect. Sawyer could guide Littlethumb, offer him suggestions, and teach him technique, but he was never to tell Littlethumb any of his artistic work was *wrong*. Elisabeth established this rule and Walter was in full support. The boy was too young to be told there was something incorrect with his creative vision. The mentorship was all about encouragement. Sawyer wholeheartedly agreed. Honestly, this rule was so in tune with Sawyer's own perspective on art it made him fall in love with Walter and Elisabeth.

"One more thing," Walter said. "These lessons are normal, creative lessons any child might take. LT enjoys art and we thought lessons would be good for him. That's all. No matter how excited you may become, we don't want you to discuss Littlethumb's gift with anyone but us. If you feel the need to talk, please, talk to us. We want to be very careful handling his talent, especially if the time comes to present Littlethumb's work to the world."

Sawyer readily agreed to this final term as well. He waffled on whether or not to tell the Brookses about reaching out to Richard Feinmann but decided to keep the call to himself for the time being. The phone call to Richard was an innocent gesture made in his initial excitement, and Sawyer didn't want to unnecessarily concern the Brookses. He had no intentions of breaking any of their rules moving forward. If Littlethumb fulfilled Sawyer's expectations there would be no need to break his pact with Walter and Elisabeth. Greatness cannot be denied or hidden. Otherwise, it would not be great.

"Please don't worry," Sawyer said. "I don't want anything to happen that could stifle what Littlethumb may be capable of. Just being a part of this, helping to nurture his greatness, that's what a teacher is supposed to do, right?" Sawyer's smile and humility were as genuine as the deep seeded anger he buried.

At the end of their meeting, the trio returned to the subject of what to do with Littlethumb's *Mona Lisa*. They agreed the painting should remain hidden for the time being. If they wanted Littlethumb's talent to remain a secret while he trained with Sawyer, they couldn't have anyone seeing the portrait and asking questions.

Sawyer petitioned the Brookses to let him deal with the *Mona Lisa*. He wanted to study the work and would ensure it was properly stored. The Brookses complied. However, being an investment counselor, Walter could not do so without protecting the asset. Elisabeth was slightly embarrassed. She didn't want Sawyer to be insulted. He assured her he took no offense. Quite the opposite, he completely understood and agreed with Walter. Photos were taken and a document created which both parties signed. The document stated the portrait was the work of Littlethumb and his solely owned property. They filmed the document up close, recording all of the wording and everyone signing. Then, as stated in the agreement, the paperwork and video were locked in a safe deposit box. Only Walter and Elisabeth knew the box's location, and they were the only ones with a key.

After his successful meeting with Walter and Elisabeth, Sawyer spent the entire weekend developing a curriculum for his apprentice. He barely slept. Sawyer designed tests for Littlethumb to provide a barometer for the boy's true aptitude and stylistic calling. These tests would also provide a large enough body of work from the kid to determine his commercial viability.

How would Sawyer package and sell Littlethumb? Despite his assurances to the Brookses he would keep his mouth shut, which he fully intended to honor, Sawyer believed he knew what was coming. Someone had to be prepared. He would respect the Brookses wishes but he also considered it his responsibility to have an appropriate plan in place for Littlethumb's talent to shine, once he was discovered.

After meeting the Brookses, Sawyer knew they didn't quite see the train coming down the tracks. They obviously recognized Littlethumb's potential gift but would need more time to accept the inevitable reality that the world would discover their son. Walter and Elisabeth were either being naïve or in a state of denial. The world would have this child. Sawyer could feel it in his bones. Still, he would bring the Brookses along at a pace they were comfortable with. In the meantime, someone had to be ready for the onslaught of attention the kid was sure to garner.

The best part of this whole deal was Sawyer truly enjoyed Littlethumb's company. He was an oddly cool little dude for a ten-year-old. Kids weren't supposed to be so layered. You could sometimes see in a child the adult they might become, but most of the time children who behaved too much like adults were annoying. Sawyer preferred kids who were kids. They were supposed to be goofy and do silly things, not behave as if they had already uncovered the nature of existence or speak with the wisdom of someone life had already punched in the stomach. Littlethumb somehow managed to be wise and childishly playful at the same time.

Considering the fact Littlethumb rarely spoke, an outside observer might easily assume Sawyer was projecting these attributes on Littlethumb. Hell, Sawyer readily assumed this idea. He was clever enough to realize he might only be seeing what he wanted in the child. Of course, he was not aware of the Occurrence, of Littlethumb's recent journey. Otherwise, Sawyer would have known he wasn't projecting at all.

9

For their initial after-school session, Sawyer placed Littlethumb in front of a blank canvas. "I want you to paint the first thing that comes to mind. Anything you want. We have an hour here together and you can use as much time as you need. If you don't finish, we can keep going next time. If you finish before the hour is up, we'll start something else. Does that sound okay to you?"

Littlethumb nodded his head.

"Great. Then have fun. If you need any help, let me know. I'll have a seat and read a little to give you some space."

Sawyer took a seat at his desk. He fussed over a newspaper in an attempt to distract Littlethumb. He was curious to see how the kid reacted, and not overly surprised when Littlethumb took no notice. The boy remained intent on the canvas in front of him.

Sawyer was mildly surprised, however, when Littlethumb did not paint anything right away. All the boy did was stand there, staring at the blank canvas. This continued for about half an hour. Sawyer was on the verge of saying something when Littlethumb finally reached for a brush.

Not wanting to see the work in progress, Sawyer intentionally positioned himself so he could not see what Littlethumb painted. He wanted the kid to feel a sense of privacy, and he also didn't want to spoil his own anticipation. Sawyer wanted whatever Littlethumb painted to be unveiled to him the same way it would be revealed to any other observer.

Once he began, Littlethumb worked swiftly. Sawyer watched as his left arm made a few quick movements with brush in hand. A few moments later, Littlethumb set the brush down and reached for his painting.

"Wait," Sawyer said. "Before you show me, I want you to give your work a name. Take a small brush and write the name in the bottom corner."

Littlethumb looked at his teacher with a curious expression, then back at his painting, then back at his teacher. He reached tentatively for a small brush, then withdrew his hand and held it to his chin. The gesture looked so charmingly thoughtful Sawyer almost laughed out loud. He didn't, however, as he did not want to hurt Littlethumb's feelings. Eventually, Littlethumb reached for the brush again before hesitating once more.

"Having trouble?"

Littlethumb nodded his head.

"Hmm. Are you afraid you'll get it wrong?"

Littlethumb nodded his head again.

"I understand. Littlethumb, you can't get this wrong. Okay? The painting is yours. You have to trust yourself. Think of what the painting means to you, maybe what you were thinking about while you were working. The name of a painting can be the most important part or mean nothing at all. It can make someone understand an emotion, or an idea, or thought process you are trying to portray, or add a layer of confusion, if that is your goal. Or, you can simply tell them the name of your picture. If you draw a picture of a dog and name it *Dog*, I would assume you just wanted to paint a nice picture of a dog. But if you paint a picture of a dog and name it *Cat*, then I assume there is something else going on, like maybe you thought naming the dog 'cat' would be funny. Do you understand?"

Littlethumb nodded his head a third time.

"Does it help?"

Littlethumb shook his head and they both laughed.

"Well then, my suggestion is to go with your gut and name it whatever you were about to before you chickened out."

Littlethumb took his teacher's playful jab on the metaphorical chin, sticking his tongue out in response.

"Hey!" Sawyer said playfully. "Watch it, tough guy."

With one more thoughtful glance at his painting, he dipped the small brush in color and signed the bottom-left corner. He put the brush down, lifted the painting by the edges, walked to Sawyer's desk, and handed the work over face-down. Sawyer cautiously took the matte board by its sides with the palms of his hands, not wanting to risk touching the painting's face. The boy's carelessness with the painting briefly inspired irritation in Sawyer, before transitioning to amusement.

Freakin' kids, he thought with a head chuckle. He flipped the painting over. A black circle decorated the canvas. The child was careful not to make the circle's outline uniform, or a perfect circular shape. Intentionally inconsistent, the line of the circle was thinner or fatter in some areas than the prevailing width. Littlethumb allowed the circle different textures as well. The line was brushed with uniformity in some places and brushed with more jagged strokes in others.

In the bottom-left hand corner, in red, the boy painted the words "Life or Death." Not *and* death. *Or* death. I have no idea what the significance was, but I believe this was a notable distinction, and so did Sawyer Pettimore.

Sawyer quietly stared at the painting, examining Littlethumb's expression with his peripheral vision. He thought he saw anticipation on the boy's face, which was understandable.

"Interesting. Very interesting, Littlethumb." He said "interesting" with an abundance of positive inflection and Littlethumb smiled. No, this wasn't exactly earth-shattering work, Sawyer admitted to himself, but from a little kid the theme was reasonably profound and delivered in a pretty cool package. Sawyer found the title's color change an interesting quirk as well. "This is pretty cool. Pretty damn cool. What do you think? Are you happy with your work?"

Littlethumb shrugged his shoulders, made a "so-so" expression with his face. He halfheartedly nodded and shook his head at the same time.

"Hmm," Sawyer hummed, soaking up the painting again. "Do you think you could make this better?"

Littlethumb stuck his bottom lip out over his top lip in a look of assured determination and nodded his head.

"Well, you can't."

Littlethumb immediately looked confused.

"Let me explain. Have a seat there." So he did, while Sawyer rested the painting on the nearby easel. "What you see there is something you created. So, you will see ways it could be made better. Make sense? Okay, good. Now, what I see is something I enjoy, sincerely. I like it. Do you believe me? Good. So, the thing is, as an artist, you will almost always see something in your work that's not quite the way you want. A painting could almost always be better or will never be quite done. It's natural to feel the need to add something. Another color, or another line. Are you with me?"

Littlethumb confirmed he was with a nod.

"So. What you have to accept is a portrait is never finished. This means at some point you have to choose to walk away. Either when you're happy enough with your work, or so frustrated you can't deal with it anymore and *need* to move on. Now, here's the kicker. The people who look at your work, they don't think like you. Most of the time, all they'll see is what is right in front of them, and then they will either like it or not. So, even if you think you could make something a little better, they will never know the difference. Those people will either think your stuff is cool, or they won't. All you have to do is be yourself. And here's the best part. Every once in a while, you will make something you will feel is perfect, and that's the best feeling in the world. You may not become a professional artist, Littlethumb, but I think you have the potential to blow some people's minds."

Littlethumb cocked his head a little to one side and considered his teacher's words intently. After a few minutes, he cocked his head in the other direction and continued his trance. Sawyer imagined the kid having some form of point/counterpoint debate in his head.

Man, I wish I knew what the kid was thinking, thought Sawyer, right before he realized he had to let that thought go. The more likely scenario was he would rarely know what Littlethumb was thinking.

After a few more minutes, Littlethumb looked at Sawyer with what appeared to be a massive expression of understanding and happiness. The boy had a big old smile on his face while he nodded his head. Sawyer joined Littlethumb in the recognition, raising his eyebrows and nodding in agreement.

"Right? This'll be fun, right?"

Sawyer hoped he'd given Littlethumb something he himself had never felt as an artist. Freedom. Littlethumb danced a little dance with his hands on his hips, rocking his butt from side to side and back to front, then offered his teacher a high-five. Sawyer heartily accepted.

"So, I don't suppose you could tell me what this means?" He pointed at the painting.

Littlethumb laughed and hid behind his desk.

IO

The weeks went by and Littlethumb's apprenticeship continued. He met with Mr. Pettimore several afternoons a week and did not tire of their work. Yep, Littlethumb's interest proved to be no passing fancy and the Brookses were happy with Sawyer's efforts in mentoring their son. Then, everything went to shit.

Just kidding. Around this time, the Brooks family received a pleasant surprise in the form of an unexpected houseguest. Well, pleasant for everyone except Walter, who was not a huge fan of the surprise visitor.

Littlethumb, Heather, and Freddy returned home from school together one day to find their favorite uncle sitting at the family table with their mother. *Uncle Dary!* Littlethumb shouted in his mind as he ran to the table to hug his wayward hero.

Samoset "Sam" Daring Bird Jones was the youngest brother of Elisabeth Brooks. He was the favorite uncle of all three of the Brooks children. In truth, he was their favorite relative, period. The kids all thought he was so cool. He wore leather and was often riding a motorcycle, and no one ever knew where he was or when he was coming and going.

Heather had a bit of an innocent schoolgirl infatuation towards her uncle. Why couldn't she find a boy her own age as cool him? Freddy fancied the idea of emulating his uncle. When the opportunity arose, he would proudly announce to his friends his uncle Daring Bird was "the shit." Littlethumb would have glued himself to his uncle's hip. He was so much fun!

The children ran to greet Uncle Dary and assaulted him with a barrage of questions: "What are you doing here?" "Where have you been?" "Why were you gone so long?" "Did you bring me anything?"

Once the kids calmed down, they seated themselves at the table with Daring Bird. The children listened to a whimsical and completely fictional tale of where and what their fantastical uncle had been and been doing since the last time they saw him. Uncle Dary always had the best stories. And while these stories of his travels were highly entertaining fiction, the children would have been equally mystified by the story of his real life.

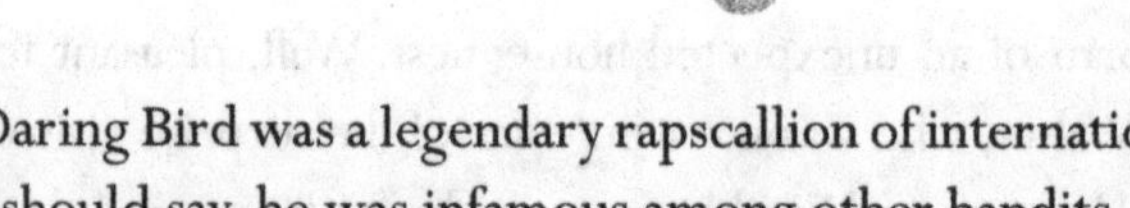

Daring Bird was a legendary rapscallion of international acclaim. Or, I should say, he was infamous among other bandits, revolutionaries, and rabble-rousers involved in the political, socio-economical, and spiritual counter-culture of numerous sovereign states on multiple continents throughout the world. International mischief-maker, that was our man.

As far as his elders in the family were concerned, young Sammy Daring Bird was a frustratingly footloose and fancy-free spirit who refused to grow up. Walter Brooks also did not care for such behavior. Daring Bird was a nice enough fellow, and he was great with the children. Walter would wholeheartedly admit this fact, but he didn't like the example Daring Bird's vagabond life set for the kids. Walter placed great value on being a contributing member of society. Of course, he simply wasn't aware of what Daring Bird was contributing.

Generally speaking, Daring Bird's family viewed him as a bit of an honest scoundrel. A harmless, well-meaning sociopath. His most common response when asked why he moved along from yet another job or domestic relationship—neither of which he ever actually had—was, "too many rules."

Though Daring Bird definitely lived by a strong ethical code, those ethics did not always coincide with the laws dictated by governments. None of his family understood or knew the full extent of his wanderings, or how he traveled internationally without a passport. Or how he paid for his travels, for that matter. He was obviously living what they all assumed must be a pretty crazy life, though most of his relatives took solace in the fact he was at least staying busy.

Stay busy he certainly did. Daring Bird was the leader of an international troublemaking organization known as the Electric Medicine Men. The E2M, as the group was known by those who knew, were "A band of spiritual brothers and sisters hell-bent on annoying the piss out of those who suck while doing good deeds for the helpless and in need."

The E2M was a Robin Hood and his band of Merry Men-esque cabal, stealing from the rich and giving to the poor. They did not only target governments, though. No, governments are not the only platform for people who suck to put their suckiness on display. The Electric Medicine Men sought to right the wrongs of the world with a broad spectrum of shenanigans. For example, they infiltrated the baby food black market and funneled thousands of pounds of stolen baby food away from the organized crime syndicates who originally stole the tiny jars of nutritional paste. The E2M moved the food into the hands of impoverished people all over the world.

The E2M would intercept stolen exotic animals intended for sale to the wealthy, who would either eat the animals or display them in some mansion somewhere to show off to other rich people. However, rather than return the animals to zoos, the group released them back into natural habitats, which gave the animals a chance to live or die on their own. The E2M ardently believed the animals should live in their wild, natural state and contribute their life's energy to the planet as Mother Nature intended, even if that meant the animals were eaten by predators soon after being released.

Most recently, the E2M stole a bunch of tamarin monkeys from a group of profiteers who had organized a heist from a European zoo. The monkeys would never know, but if not for the Electric Medicine Men, their brains would have been eaten by a sheikh and his dinner guests. The sheikh would briefly forget about his tiny penis by serving endangered species for dinner. What a big important man he was. What a big dick.

The Electric Medicine Men sabotaged shitty Hollywood movies and kept them from turning a profit. They stopped the bombing plots of terrorist organizations and re-rigged elections already rigged by fascist governments. They leaked information about military projects to the public, exposed religious figureheads for their misdeeds, and debunked numerous scientific theories developed for no other purpose than to frighten the public into buying shit they did not need. The E2M was a merry band of misfits determined to keep the cosmic balance between good and evil at least slightly tipped in the favor of goodness.

No one knew how the organization was funded. Due to Daring Bird's heritage, there were rumors the group was backed by casino money, but most people discarded the notion as too obvious, and perhaps slightly racist. The truth was, one of their members, who will remain unnamed for her own safety, was a fabulously wealthy and famous young woman. She came from big-time money and capitalized on this blessing with her own life of fame and fortune. In the public eye, she was an award-winning recording artist and actor. Behind the scenes, though, she was an international provocateur of valiant mischief, as well as Daring Bird's on-again, off-again lover. Okay, okay. "She" is world-renowned sensation Cybil "C.C." Constantine. Don't tell anyone.

On this last mission to save the stolen tamarins, Daring Bird had a premonition. His premonitions were the authentic "medicine man" part of the Electric Medicine Men. He was a modern-day shaman, a seer, and his visions often guided the group's exploits. This most recent premonition was different than his others. The vision happened during the group's escape with the stolen monkeys. Daring Bird blacked out briefly, and when he awoke, he understood he had to return to the United States to keep an eye on his sister's family. Daring Bird wasn't sure why. His vision had not shown him anything specific. He saw the faces of his sister and her family and was left with an emotional certainty. They needed him, and it had something to do with his nephew, Littlethumb.

II

S hortly before the children arrived home, Daring Bird explained to his sister the purpose of his visit. Elisabeth took her brother's premonitions seriously. She explained to him the discovery of Littlethumb's *Mona Lisa* and Littlethumb's current tutelage under Sawyer Pettimore.

"Well," Daring Bird said, "I think that's clearly the most obvious change of things, and perhaps the reason I'm here."

For the first time, Elisabeth suddenly felt some type of fear associated with the discovery of her son's talent. "Your vision, what was the emotion like? Were you frightened for us?"

Daring Bird reached across the table and took his sister's hands in his own. "I'm certain, whatever the vision intended, I did what was asked of me. I traveled to my family as I was told. This is a wonderful surprise. Littlethumb appears to be destined for greatness."

Elisabeth was not reassured and recognized Daring Bird had avoided her direct question. She was about to press him for a more earnest response when the children burst into the room. The kids ran to the table. As Daring Bird pulled his hands away to turn and receive his niece and nephews with open arms, he gave his sister a wry smile and a wink.

Arrogant boy, she thought as she smiled back at her brother. The truth was, his assurances did help. Daring Bird had always been a little more confident than Elisabeth felt was rational, but at the same time, his confidence always gave her comfort when she confided in him.

She watched as her brother further dazzled her children with some outlandish story about traveling with a circus as an animal feeder before surprisingly becoming a star attraction as a daredevil motorcyclist, the one who drives upside down in a giant, round metal cage. Daring Bird happened into the position after the previous star walked too close to the tiger cages backstage. You had to stay clear of those tigers!

Then, as things always were with Daring Bird, life got more exciting when a monkey came shrieking from his coat pocket.

Tamarins are small monkeys, and Daring Bird was still getting used to the idea of having one. The animal had been asleep for a while, and Daring Bird forgot the creature was in his pocket. As he finished with his circus story, he rose from the table to adjourn to the bathroom and then for a brief nap before dinner. He smacked his hands against the sides of his waist as he stood, as he was known to do, which excited his new friend Jojo, a cotton-top tamarin Monkey.

Jojo, a fiercely independent soul, was still getting used to his partnership with Daring Bird. The startling way he was roused from his slumber didn't sit well with him. He freaked out. The tiny warrior jumped from Daring Bird's pocket and raced around the apartment.

The monkey was barely nine inches tall and extremely nimble. He didn't cause much damage to the apartment, but catching him and calming him down required intense effort from the humans. Luckily, they were able to do so before Walter, this tribe's alpha, arrived home from work.

That evening at dinner, Daring Bird carefully went around the table extracting status updates from everyone in the household, even Walter, who Daring Bird knew damn well took issue with his life. He appreciated this fact about his brother-in-law and loved him. If he lived as frivolously as he led his family to believe, Daring Bird would have taken issue with himself. As dinner progressed, Daring Bird purposefully led the discussion to Littlethumb's artwork and the esteemed Mr. Pettimore. He expressed interest in meeting Littlethumb's teacher and asked if Littlethumb would mind his uncle visiting his next after-school session. Littlethumb enthusiastically shook his head "no".

Later in the week, Daring Bird arrived at the school. Elisabeth called ahead to let the front office know her brother was coming to meet with Mr. Pettimore. The nice, round lady at the front desk smiled flirtatiously when she handed Daring Bird his nametag and pointed him in the direction of the art room.

I suppose I would, Daring Bird thought as he walked away, *if she wanted*.

He found the art class and peered through the open doorway without entering, soaking up the room. Having arrived before the school day ended, he hoped to chat with this Pettimore fellow before Littlethumb arrived for his lesson. Pleased to find the room empty of any students, he heard someone greet him with a questioning tone. He turned to see Sawyer Pettimore stepping out of a walk-in storage closet holding an unfinished painting of a snow-capped mountain range. Daring Bird stepped through the doorway and said hello while heading toward Sawyer with his hand outstretched.

Sawyer fumbled to free a hand for shaking, but could not figure out a way to do so and hold the portrait with the care he instinctually gave any piece of art in his hands. Daring Bird noticed and pulled his hand away, gesturing for Sawyer to feel free to put the painting down without shaking hands first. The teacher sat the portrait on a nearby easel and turned to Daring Bird, who continued to speak.

"Sorry to catch you off guard a bit. I'm Littlethumb's uncle, Sam Jones." Daring Bird took Sawyer's now-free hand and shook it vigorously.

"Oh, wow. Nice to meet you."

"You too. I've heard great things about you."

Sawyer gave a self-conscious laugh. "Ha, well, the Brookses are great people, which I'm sure you know, being one of them."

"Not a Brooks, though they are great. Elisabeth is my sister."

"Oh, right. Duh. Jones. You told me your name was Jones. I suppose family is what I meant, really."

"Of course." Daring Bird finally let go of Sawyer's hand.

"So what brings you . . ." Sawyer paused for a moment, searching for the right word. "Here." He spoke casually, careful to be sure he didn't seem put-off by the visit. He continued before Daring Bird could speak. "I suppose that's a pretty dumb question, huh?" he said with a smile, scratching his head.

Daring Bird smiled and nodded his head to one side a little. "You said it, chief, not me." Both men laughed. "You know what, just to make sure we are on the same page, I came here because I was curious to see my nephew's work."

Sawyer heard the playfulness in the man's tone and responded with a smile. "Sam, you said? Right?"

"Yes, but you may call me Daring Bird if you like. Honestly, it's my preference."

"Tribal name, I assume? Interesting you didn't introduce yourself…" Sawyer trailed off as he spoke, realizing the potential for an accidental insult.

Daring Bird chuckled in appreciation. "I suppose I don't want to put people off too quickly by forcing them to deal with a guy named Daring Bird. I prefer to wait until I've made a quick, un-thorough assessment of them before I make them uncomfortable."

"Ha!" Sawyer blurted. "Oh of course. Makes perfect sense." A moment of comfortable silence followed the men's laughter. Sawyer broke first. "You want to see his work?"

"Yes, I do."

Sawyer led Daring Bird to the walk-in and flipped the light switch. The closet was lined with canvases of all sizes and shapes.

"These are all Littlethumb's?"

"Yeah," Sawyer said. "It's kind of crazy. Once he gets going, he moves fast. He's done as many as five in one hour."

"No shit."

"Nope. I mean, don't get me wrong. Many of them take longer, depending on the complexity."

Daring Bird noticed the hint of excitement in Sawyer's voice when the teacher discussed Littlethumb's work. The man's enthusiastic fervor piqued Daring Bird's interest.

"I've been working with him on exercises I've developed," Sawyer continued, "basically attempting to expose him to as many of the classic works as possible. Sometimes, I'll have him try to re-create them, either with the painting he's copying in view or from memory.

Or even blindfolded. Sometimes I have him look at a painting, then shift his focus by asking him different questions until he paints whatever comes to mind."

Sawyer went on showing the different works to Daring Bird, energetically explaining all of the different experiments which had led to their creations. Damn near every style of painting appeared to be represented, from Realism to Futurism to Ism-less. Sawyer caught himself mildly foaming at the mouth at one point and stopped speaking mid-sentence. He wiped the spittle from the corners of his mouth with his forearm and looked at Daring Bird sheepishly.

"Jesus, I must sound, hell, look like a madman. I'm sorry. I don't want to give you the wrong idea. It's just . . . it's amazing to work with Littlethumb. I mean, he's truly gifted."

"It's okay." Daring Bird spoke with an easy tone. "I understand. I can only imagine being someone invested in teaching others, only to discover you have a pupil who is brilliant. Seems like a significant responsibility." Daring Bird chose his words extremely carefully and this was not lost on Sawyer, at all.

"Absolutely. The world is full of talented people who never achieve their potential. I believe that's mostly because they aren't properly nurtured." Sawyer chose his words carefully as well. The thinnest underpinnings of competition awoke in him, deep in his subconscious.

"So what's next?"

Sawyer sighed. "The truth is, I don't know. I've been exposing him to as many styles as possible while trying to come up with creative and fun ways to inspire work from him. He shows a natural aptitude for damn near any technique he wants, often blending them together seamlessly, but none of his other works have the life of the *Lisa*."

"May I see it?"

"Oh, of course." Sawyer moved a large oil painting of a field of daffodils to reveal a tall, narrow, safe. "I keep her locked in here, and I changed the lock on the closet door without the school knowing. No one can get in here except me."

"You think that's necessary?"

"Probably not, but I'm a little paranoid. If dealt with properly, this painting could set your nephew up financially for the rest of his life." As he spoke, Sawyer unlocked the safe and removed the painting. "There will be a lot of people willing to pay large sums of money for this painting when they find out it was created by a ten-year-old kid." He held the portrait up for Daring Bird.

"Holy cows," Daring Bird said dryly, but with genuine astonishment, mouth hanging open in a stupor.

"Yeah, right? Puts a new perspective on the rest of this stuff." Sawyer motioned to the other works of art in the room.

Daring Bird agreed with a nod. "Weird. You see this, and somehow, all of the rest of these paintings seem slightly better."

"Yeah. But the funny thing is, the more you get used to the idea he's incredibly talented, and the more you stare at the *Lisa*, the more your perception of this other stuff returns to, you know, kinda meh."

"Interesting."

"Yeah. It's odd. There is something about this one that, I don't know, but whatever *it* is, it's not quite there in the others, despite their quality. I've been trying to figure out what the difference is."

"Perhaps you aren't meant to figure it out. At least, not on your own."

"I suppose that's possible."

"Let me ask you something." Daring Bird walked slowly along the row of artwork staring down at them. "Is there something fundamentally different about Littlethumb's *Mona Lisa* than the rest of these paintings?"

"Oh yes. There would be several. Many things. Big and small. Besides general style, there are thousands of subtle differences."

"No, no. Nothing too complex. Something obvious, like the type of paint. Or maybe, is this the only person Littlethumb has painted? Or woman?"

"No, to both." Sawyer's face suddenly beamed with recognition. "Holy shit. I think you got it!"

"Really? What?"

"I was literally going to sit for him for his next project, so I suppose if you are correct, I would have known soon enough. But still, you said it. Genius!"

"Thanks." Daring Bird spoke with a curious tone, holding onto the word while putting the pieces of Sawyer's statement together. "So the . . ."

"The *Lisa* is the only thing he's done of a live person!" Sawyer cut Daring Bird off in his excitement. "Sorry, sorry." He was having a "Eureka!" moment.

Daring Bird was taken aback, which did not happen often but had now occurred twice within a few moments. He was also entertained by Sawyer's outburst. "No worries." Daring Bird chuckled. "Curious, though. The real *Mona Lisa* is hundreds of years old. The woman was not sitting there for Littlethumb."

"True, very true. But she was an actual, live person when she was first painted. Maybe that's the key. Is that crazy?"

"No, not to me, and I think we know how to find out if you're correct."

12

Remember how I told you earlier Littlethumb would've seen the unfortunate bitterness buried within Sawyer Pettimore, if the boy had ever painted him? Well, the unexpected arrival of Uncle Daring Bird prevented that from happening. Instead, Sawyer asked Daring Bird to sit in as a model for Littlethumb. He wanted to test their theory on human portraits being the child's true calling and thought Daring Bird would make a fantastic subject. The unusual uncle was interesting looking, extremely handsome and roguish.

Daring Bird saw an opportunity to keep an eye on his nephew and get to know the art teacher without seeming intrusive. His initial feelings for this Pettimore guy were mostly positive, but his vision had brought him here for a reason. The situation required time for his purpose to unfold.

Littlethumb, of course, readily agreed to paint his uncle. How exciting! He got to spend a bunch of afternoons hanging out with Uncle Daring Bird *and* Mr. Pettimore? Boy, being away from his family for so long during the Occurrence had sucked pretty bad, but now that he was back, everything sure had been pretty sweet.

Work proceeded at a steady pace. Littlethumb moved quickly and did not second-guess any choices made. Sawyer was dumbfounded by his pupil's confidence. The kid created the *Mona Lisa* replica in a few nights. Amazing, but still a copy. This was an original piece and Littlethumb never started over. He never blended the colors incorrectly to match Daring Bird's skin tone or clothing. The young artist didn't flinch on the third day when Jojo Monkey awoke and inserted himself into the portrait, climbing out of Daring Bird's pocket and taking a seat on his shoulder. Littlethumb only smiled, waved hello to the monkey, and returned to the painting.

Littlethumb, Daring Bird, and Sawyer Pettimore stood in a row staring at the portrait of Daring Bird. Littlethumb held his uncle's hand lightly. Daring Bird and Sawyer did not hold hands.

"Amazing," Sawyer said. "This is amazing."

"I suppose your theory is confirmed," Daring Bird said.

"I would say so. Littlethumb, do you realize how remarkable this is?" Sawyer looked down at Littlethumb without turning his body or letting the portrait out of his sight.

Littlethumb's face showed conflicting emotions. The expression represented the conflict between honest pride and humility. Finally, he blended the two emotions together, offering Mr. Pettimore a sheepish smile of confirmation.

"Littlethumb, my beloved nephew, you have honored me," Daring Bird said. "There is no way I can be this man." Littlethumb's only response was to squeeze his uncle's hand.

In the portrait, Uncle Daring Bird sat on a low stool. His right foot rested on the stool's bottom rung, knee bent. The left foot rested on the ground with knee slightly bent as well. His hands rested on either thigh. Jojo Monkey sat atop Daring Bird's right shoulder in a fierce crouched position, his ears pinned.

What they saw, however, was the essence of a noble man. As with the *Mona Lisa* replica, there was some indefinable, undeniable quality which registered immediately as special. The indefinable quality Sawyer had not been able to explain about the *Lisa* was a statement Littlethumb's painting made about the woman's soul. Perhaps the connection was missed because she was long deceased. Daring Bird was alive and standing right there.

Sawyer quickly understood. He looked back and forth from the portrait to the man. Their colors, their physical textures, were almost reaching for one another. As if at any given moment the painting and the man would merge into one another.

Sawyer realized Littlethumb somehow had the ability to expose something holy about a human subject. Most likely, something unholy as well, he assumed, if existing within the person. Littlethumb's painting exposed the true nature of the individual. To that point, Daring Bird was clearly a king among men.

I'm not sure if *holy* and *unholy* are the correct words to describe this visual exposure of inner being, but that's how the phenomenon registered with Sawyer. For Daring Bird, it registered as uncomfortable. I think most normal, well-adjusted human beings would be slightly uncomfortable with the notion of seeing themselves in such a light.

Littlethumb was proud of his picture. He thought he did a pretty good job of painting his Uncle Daring Bird, and Mr. Pettimore agreed. Uncle Daring Bird could barely speak. Jojo seemed fascinated by the portrait as well, his tiny head poking out of Daring Brid's pocket. Yep, Littlethumb was excited about this one. What a shame Jojo Monkey couldn't talk. Littlethumb wished he could ask his tiny friend if he was happy with his representation. Then he had to pee.

Daring Bird felt his nephew tug on his hand and looked down to see the boy gingerly pulling at the crotch of his pants with his other hand. Bouncing at the knees a bit, the internationally known dance of the boy who needed to pee, his face pleaded with his uncle for relief. Daring Bird grinned.

"Sure buddy, go. Go before you burst." Littlethumb let go of Daring Bird's hand and ran to the bathroom. Daring Bird looked at Sawyer. "I want this burned. It must be destroyed."

"I'm sorry, what?" Sawyer was thoroughly caught off guard. "Why?"

"The picture frightens me. I can't see myself in such a light. Do you understand?"

Sawyer considered the question and the man standing next to him. "As much as I hate to admit it, I think I do."

"It's as if I paid some fake, cheap tarot card reader to tell me what I want to hear."

"I hear you, but it's not that, at all."

"I know. Still, I think you should burn it. I feel like part of me is in there. It must be released and returned to me."

"You do realize that's impossible, right?"

"No, I do not. Sawyer, my freaking name is Daring Bird. I am the third medicine man born to my family in the last five generations. My spirit is in that painting and I want it out."

"Don't you think that will hurt Littlethumb's feelings?"

"No." Daring Bird paused briefly. "Maybe. Either way, he will understand. If not now, he'll understand someday."

"Look, Daring Bird, I won't pretend to understand your beliefs, but I do respect you and your wishes." When the words came out of his mouth, Sawyer Pettimore truly believed them.

"Thank you."

"But, how do you think it will affect Littlethumb? Do you want him to get discouraged, or stop working?"

"Of course not." Daring Bird scoffed at the suggestion, but with a friendly tone. "He obviously has a gift, but this makes me uncomfortable, as I said before. Seeing myself in such a light is…difficult. For me to embrace this portrayal feels, what's the best word? Egomaniacal? Narcissistic? Who could humbly see themselves in such a way? Yet, it is so lifelike, I can't deny it, and I feel like part of me is in there. I can't have that."

"But what about other people? Who knows what this gift could ultimately mean, but one way or another, obviously this is Littlethumb's calling. Is he supposed to ignore the thing he's meant to do?"

"No, of course not." Daring Bird studied Sawyer intently. The art teacher made a giant leap in logical progression. He was somehow being defensive. Daring Bird found the reaction curious, but let it go for the time being. "Other people do not share my spiritual beliefs. They can form their own opinions. I won't ask my nephew to stop sharing this gift with the world. But I will ask you to burn this painting for me. Set whatever part of me is trapped in there free, please."

"Okay, I will. But what do we tell Littlethumb?"

"Don't tell him anything. I'll discuss it with him."

"Fair enough." With a deep breath, Sawyer shrugged his shoulders and crossed his arms. "Just out of curiosity, why don't you burn the painting yourself?"

"I don't think that's a good idea." Daring Bird held his chin as his nephew had done before. Sawyer noticed, smiling at the notion Littlethumb had learned the habit from his uncle.

"You know what," Sawyer said. "I'm not even gonna ask you what that means. I'll do it." He turned to shake Daring Bird's hand. I doubt he realized he was lying, but he was. "People will freak out about this. Can you imagine all the jerks in Hollywood who would want a portrait of themselves like this hanging over their bed?"

Daring Bird nodded his head with his eyes wide, bulging them for effect, and both men snickered a bit.

"Kind of crazy, huh? Was right there in front of me the whole time. How did I miss it?"

"Well," Daring Bird said, "how often do you look down to see your own nose?"

13

Littlethumb sat on the floor in his room, legs crossed underneath him, hands rested on his knees. His eyes were closed and his back was straight as a board. The commanding officers of his toy collection surrounded him. He thought about racecars.

The racecars sped off into the sunset of his mind. His next thought was of his uncle. Daring Bird left the Brooks household and found his own place in the Bronx. Littlethumb was sad his uncle left, as he didn't get to see Daring Bird on a daily basis anymore. The sadness was completely outweighed, however, by his uncle's decision to stay in New York for the time being. This made Littlethumb mega happy.

The faces of the rest of his family entered his mind. He saw Grandpa Kicking Rocks and smiled brightly. Then there was Mr. Pettimore. Littlethumb wondered about this man. They had been working together for close to six months now, and Littlethumb was beginning to develop questions about their time together. He'd come to terms with the idea he was special, at least in regards to his artwork, as all of the adults around him seemed to accept this as a fact. What he didn't understand was what this all meant.

Littlethumb wondered if Mr. Pettimore loved him, having moved his teacher into the same area of his heart where his family resided. He wondered if Mr. Pettimore felt the same way. Also, was Mr. Pettimore a good person? Littlethumb assumed he was, but the idea people sometimes deceive one another had settled into him recently, and on a deeply emotional level. The concept felt odd. He could not understand any reason for hurting another person. If everyone were kind to one another, there wouldn't be any excuse for being mean.

The image of Mr. Pettimore drifted away and was replaced by the greater philosophical question of man's inherent nature. No, my friends, the boy was not so thoughtful as to ponder in these terms, yet, but he was asking the questions. Why are people mean? Why are people starving? Why, why, why?

Littlethumb had taken to these quiet-time sessions shortly after his uncle left. Having stomped off to his room to pout when he heard the news, Littlethumb had scarcely shed a tear despite his earnest attempts to be very, very sad. Instead, he discovered he thoroughly enjoyed sitting and letting his mind wander. Not only did the world slow down for him, the meditations gave him inspiration for paintings and made him a better leader for his nation of toys.

Since his return from the Occurrence, Littlethumb had grown more and more aware of how quickly the world moved around him. Before the Occurrence, the days at school often dragged on forever. Now his days flew by in the blink of an eye. He wasn't certain why, or how, but he knew it had something to do with his journey.

Walter and Elisabeth Brooks noticed the other changes in their son. The replica of the *Mona Lisa,* his sudden artistic skill, was only the beginning. Elisabeth poked her head into Littlethumb's room on several occasions to witness the boy doing push-ups and sit-ups, or sitting in the middle of the floor with his eyes closed. She asked Walter if he had anything to do with this, which her husband denied.

Not long after they discovered their son's meditations, Walter was further puzzled when Littlethumb approached him and asked if he knew how to fight. "A little bit," he replied, ceremoniously raising the indefatigable solo eyebrow of curiosity.

Littlethumb told his father he felt it would be best if he learned a little as well, and asked if he could perhaps take boxing lessons. The boy had literally used the word "perhaps." Walter found the phrasing of the question quirky. His son's interest in learning to fight was genuinely intriguing. Littlethumb was a gentle soul, unlike his older brother Freddy, whom Walter would not have been amazed to find punching himself in the face repeatedly. Don't get me wrong, Freddy was no more psychotic than any teenage boy suffering the onslaught of copious amounts of testosterone raging through his body.

Initially, Walter figured his youngest son might suffer from bullying at school, or perhaps Freddy. When Littlethumb explained he wanted the ability to protect the people he loved, Walter was pleasantly surprised and exceedingly proud. Both parents agreed the boy was still too young for a conversation about how the world doesn't quite work that way. Thus, despite Elisabeth's trepidation, Littlethumb began taking boxing lessons.

In addition to the boxing lessons, meditations, and general calisthenics, Elisabeth noticed other new behaviors. For instance, Littlethumb reorganized everything in his bedroom and was keeping the room much cleaner. No longer did she have to chastise the child to make sense of the train wreck that was his personal habitat. Order had become a matter of personal choice on her son's part.

What she found especially curious was despite the reorganization, Littlethumb apparently came to terms with an acceptable level of messiness. He allowed himself a measure of disarray within the order he created. You might find two pairs of shoes loose in the room, but not three. No, ma'am.

Littlethumb also began to tinker on her piano when he thought no one was watching. He played the keys softly, one at a time, listening intently to their sound. On several occasions, without the boy knowing, Elisabeth watched him with a joyful heart. Finally, one day she decided to make herself known and asked Littlethumb if he might like for her to give him a few lessons. Her son playfully yelled "No!" at her and ran off to his bedroom laughing.

Littlethumb opened his eyes and looked around. Everything was still as it should be. There were times during his meditations he felt so lost in his own thoughts, when he opened his eyes, he would not have been surprised to discover he was no longer a boy but had grown into an old man. He fancied he would be a lot like his Grandpa Kicking Rocks.

Littlethumb bowed to his high council of toys, one member at a time, then took them to their normal resting places. The current chairman of the council was Sergeant Blood, a twelve-inch tall commando. The council's chairmanship rotated on a regular basis to prevent any one member from wielding too much authority.

The members were presented with a specific question to contemplate before quiet time, and now Littlethumb would poll their responses. The question was whether or not to allow Mr. Pettimore to submit one of Littlethumb's paintings into an art competition. He wasn't certain how he felt about art being pitted against other art in competition. The concept seemed odd to him.

Still, Mr. Pettimore felt the exposure would be good for Littlethumb. People needed to witness Littlethumb's talent and the competition was a good way to start. Mr. Pettimore also thought the evaluation of Littlethumb's work by strangers was critical to his development.

His parents didn't think there was any harm in participating, but they left the final decision to him. Littlethumb didn't care if other people appreciated his art. That was the honest truth. He took great joy in the fact his work pleased his parents and his teacher, and he enjoyed the painting process. Painting felt good, which was all he needed. But, and there is always a *but*, Littlethumb understood Mr. Pettimore's feelings.

Though Littlethumb didn't need the approval of strangers, if he were truly gifted, not sharing his gift with others would be selfish. If his paintings could make other people happy, Littlethumb wanted to give that to them. The Russian Wizard Arkady, an eight-inch-tall rubber Russian professional wrestler and next in line for the council's chairmanship, most eloquently expressed to Littlethumb the connection between sharing his artwork with the world and the boy's desire to love others.

"Show them what you can create, and they may love you for this. Then you will love them in return even more." Arkady spoke in his thick Russian accent. The Russian accent Littlethumb used for Arkady was a work-in-progress, but the message was clear. Arkady was correct. What if Littlethumb did become famous? Think of all the good stuff he could do.

Littlethumb could buy his friends wax packs of baseball cards and take them to Mets games. He could have sweets any time he wanted and give them to everybody else, too. He could give money to the poor, dirty people he saw on the street all the time. Plus, he could take care of his family, probably the most important reason of all, although he might be able to share enough so people around the world would stop fighting, which felt pretty important as well.

"Hear, hear!" his high council cried in encouragement.

It was agreed. Littlethumb would enter the contest, and he would paint something new for Mr. Pettimore to submit. Yes. The submission would be something inspired by his decision to say hello to the world. He was suddenly ecstatic. The adrenaline made him feel a little dizzy, so he decided to do some push-ups.

14

Sawyer Pettimore's plan was going exceedingly well. Everything was in place for a Littlethumb explosion. He cataloged enough paintings from the boy to bring in millions of dollars, as long as the collectors of overpriced art thought Littlethumb's work was hot. And they would. Sawyer's bones were certain. He could hear the lid rattling on the boil-pot. The train was barreling down the tracks? Feel free to choose your own metaphor.

Richard Feinmann made more than a few calls in response to Sawyer's voicemail about "the next Tommy Toxic," but Sawyer never answered. The messages Richard left varied from mildly interested to desperately intrigued to genuinely agitated. Sawyer coyly prodded Richard with text messages along the way and would readily admit he enjoyed teasing his old friend. He would involve Richard soon enough. If everything went according to plan, Richard would use his connections to champion Littlethumb's work among the people with big bucks.

Sawyer spent six months writing content for social media platforms, building a website, and in general creating a massive business entity waiting to be launched. The most brilliant part was the construction of multiple personas for Littlethumb. Sawyer thought these personas would help protect the boy and potentially ease the transition to fame. Uncertainty over Littlethumb's true identity would make the whole thing more mysterious, and therefore a more exciting pop culture whoop-tee-do. The misdirection would also keep the crazies from the actual ten-year-old, gifted child.

By this point in our story, Sawyer had grown quite delusional in regards to his true motivations and actions involving Littlethumb. The self-induced indoctrination to his personal cult of ambition had not taken long.

A few months before the competition Littlethumb stumbled across a brilliant trademark. He'd taken a large canvas and painted the entire surface in a rich, blood red. When viewed from close enough, depending on the quality of your eyesight, the patterns of the brushstrokes made images appear.

The images represented two opposing forces moving toward one another. A hint of black paint outlined "creatures" of varying shapes about to clash with one another. The outlines were so light in color, one might surmise the brush had previously been soaked in black paint and rinsed, with the black not completely cleaned from the brush before being dipped in the red. Thus the black leaked out under the red, faintly, yet somehow exactly where Littlethumb wanted.

What really drew Sawyer's eye, however, was the bottom right-hand corner. Littlethumb left a corner of the canvas paint-free, and in the middle of the space had placed a thumbprint in black paint. The art teacher was ecstatic, and more than a little curious. He asked Littlethumb if there was a reason he left the corner of the portrait blank. The boy could have easily made the black thumbprint over the red paint. Littlethumb responded by nodding his head.

Okay, Sawyer thought. *At least we know he did it on purpose.* He studied Littlethumb, asking his next question mostly to hear himself say the words, as he was doubtful the boy would respond with any sort of satisfactory answer. "Why did you leave the corner of the painting unfinished?" He was surprised when Littlethumb answered him in a whisper.

"A painting is never finished. You have to walk away."

Sawyer beamed with pride. "From now on, I think you should sign all of your paintings this way. What do you think?"

Littlethumb agreed with a smile.

Perfect! Not only was the thumbprint a trademarkable brand, the breakthrough immediately created a rarities collection of Littlethumb's previous work. Collectors would pay big bucks for the prodigy's earlier unsigned paintings. Hell, eventually he could have the kid do a limited run of paintings with a different signature. Maybe he could scratch his initials into the thumbprint, or something similar. Brilliant!

Everything was falling perfectly into place. How could Sawyer have ever questioned the path he was on?

Every step Sawyer had taken thus far was the placement of a domino, one after the other in line, waiting to be knocked over. The citywide Junior Arts Festival would be the tipping of the first tile. Success at the art show would generate the "from out of nowhere" feel Sawyer wanted for the mythos of Littlethumb.

Their impending triumph was further ensured when Littlethumb provided Sawyer with the ideal piece for the occasion. I will admit, in my retelling here, most anyone would've seen the entire situation as kismet, just as Sawyer Pettimore did. Littlethumb had a gift for putting forth work that fit the art teacher's schemes every step of the way.

Saturday. The art show was a week away. Sawyer bummed about his house, messing with his laundry and doing some other chores. He kept himself busy, but his mind was preoccupied. Time to return Richard's phone calls. What would he say? Or perhaps, *how* was more accurate. Yes. He knew *what* to say. He was working on the *how*.

Sawyer knew there was a good chance Richard wouldn't answer the phone. Should he leave a message or not? If he left a message, what should he say? Be blunt? "Call me?"

Or, should he excitedly apologize for messing with Richard? Speak fast and run on? This could be played in so many ways. He needed a plan of action before dialing the numbers.

"Don't overthink it," he said aloud. *Who are you kidding dickhead? You've been overthinking since eight o'clock this morning. Hell, for six months.*

He tucked a pair of clean socks together and tossed them aside, then picked up his phone on the way to the kitchen. The pasta sauce boiling on his stove needed to be checked. He lifted the top, gave the sauce a stir, and noticed the clock on the stove read noon. The art festival would open exactly one week from this moment.

Symmetry, he thought. *Cohesion. Buzzwords. I like it*. He placed the lid back on the pot. *It's time. Do it. Do it now.*

Sawyer dialed Richard Feinmann's number. The extra N was for Now, as much to his surprise, Richard answered the phone on the second ring. Sawyer heard the coarse, muted hack of a throat being cleared.

"Hello."

"Hi, Richard."

"Well if it isn't my old, mysterious pal, Sawyer Pettimore. To what do I owe this dubious honor? Calling to tease me some more?"

"No, Richard," Sawyer said calmly. "It's time."

"Time for what?"

"Time for you to find out what this is all about."

"Not interested."

This response caught Sawyer off guard. He was already taken aback when Richard had answered the phone. Sawyer gathered himself and called his friend's bluff. "Yes, you are."

Richard relented immediately. "Yes! Yes, I am. For sweet titty-fucken sake! You've been tugging at my balls for six months. What's the fucking deal?"

"Come to the Junior Arts Festival in mid-town next week and I'll show you. I'm telling you, you won't regret it."

"I already do. Because I'll come. You've got me, you dirty shit, and you know damn well." Richard respected his friend for the hook Sawyer had successfully planted in him. Might as well admit the truth. "This has been well-played, Saw. I hope whatever you're doing lives up to the hype."

"Don't worry about that, Lil' Ricky." Years had passed since either man had used an old, friendly nickname for the other. "You know what a chicken I am. You think I would do all this if I had any doubt?"

"Actually, I know you absolutely would not." Richard could hear the chutzpah in his friend's voice, which had not been there since they were arrogant teenagers. *You are seriously making a move here, aren't you?* he thought. *About damn time you manned up.*

"Good," Sawyer said. "Then show up around one. Text me when you get there and I'll find you."

"Hey, Saw?"

"Yeah?"

"I want to register you are now fucking with me for another entire week."

"Yeah, I know. I'm sorry."

"No, you aren't."

"Nope, I'm not." Sawyer smiled. What a wonderful feeling to find yourself brimming with confidence you aren't used to having, though controlling such an unfamiliar and powerful force can be extremely difficult.

"You know, I could have been out of the country, or had other plans in general."

"True, but you're rich. You do whatever you want."

"Those are both true. I've been receiving oral sex throughout our entire conversation." Richard spoke with a doctor's clinical tone, then laughed at his own joke.

"Seriously?"

"I'm not telling."

"See you next Saturday, Richard."

"Yes, you will."

Dick set his phone aside and looked down at the blond hair attached to the head buried in his crotch. She was doing very nice work, and if Dick hadn't gotten off the phone soon enough, Sawyer might have heard exactly how said work was coming together.

"Who was that?"

"Jesus Christ!" Dick said, quite startled. The young lady moved as if to look at him. He patted her head. "No, no. Everything's okay."

She continued her work and he looked around the room. He found Tommy Toxic leaning against the bar with a highball glass in his hand. "Does nobody in this damn building knock anymore?"

"Since when have I ever knocked?"

"And what are you doing? Drinking in the middle of the day?"

Tommy made a gesture with his hands that translated into any number of dismissive responses, most likely either, "Why are you acting surprised?" or "What fucking difference does it make?"

"You're thirteen years old, kid," Dick continued. "That shit will stunt your growth."

"So who was on the phone?"

"Since when do you go around asking me who I'm on the phone with all the time? Do I ask you who you're on the phone with?"

Tommy ignored Dick's question. "It was your old friend again, wasn't it? The one who says he found the new me."

Dick was surprised by the boy's intuition. He was also surprised Tommy remembered the little remark from six months ago. "How much of my conversation did you hear?"

"Enough. I want to meet this 'new me'."

"Tom, I already told you. There is not, nor will there ever be, another Tommy Toxic. You're the shit, kid. So let's say my friend is right and he has found a star. Big deal. There're plenty of stars out there. You're around them all the time."

"I know."

"So then don't be jealous."

"I'm not jealous." Tommy said this as nonchalantly as a jealous thirteen-year-old boy could. Then he finished the drink in his hand, a gin and tonic with a lime if you were wondering. "Why would I be jealous?"

"Fine, you aren't jealous. Now, would you mind getting out of here? You're kind of ruining my massage."

"Whatever, she's a skank."

"Hey," the girl tilted her head up long enough to say.

"Shh, shh, shh…" Dick patted her on the head again.

"It's more fun if you choke her," Tommy said.

"Jesus, kid."

Tommy set his glass down louder than necessary. "I'm going with you. I want to meet this fucker you're so excited about."

"Fine," Dick agreed. "No problem. Now get out of here, would ya? And stop drinking. Please. I love you, buddy. You're too young to be drinking in the middle of the day."

Tommy flipped Dick Mann the bird as he walked out with a sardonic smile on his face. In the world of Dick Mann and Tommy Toxic, this was a show of affection.

Sawyer Pettimore set the phone down and braced himself against the countertop, arms locked out in front of him. His heart raced, but with a wicked grin. He was making moves. Moves, baby. He was on his big come-up. Yes sir. He could feel the real. This shit was real. He slapped the counter with both hands and went back to his Saturday chores.

15

The day of the arts festival arrived. The entire Brooks clan took part. Normally, convincing Heather and Freddy to attend something as boring as an art festival would've been like pulling teeth with a string, but they shared the same state of excited nervousness as their parents and little brother.

Over time, Heather and Freddy understood something unusual was going on with Littlethumb's artwork. With a little prodding, their parents discussed Littlethumb's *Mona Lisa* and its implications with them. Heather and Freddy held several Q&A sessions with their parents about the situation. They also held several private conferences about the benefits of their brother becoming a rich and famous artist. Both agreed the sibling benefits would be pretty sweet.

Sawyer sent the Brookses the display number for Littlethumb's work and asked to meet for coffee before the show. At the coffee shop, Sawyer explained his game plan. He wanted the family to check out the display early, then leave the presentation to him for the rest of the day. His reasons were threefold, and he was completely transparent with the Brookses.

First, as we know, Littlethumb didn't care too much for talking. If a crowd gathered they would bombard him with questions. Second, a crowd was guaranteed to gather. Sawyer assured them if the family came back to Littlethumb's spot an hour or so after the show opened, the buzz would have already started. Third, he would help generate said buzz.

Walter and Elisabeth expressed reservations about the third part, as Sawyer knew they would. He was ready. "I understand your feelings," he said. "And I don't want you to take me the wrong way. I thought maybe we should keep Littlethumb's work anonymous for a while, to protect him, and give us a chance to see how heavy all this gets. If things pop off and flame out quickly, so be it. If for some insane reason, reactions are aggressively negative, he won't have to deal with irrational criticism. I know you have trepidation about where this could lead."

Elisabeth glanced sideways at her husband, whose facial expression exercised reserve. "It's a reasonable idea," Walter said. Walter was not completely sold on the plan. The tone of his voice betrayed his words.

"Thank you." Sawyer ignored the reticence in Walter's voice. "Please understand when I say I'm going to help generate the buzz, I'm just being forthright about the effect a great work of art by an anonymous artist could generate. In the art world, if people are lukewarm about the merits of a work on face value, if there's a mystery involved, the intrigue can make them love the work. I want to be honest with you both about the benefit and some potential . . ." Sawyer struggled for the correct word here. He was perfect in rehearsals, but suddenly his lines escaped him, and his performance had been next to flawless until this point! He improvised. ". . . side effects of going about things this way." He doubted "side effects" was the term he originally scripted, but the delivery felt soft enough.

"Sawyer," Elisabeth said, "we're nervous, too. It's okay." She reached over and patted Sawyer's hand. "We understand your enthusiasm. It's our job to protect our son, even from you when we have to." She winked at Sawyer and smiled, putting the young art teacher at ease. "Let's have some fun with this." She looked at Walter. Her words were was as much for him as for Sawyer. "If our son is meant for the world, then that's what life has given us. We have to take some joy in this and stop being so afraid. At least, I know I do. I think your idea sounds fun." She looked over at Littlethumb. "What do you think?"

Littlethumb shrugged his shoulders slightly and held his hands up with a confused expression on his face. This bit was recently stolen from his father, and the impression absolutely crushed Elisabeth. She smiled and looked at Walter who wore a coy, proud papa look on his face.

"Well I guess that settles things," Sawyer said with a chuckle.

The Junior Arts Festival was interesting enough, especially if you get a kick out of humans going about their business. Also a little surreal, to be frank. The exhibit was in a gymnasium at one of the sponsor schools, with tents and booths set up on the parking lot outside as well.

High school and college art departments recruited young talent from booths throughout the festival. Art departments aren't exactly flush with big budgets, so the booths were pretty shitty. I don't want to get into the social implications of recruiting children to schools at such a young age. Seems weird, that's all.

The eccentric humans manning the recruitment booths were a real treat for Littlethumb. He'd never seen so many soul patches, white-haired men with ponytails, and women without bras in one place, and he lived in Manhattan! Hell, he didn't know a soul patch was called a soul patch, or why those women's boobs looked so carefree. All he knew was, he loved it. All of it.

A less enthusiastic person may have found the scene slightly depressing. As mentioned, art departments don't typically generate much revenue. While aesthetically pleasing to Littlethumb, many of the teachers and department heads on hand working to fill their classrooms and departments with new recruits had already lost their fight with the world and were basically counting sheep to get to the big sleep.

To be honest, for a city the size of New York, the show wasn't super awesome. Don't get me wrong, some talent was on display for sure, but the sheer volume of work presented was less than one might have expected. For whatever reason, unlike the performance arts, painting was not often encouraged as a viable career path. Still, there were hundreds of works on display, including Littlethumb's.

The family visited his piece together. They stood with their arms around one another, soaking in what the youngest of their clan had created. He'd used a decent-sized matte board, probably three feet by two feet. The matte was painted completely white. In black paint was the outline of a torso wearing a white T-shirt. The torso was framed so the arms and neck of the body and the bottom of the T-shirt were cut off by the matte's edges. On the T-shirt in black paint was the word "hello!" in all lowercase letters, and with an exclamation point on the end. In the bottom right-hand corner of the painting was Littlethumb's signature thumbprint. Next to the painting was a small folding table upon which a placard and a magnifying glass were resting. The placard had the painting's title listed as *Nice World You've Got Here . . .*, and the artist was listed as "Anonymous Ten-Year-Old."

If you observed the painting closely, you would see the period of the exclamation point was a small metal disk affixed to the matte. If you used the magnifying glass, on the disk you would see a highly detailed, full-color miniature painting of the planet Earth. The piece wasn't Littlethumb's greatest creation but was certainly apropos, and more than intriguing enough for Sawyer to work with. The rest of the world had low expectations for a ten-year-old child. Littlethumb's piece would be a hit. Sawyer was convinced. He was also equipped with promotional efforts to guarantee success.

By noon, most the attendees of the Junior Arts Festival had arrived. Sawyer Pettimore initiated phase one, a bizarro whisper campaign. For about an hour he perused the crowd, stopping by other artists' works and complimenting them. Then he would casually tell the other observers about an exceptionally interesting piece he had seen over in aisle thirteen.

Every once in a while Sawyer returned to Littlethumb's display, calmly uttering words like "super-hip" and "ingenious" as he walked by or stood behind the other onlookers. A few times, he magically discovered the magnifying glass, discerning its purpose in front of other people and encouraging them to use the glass as well. He noticed the words "breathtaking" and "marvelous" worked nicely when observing the miniature Earth. People lined up behind him for their opportunity to use the magnifying glass and see why he was so impressed.

Shortly after one o'clock, he received a text from Richard Feinmann, stating his arrival and location near the front entrance. *Hang tight. I'm on my way*, Sawyer texted in response. On his way to meet Richard he swung by Littlethumb's booth, close enough to see the crowd around the painting had grown on its own. Numerous ponytails and pairs of low-slung titties hovered about the painting. Beautiful. Sawyer knew the buzz was official when the professionals were gathered around Littlethumb's work.

Once the necessary crowd excitement at the booth was confirmed, he made his way to the front doors. Standing near the registration table with a smaller human next to him was Sawyer's old pal. As he grew closer, he identified the smaller human as a boy. "Hello there, Richard." Sawyer stuck out his hand for a shake. Richard ignored the gesture.

"What do you say, Sawyer Pettimore? Give me a hug, damn it." Richard politely batted Sawyer's hand away and went in for a hug. Sawyer gingerly returned the show of affection.

After Richard released him, Sawyer turned his attention to the young man. Around five and a half feet tall, he was not much shorter than Richard but quite a bit below Sawyer's height of nearly six feet. He was damn near covered from head to toe, sporting an oversized baseball cap and a large pair of sunglasses. His white T-shirt read "Incognito" in large black letters.

"And with whom do I have the pleasure here?" asked Sawyer.

"This is my good friend Pauly Poisonous," Richard said. He made air-quote gestures when he said Pauly Poisonous.

"Oh, wow," Sawyer said.

"Shh," Tommy Toxic responded.

"Of course," Sawyer whispered. "Sorry. It's a pleasure to meet you." He held his hand out to shake. Tommy was way too cool for a normal handshake. He slapped Sawyer's hand and then used an interlocking thumb-grip to pull him in for a quick shoulder bump. Sawyer fumbled his way through the routine, learning on the go as awkwardly as you might imagine. Once the intros were over, Sawyer asked, "You guys want to see what this is all about?"

"I didn't come for the ass." Richard took a jokingly disgusted look around the room, eliciting an affirming groan from Tommy Toxic.

Sawyer snorted at the joke. "Well, come on then." He held out his hand, leading them to the end of the aisle where Littlethumb's painting was on display. The crowd in front of the painting had grown yet again. *Perfect*, Sawyer thought. *This is perfect*. "There it is," he said, pointing down the aisle to the crowd.

"What am I looking at, Saw?" Richard asked.

"Richard, my old friend, you are witnessing the beginning of a legend."

16

Calling a crowd of about twenty people observing a painting "the beginning of a legend" may seem a ridiculous overstatement, but Sawyer Pettimore was conducting the most important marketing campaign of his life. He led Richard close enough to observe the crowd in detail and hear the words they tossed about: "brilliant," "super-hip," "ingenious," "groundbreaking," "ahead of his or her time," "breathtaking," "masterful," "marvelous," and "shockingly original." Rumors spread like wildfire throughout the festival about a popular painting everyone needed to see and say words about, and those words most likely should be hyperbolic praise uttered loud enough for others to overhear.

After Richard had gotten the point, they found a table in the concession area. Richard sent Tommy off to get some food so he and Sawyer could have some privacy. "Look, Saw, I'm fairly impressed with the fun you've had here, but I have to admit I'm a little disappointed. I mean, it's an interesting painting and you've worked these nerds into a frenzy, but the next Tommy Toxic? C'mon, the kid is an international superstar. Even if your boy has talent, shit, it's art, Saw. Nobody gives a Dutchman's crap about art."

"Let me show you something else." Sawyer took his phone and opened a picture of Littlethumb's *Mona Lisa,* then handed the phone to Richard.

Richard looked at the picture and shrugged his shoulders. "The *Mona Lisa*. So what? Is there some metaphor here or something?"

Sawyer studied his old pal closely and chose his words carefully. "He painted it."

Richard did not respond immediately, instead taking a closer look at the picture on Sawyer's phone. "What do you mean he painted it?" he finally asked.

"What you're looking at is an exact replica of the *Mona Lisa* painted by a ten-year-old child. The same child whose work you saw on display here. This is only the beginning, Richard."

Richard Feinmann studied Sawyer's face and took another, closer look at the picture. "A ten-year-old kid?"

"Yep."

"You can't be fucking with me right now. This is legit?"

"One hundred percent."

Richard leaned back in his chair. He folded his arms together over his chest and made a squinty, thoughtful expression. "Okay, I've moved from intrigued to thoroughly interested. Now, tell me what the fuck you're thinking and stop teasing me."

"You said it yourself. No one gives a shit about art, at least not the way you're thinking. There's nobody in this country ripping up the art scene and making a name for themselves." Sawyer leaned in across the table so he could speak more softly—maybe for effect, maybe as a natural reaction to the telling of his big secret. "I've been working with this kid for over six months, Richard. He's no fluke. He's obscenely talented, and you and I will turn him into the world's first pop-art child superstar."

Sawyer sat back and put his hands behind his head. His pitch was out. Time to shut up and let Richard's mind wander with possibilities. If Sawyer had done his job well, and he believed he had, this pirate's capitalistic juices would be flowing.

Before either man spoke again, Tommy Toxic returned to the table with a tray of very unhealthy food. A giant soft drink, an unnecessarily large slice of meated pizza, and a bucket of tater tots smothered in fake cheese landed on the table with a thud.

"Jesus Christ," Richard said. "You know that garbage is bad for your skin, right?"

Tommy shrugged his shoulders, took a large bite of pizza, and spoke with his mouth full. "Do you know how bad it sucked waiting in line for this shit? I can't believe people live like this."

Richard returned his attention to Sawyer. "I want to meet him. Is he here?"

"Yes."

"Call him over."

"Call who over?" Tommy asked.

"The next you." Richard spoke with a dry, sarcastic tone, but the seeds of possibility were planted in his mind. His tone was more for the benefit of Tommy, hoping the kid wouldn't take this too seriously and get offended, defensive, or in general become a pain-in-the-ass about the whole situation. All of which were bound to happen one way or another anyway.

"Aww, not this shit again," Tommy said. He looked at Sawyer. "What exactly do you think you've got going on, big shot?"

Sawyer was taken aback by Tommy's cold stare and shrewd nature, but he recovered quickly. "I've got a phenomenon waiting to happen. You can slap your name all over it and make a bunch of money, kid." He almost didn't believe the words coming out of his own mouth.

Selling the concept to Tommy Toxic was never part of his plan. Sawyer never thought he would suddenly be turning the human child Littlethumb, whom he genuinely cared about, into a commodity to be pitched to a thirteen-year-old rock star. A thirteen-year-old rock star who somehow scared the crap out of him.

"Well then, like the man said. Call him over." Tommy took another drink of his soda and raised a single eyebrow at Sawyer.

Sawyer was thoroughly prepared for Richard Feinmann, or the Dick Mann version of Richard Feinmann, whichever arrived. He was not prepared for this aggressive teenager. Rattled as he was, he managed to take his phone and shoot a note to Elisabeth and Walter. They responded after a few minutes.

"They're on their way," he said. He leaned forward again as a show of discretion. "Tommy, Littlethumb has an older brother and sister. Do you think . . ."

Tommy cut Sawyer off. "What the fuck is a Littlethumb?"

"Oh, the artist's family is Native American. He's a young boy. His name is Littlethumb."

"That's pretty fucking cool." Tommy gave himself an affirmative nod. "I hate him even more." Both men laughed at the joke. Tommy wasn't joking.

"Littlethumb is probably too young and, honestly, a bit too weird to know you, but I'm sure his brother and sister will be blown away by your presence."

"Most likely."

"I was wondering if I could discreetly let them know who they're meeting? I'm sure it'll be a big deal for them."

"Be cool. Low key. I don't want all these losers grabbing at me and shit."

"Fair enough. I'll make sure they understand they have to keep their excitement to a minimum." Although he knew Heather and Freddy would legitimately be excited, Sawyer said this with a slick sarcastic tone for Richard's benefit, who responded with a smirk. Sawyer looked back at his friend with an expression of his own which quite clearly stated, *nice evil little bastard you've got here*.

"Okay," Sawyer continued. "One last thing. In general, I want them to think I invited you down because we're friendly and I thought you'd enjoy meeting one another. Littlethumb's parents don't fully understand how big this could get yet, and I want to ease them into my plan, so they aren't scared away. Is that cool?"

"Whatever."

"Hey!" Richard smacked Tommy on the shoulder with the back of his hand. "Show my pal some respect here, knucklehead. Be nice to these people, would you? You don't have to be a dickhead to everybody."

"All right, all right," Tommy said. "I'll be nice."

"Thank you." Richard looked at Sawyer. "So you have a plan?"

"Of course I do. We'll have to discuss the details later, though. Right now, I need a small favor from Mr. Toxic here, if he's game."

The Brooks family arrived and introductions were made. The adults chatted about what a neat little event the festival was. Richard played the scene real cool with regards to praise for Littlethumb's work, careful not to put off a creepy exuberance. Though he did force Walter and Elisabeth to acknowledge there was quite a stir over their son's painting.

While getting to know one another, the Brookses asked Richard what he did. He sheepishly admitted to working in the entertainment business and revealed his alter ego, Dick Mann. Richard Feinmann could be disarmingly charming. He emptied his reservoir on Walter and Elisabeth Brooks.

Sawyer was correct. Littlethumb did not understand who Tommy was. He understood Toxic was famous because Heather had a poster of him on her bedroom wall, but Littlethumb was too young to think meeting a famous person was a huge deal. Or to understand the difference between a bit of fame and being truly famous. Tommy Toxic was international, and if you don't know, ya betta stab somebody.

The two boys shook hands. Tommy quickly taught Littlethumb a slight variation of the handshake he used with Sawyer, then they studied each other intently. The punk rocker stood with his arms crossed, sizing the smaller child up. The artist stood with his head cocked to one side, wondering why the bigger boy was looking at him that way. Tommy was wondering how much he already hated this kid. Unfortunately, Tommy Toxic was born with an instinctual aversion to kindness.

<h1 style="text-align:center">17</h1>

Thanks to Tommy Toxic most of the local prime-time news broadcasts reported on the events at the Junior Arts Festival. Other than a handful of live performances, Tommy had been out of the public's eye for most of the previous year while secretly dealing with his unfortunate teenage skin and planning his upcoming tour. When he made his surprise appearance at the art festival, footage recorded by the attendees quickly hit the Internet. There were also several audiovisual clubs from local schools on hand to record broadcasts for their student television networks. What a day for those lovable geeks.

Tommy was seen standing on a table tossing coins and dollar bills at the crowd, starting a massive food fight, and surprising an infatuated teenage female with a kiss, thereby breaking every other teenage girl's heart in the room. The lucky girl happened to be Heather Brooks. This was not part of Sawyer's plan and the incident almost ruined everything. Walter and Elisabeth were not pleased. Still, they didn't blame Sawyer and Richard apologized profusely for Tommy's behavior.

105

Years later some historian with too much time on his or her hands would go back and review footage of the event. He or she would discover Littlethumb was there all along, standing next to his father, holding Walter's hand and using his other hand to cover his eyes, peeking through cracks in his fingers as a large crowd took pictures of Tommy Toxic kissing his sister.

All of the news stations that covered the story showed footage of Tommy taking questions from the student reporters. They inevitably asked Tommy which piece on display was his favorite, which was Littlethumb's, of course. When asked what he liked about the painting, Tommy was dramatically hip. "Just look at it. If you don't know why this is awesome, you're fucking lame."

Now I ask you, with such a powerful endorsement who would be cool and aloof enough to refuse to acknowledge the painting's awesomeness? Or be respected by anyone for expressing a dissenting opinion? Maybe three or four people on the planet could have out-cooled Tommy Toxic right then and none of them were present.

Littlethumb's painting won best in show. One local television station picked up the story before the festival was over and immediately moved a field reporter to cover the commotion. The reporter, Alexi Lawson, arrived shortly after the prizes were awarded. As planned, no one was around to accept the ribbon for Littlethumb's work. The award was hung from a corner of the painting.

Unable to get anywhere near Tommy Toxic with the throng surrounding him, the intrepid Ms. Lawson turned her attention to the anonymous piece of art. "John, perhaps the bigger story here—yes, even bigger than Tommy Toxic showing up to have some fun—is the work of art that won best in show. According to its billing, the painting was created by an anonymous ten-year-old child. Many of the local artists and art teachers attending the festival are using words like 'iconic' and 'child prodigy,' *if* this was indeed created by a child, which is still in question as the painting's registration card is incomplete. When asked how the painting was accepted into the festival without any information regarding the artist, one official told me, 'Because this is a Junior Arts Festival. We want these kids to be interested in art. If someone wants to submit a painting anonymously, who cares?' Well, they care now, John. With the stir this painting has created, no doubt with the help of Tommy Toxic's endorsement, everyone is asking the same question: Who is this secret artist?"

Anchorman John smiled intently from his news desk. He liked this new field reporter. "Wow. I know I'm intrigued, Alexi. Do you have any idea what will happen if no one shows up to claim the painting?

"A festival official told me if no one claims the painting, for the time being it will get stored with other materials from the annual festival. No long-term plan has been made as of yet and eventually the festival's board would have to vote on the painting's fate. The official finished by saying if the painting was never claimed, he presumed it would most likely be hung somewhere."

"Well that makes sense." Just in case she didn't believe him, John gave an assuring nod. "Now, Alexi, if someone shows up to claim the painting, how will they prove it's theirs?"

"I wondered the same thing, John. Luckily, the small paper placard with the name of the painting and the painting itself have been branded with what we think are thumbprints. By the size of them, we believe both marks were made with a child's thumb." The reporter held the placard up in view of the camera.

"Have the police run the fingerprint?"

"We are on the same page today, John! I asked that very question and was told nobody thought running the fingerprint was necessary or a good use of police resources."

The news anchor laughed. "I suppose that's true. Interesting story, though."

"Indeed it is, John. A fun little stir on a lazy Saturday afternoon here in Manhattan. Will this child-sized local mystery be solved? Is the next Vincent Van Gogh hiding somewhere in New York City? For News Channel 15, I'm Alexi Lawson."

Thus, the legend of Littlethumb had begun. Of course, no one knew who Littlethumb was yet, or the name Littlethumb for that matter, but the foundation was laid. News of the story and the painting hit the Internet and gained momentum, at least within art circles. Sawyer monitored anything he could find on the festival or any discussion of the painting. He posted comments on those sites to perpetuate the conversation and interest.

When things were about to die down, which was about two hours after the story made the news, he cleverly dropped Littlethumb's name into the comments sections of any posts he found about the painting. This tactic spurred the conversation and eventually, "Who is Littlethumb?" became a thing. Once people started searching the name, lo and behold, they found all the fake social media content Sawyer created. Guess what was plastered on every fake profile?

"Who is Littlethumb?"

Once Sawyer's plan hit this point there was no going back. The Brookses would be uneasy. Sawyer knew this and was prepared. The online campaign was crafted in a fashion which made tracing things back to their son damn near impossible. Littlethumb's birth certificate was registered with his given name from his parents, not his tribal moniker. Sawyer had asked Elisabeth about this once in passing while his scheme was in development.

Although Littlethumb's schoolmates knew him as Littlethumb, most of them didn't know anything about the Arts Festival whoop-tee-do, didn't care, or were entertained by being a part of the secret. Discovering Littlethumb's true identity would have been difficult for any seriously curious person. Not impossible, for sure, but certainly not easy.

Sawyer understood how fickle the American public was. Sustaining long-term success took one of two things in this country: A product of actual quality and substance, which was still no guarantee of success. Or, a gluttonous use of every available outlet to keep yourself in the public eye, which worked every time. You could be a completely pointless, unintelligent, good-for-nothing human being in this country and stay famous if you kept everyone watching. But if you combined a quality product *and* enormous exposure? That's how empires are built.

As he sat at home on the night of the arts festival, watching replays of the evening news stories over and over, marveling at the stir he created and fantasizing about what was to come, Sawyer knew he had found his calling, though no one might ever recognize the artistic brilliance but him. Richard would probably understand. This entire phenomenon was one giant work of living, breathing, concept art. Sawyer Pettimore's magnum opus.

18

It should come as no surprise "Who is Littlethumb?" t-shirts were available for sale within days of the art festival. Very little nudging was needed from Sawyer to convince Richard to bankroll printing the shirts. The costs were a drop in a bucket to Richard. Tommy Toxic even wore one of the shirts during his performance at an awards show in Los Angeles.

Despite how irritated he was with the amount of attention Richard was paying all of this Littlethumb bullshit, Tommy received a cut of the agency commission. Not much yet, but it would be, and when Tommy was seen wearing the shirt on television he helped take the Littlethumb phenomenon nationwide.

As the Internet traffic grew over the mystery of Littlethumb's identity, Sawyer and Dirty Dick Mann went to work with one of the more crucial elements of Sawyer's plan. The extra N was for "networking." Dick Mann reached out to rich and famous acquaintances and explained he could let them in on the Littlethumb secret, which went far deeper than the media reported.

If Dick's acquaintances were intrigued, Dick requested a personal meeting. He would fly to his friend and show them a picture of the portrait Littlethumb painted of Daring Bird. Then he would explain, if the party were interested, they could throw a bid into a silent auction to have the boy paint their portrait. Whoever had the highest bid would get their portrait made first. The next highest bid would be painted second, and so on. Dick would only accept the top ten bids at first, creating a limited run. They didn't want the market oversaturated early.

One tricky little detail to be planned was the handling of Walter and Elisabeth. Once again, Littlethumb's parents would have to be convinced something was a good idea. Sawyer might have labored over the situation, overthinking the correct things to say. Not Dick.

"It's a lot of money," Dick said, and that is what Sawyer told the Brookses.

Sawyer explained to the Brookses that, having seen the news about Tommy Toxic attending the arts festival, a very wealthy individual put two and two together and reached out to Dick to find out if he had any connection to Littlethumb. The person pressed Dick, wanting to know if he could meet the artist and possibly sit for a portrait.

Of course, Dick told the person no. He had no connection to the "whole Littlethumb thing," so meeting wasn't possible. But, Dick wanted to relay the message to the Brookses as he didn't want to be overly presumptuous. This was the first time Sawyer had flat-out lied to Walter and Elisabeth. Honestly, he was so caught up in the moment he wasn't aware he was lying.

On a quick side note, Tommy told Dick he wanted to be the first person Littlethumb painted. "Tell me the highest bid and I'll beat it. I want to be first."

Dick told Tommy that wasn't going to happen. He explained the first portrait couldn't be of someone from the discovery camp. They needed an outsider, for marketing purposes. Some other wealthy jerk had to pay a premium to be the first if they wanted to make the plan as profitable as possible. Despite the reasoned explanation for denying his request, Tommy Toxic was royally pissed off.

Walter and Elisabeth immediately rejected Sawyer and Dick's plan. Sawyer was prepared for that outcome. "Okay. No problem. I completely understand."

A week later Sawyer called Elisabeth and explained to her the anonymous person had called Dick back and was begging to meet Littlethumb. Just to meet him. The person would travel anywhere he needed to, or pay to bring Littlethumb to him. Elisabeth said she thought the request was very strange. Sawyer reassured her there were people in the world who were truly this passionate about art, and he was certain the person was not strange. In fact, he told her the person's identity, brilliant French architect Jean Luc Ricard. Ricard was in his sixties, a billionaire, and not at all bothered by questions about science fiction television shows.

Sawyer didn't press too hard but he did lean on Elisabeth a little. "At least do me a favor and talk it over with Walter and LT," he said. "It could be a cool experience. And, I don't want to hide from the elephant in the room, Elisabeth. If Littlethumb did want to paint Jean Luc, the man would be willing to pay a small fortune. None of your children would ever want for anything ever again. I can't imagine what that would be like for Littlethumb. To provide so much for his family at such a young age."

Elisabeth saw right through this bullshit and she was not pleased. Elisabeth Brooks was rarely a profane woman. "What the fuck, Sawyer?" she said.

"I'm sorry?"

Elisabeth didn't respond. She bit her tongue for a moment and calmed down. "I'm sorry, I had a stressful day. I apologize."

"No, no. It's okay. I'm sorry. I shouldn't have pressed you."

"No, you're right," Elisabeth relented. "The truth is, a lot of good could come from this if handled correctly. If the guy was that disappointed, I will talk to Walter and Littlethumb."

"Okay. Great. Let me know." Sawyer spoke with an intentional level of sheepishness in his voice.

Elisabeth knew right then she no longer fully trusted Sawyer Pettimore. Being the woman she was, she made every effort to give the man she considered a friend the benefit of the doubt, but the seed was planted. Even so, despite whatever his motivations were he did have an interesting point. What if something terrible happened to her and Walter? The kids had family they would go to, but who knows what sort of financial burden they might create for whoever took them? Or, what if Walter and Elisabeth became incapacitated medically and lost the ability to earn a living?

It is so easy to think of all the good that can be done with money.

Jean Luc Ricard turned out to be a charming, gracious, lovely man. When introduced, Littlethumb sat on his lap and put his arm around Jean Luc's neck, staring up at the man's face intently. A smile took shape on his face. He looked at his parents and gave them a thumbs-up with a big, affirmative nod.

Littlethumb painted Jean Luc in two days and sent him back to France mesmerized with his own image like never before. Walter and Elisabeth deposited the very sizable check from Jean Luc into a fund for their three children. Life moved on as normal as possible and Littlethumb continued to work with Sawyer on his regular schedule.

Sawyer and Richard knew they had to move things forward to maintain momentum, but at the same time, the men had to be careful not to become too pushy. They waited a month after Jean Luc's portrait was completed before broaching the subject of another potential model for Littlethumb. This time, however, the person was Tommy and the portrait wasn't for money. This was the perfect way to get Walter and Elisabeth further acclimated to the idea of Littlethumb continuing his portrait work. Tommy's was the request of a hopeful friend, not of some unknown rich person. Plus, Tommy threatened to expose Littlethumb's identity if Sawyer and Richard didn't agree to let him be painted next. Sawyer did not tell the Brookses about Tommy's threat, but that's how it went down.

Walter and Elisabeth were surprised when Littlethumb was hesitant about the situation. He didn't say so out loud, but they could see the reticence in his body language. Despite his hesitation Littlethumb agreed, if for no other reason than his sister Heather pleading, "You have to, you have to, you have to!" over and over with a crazed expression on her face.

Littlethumb painted Tommy the following week. The work took three days. When he was done, Littlethumb craned his head out from behind the canvas one last time and stared at Tommy, then back at his portrait. He touched his brush to the canvas one last time then put the brush down and moped out of the room with his shoulders slumped, tears slowly moving down his cheeks.

"What's his problem?" Tommy said with a laugh.

The adults in the room stared at the portrait with pained expressions. Elisabeth Brooks finally said, "I'm so sorry," and left the room.

Walter turned to Dick Mann and started to speak, but instead contorted his face in an expression that said one hundred things at once, not the least of which were, "that's fucked up," and, "I'm sorry." He followed after his wife and child. Dick Mann lit a cigarette and shook his head.

"Let me see that thing." Tommy hopped off the stool and walked over to the painting. An evil grin lit up his face. "This is fucking awesome."

Littlethumb learned something that day. Unfortunately, he could see things in people that made him very sad when he painted them. He didn't like this.

Despite his outward exuberance, somewhere deep down inside Tommy didn't like the painting any more than Littlethumb. Subconsciously, Tommy was hurt. He was still just a boy, after all. Regardless of his reputation and desire to be seen as a deranged rock-and-roll psycho, part of him registered the painting as a personal attack. Until this point everyone, including Tommy, thought his evil was all an act. He wasn't ready to recognize or believe what Littlethumb's painting very clearly stated: Tommy Toxic had demons in him.

After Tommy's portrait Littlethumb refused to paint anyone who made him uncomfortable. He would be sweet to the person, shyly offer them a hug and a peppermint and shake his head, "no." Then he would leave the room. Any rational person found difficulty in taking offense at the shyness of a child, so Littlethumb's rejections never became a big deal. Mostly, the person quietly left disappointed.

Sawyer's plans went phenomenally well, aided by some thinking on the fly and help from Dick Mann. A Littlethumb portrait quickly became an ultra-elitist status symbol. Of all people, the President of the United States had a covert sitting, having been told about the situation by a very wealthy campaign supporter who was a recent subject for Littlethumb, subject number seven to be exact. The president's request was eagerly granted, although I'm not certain when the work was finished the president was too excited about Littlethumb's portrayal of him as being made from metal, or the numerous strings the boy painted coming up from his body.

Meeting the president was definitely a big deal for the family. Walter and Elisabeth both voted for him and were ridiculously embarrassed at Littlethumb's depiction.

"Oh, my God," Elisabeth said. "I'm so sorry."

Despite their embarrassment, holding in their equal levels of amusement proved impossible. She and Walter both chuckled while they apologized, which of course led to more apologies for all the laughter. The president, being the dynamic, affable, charismatic leader he was, joined in the hoos and haas. "You know, whether I like it or not, in a lot of ways your son is correct!"

19

Daring Bird's move to the Bronx was born of necessity. All things being equal, he would have preferred to keep his nephew in line of sight on a daily basis, but he also had international matters to deal with. The plan was to live far enough from his family and in a shitty enough neighborhood so as to prevent anyone from casually dropping by his apartment. If anyone did, they were sure to ask questions about all the computers and other pieces of advanced technology. What was he using all that stuff for, anyway? And how could he afford such equipment on a janitor's salary?

Before the nonsense at the arts festival he seriously considered taking his leave of New York. Despite his desire to keep an eye on his sister's family, he'd almost convinced himself his duty to the vision was fulfilled. Quite a bit of time had passed and nothing bad had happened to Littlethumb. There was a solid chance his presence had already averted any potential calamity. Then the arts festival came and went. The significance of that day was not lost on Daring Bird. He didn't want to upset Elisabeth, so he hadn't made a big deal out of the event in front of her, but when he saw the news reports he knew shit would get crazy. La caca was about to hit el ventilador.

As is often the nature of life, Littlethumb's explosion into fame could not have come at a worse time for Daring Bird. The Electric Medicine Men were under considerable heat. A bounty was out for their discovery, capture, or execution. Apparently, several of the criminal organizations the E2M had crossed finally realized they were under siege from the same troublemakers. These syndicates decided to pool their resources and figure out who these E2M fuckers were. As soon as the intel of the bounty had reached Daring Bird he sent his men into hiding. Luckily, the E2M were very good at concealing their identity, and these particular enemies were overseas.

With a price on his head, Daring Bird was torn between leaving his watch over the family and potentially putting them in danger. Living in New York City was hiding in broad daylight, true enough. And he was not an anxious, overtly negative, doom and gloom type person. In fact, quite the opposite. You could not invest your life into running around attempting to make the world a better place if you weren't filled with hope and a dauntless spirit. Daring Bird was a power-of-positive-thinking kind of guy, but his adventures also instilled in him a heightened sense of vigilance. There were millions of people in New York to be lost among, but he was still further aboveground than he preferred. Especially when villains were out to get him.

In the end, despite his mixed emotions, Daring Bird chose to remain close to his sister's brood a while longer. Even if the poop hitting the fan was a fun loving, healthy poop, Daring Bird still had to stick around to make sure his family was safe. If the spirits had felt the need to send him the vision then he needed to see the mission through, and it didn't feel complete yet. Of course, one problem with visions is they don't explain themselves to you.

As the months following the arts festival passed the Littlethumb phenomenon only gained momentum. Daring Bird created a tracking program to run a ticker on the number of times the word "Littlethumb" appeared on the Internet. The ticker eclipsed one million searches in short order and the number grew steadily. To this point the art teacher had done an admirable job of maintaining Littlethumb's anonymity, though he was also driving the narrative and that made Daring Bird leery. If Pettimore or the greasy agent did anything harmful to his nephew, they would have Daring Bird to deal with, which they would not enjoy.

Shortly after Littlethumb painted for the president, Alexi Lawson, the reporter who broke the story at the arts festival, ran a follow-up story on the ever-growing Littlethumb fascination. Daring Bird was on his couch spooning stew into his mouth and channel surfing when he saw "Who is Littlethumb?" on the banner at the bottom of the television screen. He cranked up the volume.

The reporter lady was familiar. She was the same chick from before, only now she was at the news desk giving the story. *Must have got a promotion*, he thought.

". . . and if you happened to see our story six months ago, you were in the know early for what has become quite the Internet sensation. But it's not just an Internet sensation anymore. An anonymous source contacted me with an inside scoop on how far this Littlethumb fixation has traveled, as well as an amazing photo of another painting supposedly created by this supposedly ten-year-old child. You won't believe your eyes when we return."

A commercial, of course. The channel went to advertising as Daring Bird called Elisabeth, who answered after a few rings. "Are you home?"

"Yes."

"Anybody else around?"

"Not really. The kids are goofing off somewhere."

"Turn the TV to News Channel 15. They're talking about the kid again."

"What? Why?"

Daring Bird heard his sister's television come to life on the other end of the line. "I don't know. They teased the story and went to commercial. Will be back on any . . . oh, here it is."

"Welcome back. Before the break, we revisited a story from the Junior Arts Festival several months ago. If you have yet to hear or read the words 'Who is Littlethumb?' you may want to take your pulse and make sure you're still alive. The phenomenon surrounding the unknown artist named Littlethumb and his or her amazing works continues to grow since our story last spring. I have an exclusive new update on the Littlethumb story. What I'm about to show you may seem unbelievable, but I've been assured by my source it's one-hundred percent authentic."

A picture of Littlethumb's *Mona Lisa* flashed onto the screen. Daring Bird's mouth dropped open and he mumbled the words, "Son of a bitch," with a mouth full of stew. On the other end of the line Elisabeth grunted and frowned at the television.

"I know what you're thinking," the reporter continued. "What does Leonardo da Vinci's *Mona Lisa* have to do with this? Well, this is not Leonardo's painting. What you see is an exact replica painted by a ten-year-old child. I received no gender information on the child but I was assured by my source Littlethumb is indeed ten years old, and there are numerous witnesses who can corroborate Littlethumb painted this amazing replica, revealing the extent of the young artist's gift."

"I'm going to kill him." Elisabeth spoke calmly, resisting the emotional tempest brewing within.

"My source also tells me there are a handful of very wealthy and famous people who have already paid outrageous amounts of money to have their portrait painted by the mysterious artist. According to the source, the opportunities were rewarded by highest bid and the hopeful models had to sign a contractual agreement to keep Littlethumb's true identity a secret. Upon meeting with the hopeful subject the artist either agrees to paint them, or if not, politely shakes his or her head, offers the would-be model a hug, and leaves the room."

"They forgot the peppermint," Daring Bird said. This comment made Elisabeth laugh. He chuckled with her. On the television the lead anchor also chuckled.

"What a curious story, Alexi," the anchorman said.

"Yes it is, John. Both curious and extremely profitable. We're talking about people paying millions of dollars to have their portrait done by a child. In addition, I have no idea how my source gained a photo of the artist's *Mona Lisa*, as its whereabouts are currently unknown. Meanwhile, the award-winning work from the Junior Arts Festival still sits unclaimed in a storage facility. The word 'Littlethumb' is currently the most frequently searched term on all the major Internet search engines, and to top the whole mystery off, my source told me even the President of the United States sat for the secret artist!"

"Wow! No kidding. Pretty amazing stuff, Alexi."

"Thanks, John. I certainly think so and apparently most of America does too. Now we're all left with one very intriguing unanswered question. Who is Littlethumb?"

The broadcast went to commercial again. Daring Bird turned off the television. "I'm coming over," he said to Elisabeth. "Call Pettimore."

You probably won't be surprised to learn Sawyer Pettimore had a good explanation for the news story. He'd been blackmailed and didn't know else what to do. One day after school he caught a school janitor in the storage closet filled with Littlethumb's artwork.

Littlethumb had left after finishing their painting session. Before locking up his classroom, Sawyer went to urinate. When he returned he found a janitor in his supply closet. The safe with Littlethumb's *Mona Lisa* had been locked, Sawyer was certain. The janitor swore the safe was already open when he entered the closet. Either way, the *Lisa* was exposed.

Realizing he had stumbled upon something secret, the janitor wanted money to keep his mouth shut. Sawyer agreed to pay him five thousand dollars but he didn't trust the man would remain silent. So, after he paid the janitor off he leaked the information to the reporter. Aside from the photo of Littlethumb's *Mona Lisa*, everything else in the news report could already be found on the Internet if someone looked hard enough. Sawyer figured if he stayed ahead of the story he could control the exposure. With the information already out, hopefully the janitor would take his five grand and go away.

You have to understand, Walter and Elisabeth Brooks weren't naïve. Sawyer had become family. The three of them spent many nights discussing over food and wine the development of Littlethumb, and they became fast friends as a result. They wanted to believe him. Yes, doubt about Sawyer had crept into Elisabeth's mind but she actively combatted the feeling. She felt guilty to be suspicious of a loved one.

Unfortunately, her suspicions weren't without merit. Though Sawyer Pettimore sincerely cared for Littlethumb and the Brooks family, he was blind to the reality of his own machinations. Because he meant Littlethumb no harm, he assumed no harm would come. He was simply creating. Sculpting life. That's what artists do.

Daring Bird, being the man he was and despite his power of positive thinking mantra, reserved a certain level of pragmatic skepticism for any situation. This was no different. He found Sawyer's janitor story implausible and voiced his concern to Elisabeth. The cagey uncle no longer trusted the teacher. For once, this was something Walter and Daring Bird saw eye to eye. They didn't care if Sawyer had good intentions, or if he was good-hearted, or if he truly loved Littlethumb and the family. There is a weakness inherent in most men which allows them to ignore all the goodness of their being and instead behave like monsters.

20

When the photo of Litttlethumb's *Mona Lisa* became public the mystery of his identity went international. I suppose on the Internet all content is somewhat international. Making the network news in a foreign country was a different level of fame. For example, when the story of Littlethumb's *Mona Lisa* exploded, Alexi Lawson immediately fielded offers from all of the major cable news channels. She was smoking hot and read copy well.

Whoever hired her would be excited to discover she also liked to fool around with her superiors. Perhaps her new boss wouldn't be interested. They might be someone in an honest, committed relationship. Or her new boss could be a homosexual male, though Alexi had gotten to a few of those dudes already as well. It certainly wouldn't matter if her boss were a woman, that's for sure. She preferred chicks from time to time.

Sorry. I digress. Yes, there was a time in my life when I had a huge crush on Alexi Lawson. She was an unabashed, beautiful spirit. This will most likely be edited out.

Back to the story. Despite the excitement over Littlethumb's *Mona Lisa* and his reported mingling with the world's rich and famous, the "Who is Littlethumb?" phenomenon could have easily fizzled out if not for one detail. Littlethumb was amazingly talented. He would be famous forever unless he actively chose to hide his talent from the world. By all accounts, his anonymity ship had sailed. If his family had burned the rest of his work and he stopped painting, the name "Littlethumb" might have faded into obscurity. Maybe.

Attempts to discover Littlethumb's identity escalated. I give Sawyer Pettimore credit. He did a masterful job of misdirection. He created so much false information no one came close to uncovering the truth. If anyone tried long enough and had the resources, they might've figured the puzzle out eventually, but they wouldn't have time.

For Walter and Elisabeth the revelation of Littlethumb's *Mona Lisa* was perhaps the best thing to happen. Once the painting became public knowledge, a particular fear of the unknown was removed from the equation. The reality was Littlethumb's life had not changed much to date, which is what they had wanted. Sure, he met a handful of famous people, but he was still too young to care. Otherwise his daily and weekly routine stayed the same. He attended school, painted, took his boxing lessons, and spoke very little.

These news reports emerged nearly a year after Littlethumb painted his *Mona Lisa*. The family had spent the year acclimating themselves to Littlethumb's extraordinary talent, and to incredible wealth. Payments for Littlethumb's portrait work made the Brookses remarkably affluent overnight, though to their credit they didn't behave extravagantly. Walter and Elisabeth were thoughtful people who wanted to be wise with the money. They also had to maintain Littlethumb's anonymity. Strength of character kept the family on the right path.

Elisabeth and Walter were in the kitchen prepping dinner. Littlethumb secretly watched his parents. Observing his parents unnoticed was a sneaky habit he thoroughly enjoyed. Most of the time they seemed genuinely happy with one another, happy overall, really, and watching them move around each other comforted Littlethumb. Walter and Elisabeth caught him spying every once in a while, which always caused an entertaining commotion. Sometimes Littlethumb got caught on purpose.

Tonight, however, Littlethumb was not trying to get caught. He wasn't in the mood for a commotion. Nope, he just wanted to relax and allow his parents' warm interactions to soothe his stress. Elisabeth and Walter spoke about their workday while also carrying on the functional dialogue needed to prepare a meal.

His mother was in mid-sentence as she turned to open the refrigerator. Before doing so, her words trailed off. She placed her hands over her belly and silently stared. Affixed to the refrigerator door was a painting by Littlethumb. One of her hands moved to her lips and she turned to look at Walter.

"Do you still wonder what happened?" she asked. The painting was a rudimentary depiction of a stegosaurus. Littlethumb gave her the picture shortly before the Occurrence. "This picture was the last thing I remember him painting before the *Mona Lisa* happened. Do you ever wonder why he went to bed one night a normal little boy who made bad dinosaur drawings and woke up the next day capable of painting like a master?"

"Of course I do. You know I do."

"I know but I like making sure I'm not the only one."

Walter stopped chopping vegetables and pulled Elisabeth in close. "You know, all in all, I think things seem to be going extremely well."

"Yeah, they really are. There's no denying it."

"Nope."

"Do you think, maybe," Elisabeth hesitated. "Maybe we should quit our jobs and manage this situation full time. We can't hide him forever, and to be honest, I don't like waiting around, unsure when people will find out who he is, and who we are. The idea of dealing with all of that madness suddenly. The anticipation is too nerve-wracking. It's starting to drive me crazy. Isn't it starting to drive you crazy?"

"Eh. You know how I am." Walter was proficient at compartmentalizing life. "But, I don't think it's a bad idea to take control of the things we can. The situation has certainly escalated well past a point of no return."

"Right. We decide when and how the world will meet our son."

Littlethumb wondered sarcastically if he got any say in when and how the world would meet him, then smiled and thought about how much he loved his mom and dad.

"It's settled then," Elisabeth said. "High five."

Walter slapped her high-five but did not let go. Their fingers intertwined and they kissed. The kiss was slow and gentle while alluding to future aggression, perhaps later that evening. They returned to the business of cooking and conversation.

"We need to start a charity."

"I wonder how Mark is going to react if…when I quit," Walter responded, back to chopping. Mark was Walter's non-descript boss.

"What do you think will be the best way to tell people, for Littlethumb?" Elisabeth was now wandering in a circle with a colander of fresh snow peas. "I know things will be crazy at first."

Walter reached over and rescued the snow peas, resting them on the counter. "I'm not sure. But however we tell people, once it's out there you and I must have a plan. We have to stick to our guns when it comes to interviews and all the rest of the bullshit."

"Right. I wonder if Sawyer has any ideas on how to reveal Littlethumb's identity."

"Are you kidding?" Walter's response was not overly sarcastic or negative. His tone was exactly the right amount of both.

"Ha, right. That was a dumb thing to say." Elisabeth shook her head. "Speaking of young Mr. Pettimore, what do you think we should do about him?"

"Sawyer's fine. We've kept him reined in for the most part so far, and we'll do so moving forward." Like many others, Walter was blessed with the ability to state with confidence ideas of which he was still attempting to convince himself.

"I know he loves Littlethumb. I can tell. But sometimes, I think he might not be, I don't know." She passed behind her husband, brushing her hand across his back along the way. "I wonder how he'll react to all the attention he might get."

"I know," Walter said. "But in the end, he isn't our biggest concern. Whether we like it or not, we have to be leery of him and remain cautious. As fond as I am of Sawyer, if he does anything to hurt my son I will fuck him up."

"Walter Brooks!"

"I'm just saying . . ."

Don't forget, Littlethumb was still listening, and he was delighted with his daddy. I wish you could've seen his face. I can tell you, his eyes were wide and his mouth was wide open. Unable to hold back any longer, he jumped up and ran into the room with his arms spread open like an airplane. Littlethumb twisted and turned until he found a straight line to Walter's side and crash-landed into a hug formation, arms tightly wrapped around his father.

Sawyer was more than a little surprised when Elisabeth called him with the plan to unveil Littlethumb's identity. Wait, "Plan" is not quite correct. "Intent" is more accurate.

The time had arrived for the Brookses to introduce their son to the world and see what happened next. Sawyer had been prepared for Walter and Elisabeth to need significantly more coaxing to be ready for this. The fact they reached this decision much sooner than he expected, and of their own accord, was further validation he was going about things correctly. Elisabeth wanted to hear his ideas about the reveal. Sawyer had been visualizing the possibilities for a while and did not hold back his enthusiasm for their decision, or the fact he was prepared with several different scenarios.

A traditional press conference was the first idea to get nixed. Boring. Next, please. They discussed a surprise revelation to catch the media off guard. Perhaps an organized wild goose chase which could extend the process into a slow reveal? Not bad. That could be a lot of fun. They could pick a specific journalist for a one-on-one interview. Blah. They could play one last joke on everyone, revealing Littlethumb to be some-one else and having a big "gotcha!" moment before finally introducing him. Better. This led to big laughs when Heather proposed the idea of presenting Jojo Monkey to the world as the amazing Littlethumb. Jojo, who was present at the time, appeared to get the joke.

In the end, they decided an exciting way to introduce Littlethumb would be an invitation-only gallery opening of his work. The scenario was one of Sawyer's dreams. He was beyond exuberant when Walter and Elisabeth brought the idea up on their own.

<h1 align="center">21</h1>

When his parents asked about his interest in an exhibit, Littlethumb did not respond right away. Instead, he made that thoughtful little face of his. Walter and Elisabeth both knew the meaning of the expression.

Elisabeth leaned forward and said, "Why don't you think about it and let us know?"

Littlethumb retreated to his room and sought the advice of his toy collection. He sat quietly with the council in front of him. At this point, his high council was under the command of its first female chairman. I suppose I should say *chairperson*? No, that's not fair either. Is *chairwoman* a word? Has to be. Anyway, Catrina Courage was the leader of The Courage Girls, a teenage group of superhero chicks, and she was also in the middle of her stint as the head of Littlethumb's high council. Not surprisingly, Catrina reminded Littlethumb of his mom.

The council agreed the art show sounded like a lot of fun. A few reservations were voiced during the meeting, but overall the idea was well received. Once the decision was made, Littlethumb informed his parents he was on board. He opened his door and whistled. When they looked over, he held his hand out with his thumb up and an affirmative nod of his head.

His father said, "Okay then," and both his parents nodded an affirmative back at him in unison, wearing intense facial expressions. Their affirmation acknowledged, Littlethumb returned to his room to get a few sit-ups and push-ups in before bedtime.

Dick Mann would announce Littlethumb's exhibit to the world. There was no press conference or promotional release. A more subversive approach was taken. Dick casually mentioned the event to paparazzi gathered outside his building one day. Within minutes his phone started ringing. He was besieged with calls from members of the media who wanted more information and social elites who wanted an invitation.

At Freddy's suggestion the exhibit was planned for the night of April Fool's Day. He thought making people wonder if the event was some sort of trick would be fun. Dick gave the kid high marks for the idea. One hundred of Littlethumb's pieces would be on display for purchase. All profits would go to charity. As the cherry on top, Tommy Toxic and The Pond Scum would perform during the first hour of the show.

The exhibit was about two months away, which left plenty of time to plan and create a guest list. Any A-list celebrity who happened to be invited shat on their previous schedule to attend Littlethumb's opening instead. Meanwhile, upon the show's announcement, most of the media gave up their search for Littlethumb's identity and began speculating about the art show. The careers of numerous interns were made or broken while trying to provide talking heads with new information to report on the exhibit.

The coverage was endless. Who was invited? What would they wear? Who would cater the event and what food would they serve? Who would decorate? Speaking of which, where would the event take place? At the time, Littlethumb and his family didn't pay much attention to the media coverage. The family kept the television turned off, went about their normal business as much as possible, and spent time helping Littlethumb select paintings to display in the show. Littlethumb had compiled quite a portfolio.

Exhibit day arrived. Speculations the whole thing was a hoax hit their apex. Meanwhile, the exhibit's location remained unknown. On the morning of the event, Dick Mann announced via his website that he had purchased an abandoned building on the other side of the East River, in Astoria, and was going to turn the property into an art space. Lofts would be available for young artists to rent on the cheap so they could practice their craft. The building's first floor would house galleries where their work could be displayed for purchase.

Dick was a progressive thinker who understood investing in the city's trendy youth would eventually make him a fortune. Kids would dig hanging out in the neighborhood where these artists lived. After the kids deemed the area a cool place to be seen, eventually, people with money would think hanging out in a shitty part of town was cool too. Once the money started flowing, if you owned real estate or businesses in the area you would make a fortune. He'd seen this happen so many times before. Neighborhoods rose and fell in his hometown over the course of his life, making some men rich while sending the over-invested to the poor house.

Anyway, the cherry on top of Dick's big announcement was his building would also be the location of Littlethumb's exhibit. The invited guests received the address shortly after his announcement. Anyone else was welcome to stand outside the building to cheer the event and watch the guests arrive, but they had to figure out the building's location on their own.

Remember, Dirty Dick Mann loves you, but the extra N is for naughty.

Of course, Dick leaked the address to the public. No reason to risk people not finding the place. As rumor spread throughout the city, by early evening, an enormous crowd gathered in front of the building. Reporters flocked to the scene. People still questioned if the whole thing was a hoax. Many people wondered if they had been tricked and the real party was happening elsewhere. All speculation came to an end when the first celebrity arrived in a 1939 Packard hearse. Smoke billowed from the doors as they opened. There was a quick hush of anticipation as the crowd waited to see who had arrived.

Tommy Toxic and The Pond Scum triumphantly exited the Packard amidst the smoke, a smashingly dressed groupie on every arm. The crowd went crazy. The two women on either side of Tommy were both old enough to be his mother, but they were pawing at him like he was the Greek god Eros.

Other celebrities followed. Of specific note to you, dear reader, was the lovely C. C. Constantine. Daring Bird inconspicuously ensured her inclusion on the guest list. Their opportunities to see each other in person were rare.

Not all the attendees were celebrities. Many guests were fabulously wealthy, but relatively unknown to the public, while the

Brookses insisted common folk be in attendance as well. Family and colleagues were on the list. Special guests such as cancer patients and children from a local orphanage were invited. Overall, between two hundred and fifty to three hundred people attended the opening.

The building itself was an old, four-story brick factory that backed up to the river. I believe it may have originally been a fishery. Converted into lofts years earlier when there was speculation the neighborhood would gentrify, another real estate deal had fallen through causing the area to stay low-rent. Thus, the owner turned the floor space into a bunch of tiny, shitty apartments with a couple of community bathrooms on each floor and then let the place go to hell. By the time Dick Mann bought the building it was abandoned once again.

The exhibit was on the fourth floor, which Dick had converted back to open loft space. The building had only a single, large cargo elevator. As the guests entered they took turns waiting on the red carpet for the elevator. When they reached the fourth floor they were greeted by coat attendants, champagne, and a fantastic view of Manhattan. An hour of mingling with music and cocktails began the evening.

None of Littlethumb's paintings displayed a price. Each piece was to be sold through silent auction, with a starting bid listed on each painting's informational placard. Littlethumb's *Mona Lisa* was on prominent display in the center of the room but was not for sale. The painting was there to remind people of the young artist's capabilities while they placed bids on the other paintings.

Once everyone was inside, Dick Mann called for their attention.

"Greetings, greetings everyone. Thank you very much for attending. What an exciting evening, and what a handsome room! I see several of you out there I haven't had the chance to dance with yet, and if your reputations are as true as mine, we should definitely be dancing. And by dancing, of course, I mean screwing."

Most everybody laughed. That was Dick Mann for you. As a younger human I often envied those lovable rogues who are able to get away with being sexual scoundrels, until I realized being "that guy" was a full-time job.

"I don't want to take much of your time blabbing away," Dick continued, "when there is wonderful art, music, delicious food, and expensive booze to enjoy. But I do want to take a brief moment to introduce you to an old friend of mine. In many ways, he's the reason you're all here tonight. A fine artist in his own right, my good friend Sawyer discovered the amazing Littlethumb. Ladies and gentlemen, please put your hands together, as I take great pleasure introducing you to Mr. Sawyer Pettimore."

This was a big moment for Sawyer, one he had always dreamed of, though in his dreams it was his art on display. Sawyer made a brief speech, thanking everyone again for attending and making sure they all understood the paintings were to be sold by silent auction. He explained Littlethumb would be introduced a little later in the evening after spending some time mingling with the crowd incognito.

"That's right. Our guest of honor thought it might be fun to spend a little time wandering the room, so you might want to be careful what you say. You never know who could be listening." A brief rumble of appropriate crowd noise confirmed the guests all thought this was fabulous. "So," Sawyer continued. "Let's get things started shall we? Ladies and gentlemen, please put your hands together for Tommy Toxic and The Pond Scum."

Tommy had recently decided to expand his repertoire musically. He penned an acoustic album and stripped down his punk caterwauling in an effort to show his more thoughtful, deep, romantic side. The problem was he didn't have that side. Also, he wasn't a skilled vocalist. He could be a punk and scream and do playful, crazy things with his voice. Trying to carry an actual tune in a bucket proved impossible for him.

The set was not well received. To be frank, the band was awful. They were all super high on an assortment of drugs and out of sync with one another. When Tommy realized how poorly the set was going he got rattled and forgot some of his lyrics. He went on a multi-instrumental solo rant, kicking the rest of his band off stage. He played everything, drums, guitar, bass, ignoring the silence when he put one instrument down and moved to another. The set finished with Tommy stomping around the stage smashing his guitars and calmly asking the audience, "Is this what you want?" Then he flipped everyone his middle finger, bowed, and left the stage. People applauded because he was Tommy Toxic, but not the way people were *supposed* to applaud Tommy Toxic.

When his show was over Tommy was earnestly disheartened. It was bad enough everybody was sucking off this Littlethumb kid, but to blow his opportunity to steal the spotlight and make sure everyone remembered who the real star was? To fail so miserably? The thought was more than Tommy could bear so he went looking for comfort from the only person he almost trusted. "They hated me," he whimpered.

"I warned you, kid," Dick said. "People don't like new shit. People want the same shit over and over again. And why is that?"

"Because people are stupid."

"That's right. People are stupid."

"But I wasn't any good."

Dick looked down and saw tears well up in Tommy's eyes. Tears and anger. "Hey kiddo, look, if you want to make those songs, make those songs. You're Tommy fucking Toxic. People may need some time to get used to the new style, and you'll have to practice to make shit sound right, but you have all the resources in the world. It'll just take some time."

"I don't want to be here anymore. I'm leaving. Will you leave with me, please?"

"What? No. I can't do that. I'm the freaking host, kid. It's almost time to introduce LT."

"Please don't stay. Come with me."

Dick had honestly never seen Tommy behave this way, and he took note. "Why don't you stick around here with me?"

"I don't want to be here anymore," Tommy repeated. "I have to go. Please, come home with me. This party sucks." He sniffled as he spoke and ran his forearm across his face, trying to hide a few tears escaping his eyes. Tommy Toxic took Dick's hand.

"Sheesh. What's with you, kid?" Dick said, pulling his hand away. He softened instantly, putting both hands on Tommy's shoulders. "Look, tough guy, go ahead and get out of here. I'll be right behind you in a couple of hours. When I get home, we'll smoke a bowl and watch a movie together, or play some video games or some shit. Let me get through this nonsense and I'll leave as soon as I can. Okay?"

Tommy remained silent as he looked up at his surrogate father. His bottom lip quivered briefly then he steeled his chin, nodded, and turned to walk away. Dick turned his attention back to the events at hand as Tommy headed for the stairs leading to the building's roof. A helicopter waited for what was supposed to be his grand exit. Do you have any idea how disheartening life can be when you're leaving a party via helicopter from a rooftop and no one bothers to watch or cheer or wave goodbye?

During the first half of the party, the Brooks family mingled inconspicuously. Knowing their secret, they were unabashed about presenting themselves to the famous guests. Walter or Elisabeth would say hello and introduce their family to various people, presenting their children as, "Our oldest Heather, our son Freddy, and our youngest," always stopping without having given Littlethumb's name. Then the family would chuckle or snicker at their secret joke.

Guests reacted in various ways. Some didn't notice the odd introduction, as they were too self-absorbed to care. Some would laugh with the family, purely out of social conditioning, with no idea why they were laughing. Some would ask the youngest child's name only to have the subject changed by Walter or Elisabeth. A few guests bent down to ask Littlethumb directly.

"And what about you, little fella? Do you have a name?"

Littlethumb would smile and nod, and maybe giggle a little. Typically, the adults found his behavior curious and chuckled with him.

When the witching hour for the big announcement arrived, Sawyer called for everyone's attention and introduced Walter Brooks. Walter greeted the guests again and thanked them for coming. Without further ado, he introduced his son. The crowd applauded and cheered. "He's really a child!" "I knew he was a boy!" "I still don't believe it!" "Hey, I met that kid!"

Walter stood with his arm around Littlethumb's shoulders. "Now, my son is a quiet child and this is, as you might imagine, very new to him and to all of us. So, Littlethumb will not be available for questions.

However, we think we have something more fun in store for you. I will answer any questions I can for a few minutes. Then, in order to prove our son is indeed the artist you are looking for, Littlethumb will pick someone from the audience and paint their portrait right here, this evening."

The crowd applauded this revelation with a bevy of oohs and ahs.

"Now," Walter continued. "Littlethumb may not finish the portrait tonight. We will see. If he doesn't finish, we'll make sure to schedule a session to complete the portrait at a later date. So, at this time I will take your questions while LT makes his way around the room to choose his model. I ask you to please respect the process and allow him to move about freely. Please don't take it personally if you aren't chosen. There are nearly three hundred people in this room and he's only picking one of you. Let's all keep this positive, have fun, and be happy for the lucky winner."

Walter Brooks exuded confidence and kindness, commanding the attention of even the wealthiest and most influential guests in the room to respect his wishes in regards to his son. He looked down at Littlethumb and said, "All right kid, go have fun."

Littlethumb left his father's side and moved about the crowd, looking for the subject who inspired him the most. Walter answered questions about his child from the media and other guests. After about ten minutes Littlethumb chose a wild-eyed young girl from the group of orphans for his subject. As he led her through the crowd, the room was rocked by an explosion.

Early accounts of the tragedy had little information. Breaking news reports followed the incident, interrupting regularly scheduled programming. Firefighters had arrived at the scene and were battling the blaze. Police had successfully moved the crowds outside to a safe distance. Due to the enormous amounts of paint and alcohol in the loft, by the time fire crews had arrived they were unable to stop the inferno.

The firefighters contained the fire by hosing down the surrounding structures. As the battle wore on the firefighters, police, emergency medical teams, and crowd of onlookers all watched as the building burned through the night. The next day, news outlets reported only two people survived the fire. The survivors' identities remained undisclosed. Everyone else inside had perished.

Part II

22

You know how when you sneeze, if your eyelids are somehow open your eyeballs will supposedly pop out of your head? Not true. The world freezes. Okay, maybe not every time, but that's what happened to Littlethumb. In hindsight I don't think his open eyelids had anything to do with the situation. That was pure happenstance. And his eyeballs certainly didn't pop out of their sockets.

We are in the past again, as far back as this story will go, in the Brooks' apartment on the day of the Occurrence. Littlethumb has just sneezed. He was standing in the bathroom with the faucet running as he wetted his hair for combing. He was about to step over to the toilet for a pee when it happened. Truth be told, it wasn't even a powerful sneeze.

The first thing he noticed was the water pouring from the faucet suddenly stopped. A stream of water floated between faucet and basin. Littlethumb mouthed the word "whoa" and passed his hand through the water. His hand emerged from the stream wet, but the water otherwise remained in place, suspended in midair.

Littlethumb was suddenly frightened. He opened the bathroom

door and stuck his head into the hallway. Silence. He looked up and down the hallway. Still no noise. Very disconcerting.

Out of the bathroom he crept. The air felt different somehow. Scary. He tiptoed to Heather's bedroom, the next closest door, peeking inside to find his sister frozen in mid-step. A tug at her shirt did not insight reanimation. An arm moved a little when he pulled but the rest of her body remained motionless. Littlethumb's lip quivered as tears puddled behind his eyes, but before he fell into a panic he forced himself to move on and examine the rest of his family. He found his brother and father in the same catatonic state as his sister but was able to maintain his courage. When he saw his mother, he broke down, right there on the kitchen floor.

As the tears eventually began to slow he was struck by a startling recognition. Littlethumb knew if he opened the door and left their apartment, everywhere else would be exactly the same. He was alone.

After the first wave of tears had fully passed, Littlethumb remained on the floor staring at his mother and sniffling for a bit. Inevitably he asked himself questions. First and foremost, was his family still alive? Though afraid of what he might find, he stood up and walked over to his mom to find out if she was still breathing.

There wasn't much to ascertain from ground level so he pulled a chair from the kitchen table over in front of Elisabeth. He stood on the seat of the chair and looked into her eyes. They seemed the same as before. Littlethumb had recently seen the open eyes of a dead person for the first time. After returning from a rainy Satur-day afternoon movie, the family had found Kicking Rocks forever asleep in his rocking chair, eyes wide open. His mother's eyes didn't look like Kicking Rocks' had. They looked alive, a glimmer of hope.

Littlethumb placed his ear against his mother's chest and wrapped his arm around her back, holding his head tightly against her as he listened intently. A heartbeat! The sound was faint but definitely there. This brought a smile to his face. Something crazy was happening, but at least he knew his mother was alive. Sort of.

Littlethumb listened to his mother's heartbeat again. Yep, still there. The soft, rhythmic thump was music to his ears.

Upon further examination he noticed something odd. The sound was faint but not weak, as if his mother's heart was beating strongly but from a great distance away. Littlethumb found this extremely curious, then realized he should check to see if the rest of his family's hearts were beating as well. His natural inclination was to believe they were and he moved quickly to discover if he was correct. Once he confirmed the rest of his family was still alive, Littlethumb wandered into the den and flopped onto the couch.

No TV? Well that sucks. He looked around the room. None of the clocks within view were changing time, which made sense under the circumstances, he supposed. But what was he going to do?

I'll tell you what he did, he fell asleep. All the emotional intensity wore him out and eventually Littlethumb dozed off on the couch. After a long, much needed nap, he woke up and reviewed the situation. A quick status update confirmed he could still hear his family's hearts beating, so that was good.

With his family's vitals checked, the notion suddenly struck him to look out the window. He opened the blinds and surveyed the street below. Nothing moved. People were frozen mid-step, cars were stuck in place, cyclists were perched motionless on their bikes, birds were suspended in mid-air, and dogs were stiff as a board, tails motionless. Previous theory on the outside world confirmed.

As he soaked in the reality before him, Littlethumb's stomach grumbled. Unaccustomed to feeding himself, he wondered what he would eat, then realized he could eat anything he desired. Wait a minute. Not only could he eat whatever he wanted, he could *do* whatever he wanted. Who knew how long this would last? Everything could unfreeze at any given moment. Littlethumb decided he better take advantage of this situation. He started by eating an entire bag of powdered sugar donuts.

Littlethumb tore through the house and got into all sorts of trouble a ten-year-old might get into when home alone: sister's diary, brother's comic books, parents' everything! The unadulterated jubilance of silliness unbound. Nonsense was blabbered at normally inappropriate decibels. Jumps were jumped on the bed. Circles were run in circles until dizziness wrestled him giggling to the floor.

Yes, playtime was a blast. For a while. Eventually, reality set back in and the quiet dampened his mood again. Then he busied himself with cleanup, leery his parents might suddenly return to life and ground him. No trace was left of his escapades.

I cannot tell you how long he was in this other realm. I don't know. The sun never set and the clocks didn't move, making the passage of time difficult to measure. When Littlethumb slept, he never knew for how long. I suppose he could've tracked time by keeping a continual count in his head and making a record in a notebook, but he didn't. He was a child after all, and there were so many things to think about.

Eventually, Littlethumb felt a significant amount of time must have passed. He had fallen asleep on several occasions. Every time he woke, his family seemed no worse for wear. Still frozen, hearts still beating. In what I can only assume were the first several days, his emotions spiked in several directions. Obviously he had some moments of unmitigated joy, as any child might with the sudden realization they have complete freedom. However, these moments of joy quickly spiraled into the chasm-like depths of fear any child might feel with the sudden realization that no one was around to protect them.

As he grew more accustomed to the situation, two concepts became clear. First, he had no idea if and when his family would get out of their frozen state. (Or if he would ever return to them, depending on how you choose to view the circumstances). Second, he felt the presence of something else. The air felt different, as if some formless creature Littlethumb couldn't see was nearby. He felt like it was reaching for him, whatever *it* was. Understandably, this frightened him.

Littlethumb decided the best way to deal with this situation was to set out on a quest. He would leave his home and have an adventure. Travel the world, journey to the ends of the Earth if he so desired, and return home a man. A note would be left for his family just in case the world unfroze while he was away. So that was the plan. The decision was made. He would prepare for adventure. But first, a mission inside the building.

There was a lady who lived on the second floor he saw fairly often. Sometimes she was coming home at the same time as him and they wound up on an elevator together. Littlethumb was always disappointed he only got to ride with her for one floor. She smelled nice and he thought she was pretty. Without fully understanding why he was so compelled, before he left for his journey he would venture downstairs and get a look at those boobies.

Get a look at those boobies he certainly did. Oh, and he traveled this entire world alone for an unspecified amount of time. I'm sure you can imagine on your own all manner of things a boy could do and discover when left to his own devices on a planet frozen in time. Well, he did those things, and if you run out of your own ideas of all the fun that could be had, ask the reader next to you what they imagined, or would imagine if they haven't read this far yet. If the reader next to you is a guy, I bet the answer is more boobs.

The sun never rose or fell as he travelled, but instead continuously cast the glow of early morning. Until, of course, Littlethumb was on a different part of the planet. There were lands he traveled forever frozen at dusk, others midday, and others the darkest of night. No surprise his journeys through the dark places were the scariest.

Although he slept, Littlethumb's urges for food and rest were sporadic at best. The longer the world remained frozen, the longer Littlethumb could go without either. He didn't grow physically during the Occurrence, and despite hours upon hours of silent contemplation he remained a child emotionally as well, albeit an increasingly thoughtful one.

I've played with some math regarding the duration of Littlethumb's adventure. The Earth is a little under twenty-five thousand miles around at the equator. If Littlethumb had walked ten miles a day, he would've needed four and half years to circle the Earth. Now, he was able to use bicycles, skateboards, rowboats, and many other types of self-propelled machines that sped travel up considerably, but if you balance that against the fact he was a child who didn't cover much ground when he was forced to walk, and was not always travelling a straight path, I believe he might have been in this frozen world all alone for up to five years.

During his journey Littlethumb made two significant discoveries. First, the presence he felt in his home had followed him. No matter how hard he tried to outrun the specter, the uncomfortable feeling always came back. He feared an evil spirit stalked him, though the presence didn't particularly feel evil. The feeling was more off-putting than evil. Creepy. That's the word. He feared a creepy spirit stalked him.

Second, and perhaps more importantly, over time Littlethumb realized he could perceive more than the physical world. The light and the darkness inside living creatures became visible. Littlethumb sensed the light and the dark were good and evil. All of the frozen animals were nothing but light. Plants? Light. The only darkness? You guessed it, people.

For most people their internal auras were at least a little more light than dark, but the forces were amorphous and always trying to spread. The darkness consumed some people, and the light consumed others, but most of us simply looked grey.

As time wore on, the looming specter that plagued his journey seemed to grow larger and closer to Littlethumb. He felt its presence more strongly and frequently. The time had come to confront his stalker. The question was, how?

Many miles later, Littlethumb was in Asia, having recently crossed into Northwest China when he decided to abruptly turn around. This wasn't the first time. He had whirled around on numerous occasions to no avail, yelling, "Ha!" or "Who's there?" only to find silence in response. This time his sneak attack worked. He spun on his heels, holding his walking staff in front of him in an attack position. There, caught by complete surprise, was Grandpa Kicking Rocks.

No, Kicking Rocks had not been haunting his grandson. As it turns out, after his death, Kicking Rocks awoke in a spirit world. Having seen the sadness in his family, and especially in Littlethumb, Kicking Rocks refused to leave them and move on to whatever the real afterlife was. Thinking they can somehow comfort loved ones they've left behind is a typical mistake made by the newly dead. Everybody knows there are all kinds of ghosts who hang about, refusing to move on to their next life. What no one knew with any appreciable level of certainty though, until Littlethumb, was the existence of a place between our world and the afterlife. The spirit world he discovered is conceptually similar to purgatory but without all the dogma about sin.

Kicking Rocks explained that although Littlethumb was pulled into the spirit world, Kicking Rocks hadn't been able to communicate with him. Attempt after attempt, he tried and tried to no avail, and eventually Littlethumb started running from him. Every time he felt like he was close to making contact, Littlethumb would get spooked and take off. Over time, Littlethumb's connection with the spirit world must have grown stronger. They both agreed that's why he began to see the lightness and the darkness in people, and why he'd finally seen Kicking Rocks. Their theory was further validated as

Littlethumb began to see more and more of the ghosts floating about our world.

To this day I don't know how or why Littlethumb wound up there, though Kicking Rocks frequently apologized for the incident. He'd been attempting to contact Littlethumb, to say goodbye and tell the boy a final thing or two about life, and must've somehow pulled him out of place. "I wanted to help you fulfill your destiny," Kicking Rocks said. "I tried to contact you from the spirit world and I must have somehow pulled you out of place, between the worlds of the living and the dead. Sorry about that."

Kicking Rocks might have been convinced he was at fault but Littlethumb didn't think his grandfather had caused the Occurrence. No, Littlethumb was convinced the event had something to do with his wide-eyed sneeze.

If Littlethumb's connection to the spirit world had grown, Kicking Rocks worried his connection to the living world might fade. Thus, they decided to travel back home to New York. Neither was quite sure what would happen when they got there, but they didn't know what else to do.

As they made their way, along with many other questions, Littlethumb asked what his grandpa had meant about Littlethumb's destiny. Kicking Rocks admitted he had no idea about the boy's destiny and explained how disorienting the transition is from life to death.

"When you realize you're somehow still alive, that you've beaten death and are somehow still you, this can make you feel more important than you are. I was filled with many grand notions. One of which was that you were destined for greatness, and I would help you fulfill your destiny." When Littlethumb asked him what destiny was, Kicking Rocks said, "I'm not certain. I'm sorry. I was a crazy old dead man who thought he had cheated death. Don't get me wrong, boy. You are a different breed. I've always known that. I knew you were special when I was alive."

Littlethumb thanked his grandpa, then explained to Kicking Rocks he still didn't understand what destiny meant. Sure, he was in some special place between the real world and the spirit world, but he was still only ten years old and literally did not know the meaning of the word destiny. Kicking Rocks laughed and told him to look the word up in a dictionary when he got home.

They eventually made their way back to New York City. Although he adored his grandfather and was hesitant to say goodbye again, Littlethumb desperately missed the rest of his clan. He wanted to know the world would move forward again, that his family would be okay. When he and Kicking Rocks arrived at the apartment Littlethumb was pleased to see everyone still safely frozen in time, hearts beating from somewhere off in the existential distance. Littlethumb wondered aloud how things would get back to normal.

"I'm not sure," Kicking Rocks said. "I think perhaps they will get back to normal because they're supposed to. I believe my time here is over. I need to finish my journey to wherever I'm going, and you need to finish yours as well." Kicking Rocks paused as Littlethumb spoke, then replied to his grandson, "That's right. Can't leave the game on pause forever."

Their last bit of time together was spent quietly, much like when Kicking Rocks was alive. The old ghost man explained a whittling technique to his grandson he'd meant to teach him before being caught off guard by death, then watched the boy practice the carving motion until he began to yawn. If Littlethumb was tired, Kicking Rocks suggested it might be a good idea for him to sleep in his own bed. The boy agreed, and they headed for his room.

For some reason Littlethumb put on the same pajamas he was wearing the morning the world froze. He crawled into bed and tucked himself in as his grandfather watched. Being a ghost, Kicking Rocks couldn't do much to help with the blankets. Once Littlethumb was snugly under the covers, Kicking Rocks wished his grandson well and began to leave. Before he could float out of the room, Littlethumb asked Kicking Rocks to stay until he fell asleep, a request to which the old, dead grandpa readily agreed. Littlethumb kept his eyes open, chatting quietly with Kicking Rocks for as long as he possibly could, until eventually, sleep laid its mighty will upon him.

23

I'm taking you back to the much more recent past…

We've returned to the Coney Island boardwalk. At the end of a slow day Smith, our caricature artist, gathered his things to head for home. He motioned a farewell to the cotton candy guy and headed off on foot, arms full.

Smith lived above a twenty-four-hour, greasy spoon diner in a noisy shopping district. Inside his apartment was larger than you might expect, as the space had originally been two separate units. A few years after he moved in the renters in the unit next door had vacated. Smith put his name on the lease and combined the apartments.

You might be surprised to learn the rooms were filled with high-end computer technology, gadgets, gizmos, beeping things, and pulsing lights. Or you might not be surprised at all. Either way, this stuff filled many rooms of the apartment. The living room resembled a command center of some sort. In the far left corner a computer server sat in a padlocked cage. One side of the cage was painted to resemble a bulbous-headed alien brandishing a ray gun. All of the windows were fully draped, which was a bummer. The artificial light that filled the room was lame, but the shading was a necessary evil. No need for prying eyes.

Cathouses were strewn throughout the place. Monkey bars hung from the ceiling by chains. There were rope swings as well. Over in the corner a diminutive, elderly monkey slept on top of one of the cathouses. At the sound of Smith's arrival, three younger monkeys filed into the room to greet him. Sir Alister Pickney, Stevie Two-Sharks, and Zeus formed a straight line and saluted the arrival of their pack leader with tiny monkey paw to tiny monkey forehead.

Smith set the tools of his day job down by the front door and kicked off his shoes. Then a quick check on the old fella in the corner. He laid his hand on the monkey's side belly and felt the slight up-and-down breathing motion. Good, still alive. Smith patted the little guy gently on his head, careful not to wake him.

When he turned to walk away the other monkeys confronted him. They made combat maneuvers. With a screech from Zeus they attacked. Smith raised a forearm to protect his face. With one hand, he intercepted a monkey in mid-air. Tamarins are small creatures, maybe a few pounds fully grown. Their attacks, although not without fervor, were easy to defend. And a lot of fun. Smith made his way to the kitchen, wrestling his friends along the way.

You might be wondering about all the poop and whether or not the place stunk to high heaven? The monkeys were trained toilet artists, so the poop was not a problem. Their body funk was a different story. Smith went through a lot of incense and candles.

Once dinner was served and eaten, Smith made his way to one of the many computers in the main room. With a shimmy of the mouse, the computer hummed back to life.

Our caricature artist had a second job. Smith was the founder and sole operator of the One Dollar Prayers charity and the onedollarprayers.com website. Onedollarprayers.com was a website where a user could donate a dollar and make a prayer request. The dollar would get donated to charity, and the prayer requests would be honored daily. Smith designed the website and built its following. He also did the praying.

Calling Smith's spiritual exercise "praying" probably isn't the most accurate description. Meditation is more precise. Either way, Smith printed the prayer requests daily, read them, sat with them quietly in the small bedroom he had designated a meditation area, and at the end of each session he burned the list.

One hundred percent of the money donated to the website was funneled directly to a charity. Smith paid the operation fees out of his own pocket. For the first three weeks of every month, users submitted nominations for eligible charities to the website. On the last week of every month the users voted on which organization would receive the money. To ensure the donors knew where their money was going, all of One Dollar Prayers' financials could be viewed on the website.

Smith remained anonymous as the charity's administrator. The website had developed a modest regular following and received thousands of daily hits worldwide. Nevertheless, as popular as onedollarprayers.com had become, with the amount of nonsense there was on the Internet the site broadly went unnoticed. Despite the charity's financial transparency, if someone were to research One Dollar Prayers' origin or ownership, they would get lost in a never-ending loop of umbrella companies. Not that anyone ever bothered.

Smith printed the day's list of prayer requests and prepared for his evening quiet time. As he walked to his meditation area, along the way he left his beach hat and lanyard on a hook in the hallway. Removal of the lanyard revealed a small key hung on a thin chain around his neck. We'll get to that later.

The mediation chamber was sparse, and dark. The windows were shaded like the rest of the apartment. There was no alter or statue. No idols, totems, or decorations of any kind. Just a rug for the man and several pillows for the monkeys. Before he sat down and closed his eyes, candles and incense were lit. As Smith prepared the young ruffian monkeys joined him, taking the lotus position on their pillows.

Honoring the prayer requests made the charitable organism function properly. The website generated a good deal of money. Performing the prayers was Smith's duty and maintained the spiritual circle he'd created. In order to prove to the site's followers their prayer requests were being honored, Smith filmed the evening sessions. He posted the video live on the Internet. Anyone who so desired could join him online in that evening's meditation session, which he encouraged. The more energy provided to the exercise the better. During the tapings the camera showed Smith from behind and at ground level, sitting peacefully with his shrine of live monkeys before him.

Smith also had a camera filming the monkeys while they meditated. Those clips were posted on an Internet video-sharing platform under the name "Meditations with Monkeys." The monkeys' channel had more followers and received more hits than onedollarprayers.com, which Smith found hilarious and depressing at the same time.

Once meditations were finished Smith headed for his studio. If Smith were one to talk, he might have admitted to the monkeys he was having trouble getting the little girl's nanny out of his head. His voice wasn't necessary though. I think the room full of paintings of her, which had accumulated since the day they met, spoke loud and clear. Smith switched on the light to his studio and scanned the room. Everywhere he looked her face was staring back at him. He sighed the sigh of ten thousand lovelorn nerds. What the fuck was he going to do about this?

For the time being, Smith was going to paint. He sat down at a piano in the corner of the room and played several notes. Handwritten sheet music rested on the piano. Unusual symbols were scrawled on the sheet music in its own format, not standard music notation. Smith played a few notes for inspiration. The exercise was intended to strike an immediate emotional chord within him. The mechanism never failed. Smith stood and moved to his painting station, a fresh canvas already waiting for him. He closed his eyes for a moment, breathed deeply, and opened them again. Why bother trying to paint anything else?

The artist worked feverishly, almost in a hypnotic state. Paint flew with urgency, desperation. The brush wasn't an instrument to utilize but rather a sage. An inanimate prophet determined to show Smith the secrets of his heart.

And there she was. This time Smith was staring at her from afar. She was a shadow in the distance on the beach, looking back at him and encouraging him to chase after her.

That was the problem, though, wasn't it? There was no way of chasing after her. He should have acted when he had the chance. Of course, he had no idea she would haunt him like this. How could he have known? Sure, she was gorgeous, she couldn't speak or hear, and she had probably the most beautiful aura he'd ever seen. So yeah, she was the perfect woman for him, but that's a lot to process in, what, the ten minutes she was standing there? Fuck!

This was what life had been for days now. The woman's name and face commandeered his mind, with marching orders on his heart. Maria. God, she was magnificent.

Anyway, with yet another painting of her finished he left the canvas to dry, turning off the studio lights as he vacantly ambled back into the family room where the monkeys were watching television. The old fella was awake, sitting on the couch with the remote next to him. The other three respectfully sat in a row to their senior's left. Don't get too excited. They didn't know how to change channels, though Smith had taught them how to push the button that turned the magic on.

He flopped down on the couch with his pals. What was she doing to him? He knew damn well what she was doing to him. This was an artist who lived a life of stoic solitude. A man and his monkeys. His emotions were not to be stirred like this. Besides, there was absolutely no way on this giant planet to find her, you jackass. You let her walk right away. Chicken shit. That's what that was. So, Smith came to the same realization he had come to every night since the Fourth of July. He'd blown it.

There was a good chance he'd met the woman of his dreams. Whether he was interested in meeting her or not was irrelevant. You don't get to choose everything in life. Sometimes, life insists you take things as they come. Yep. He'd blown it.

The only way he would see her again was if she came looking for him. That was the unfortunate truth. You were supposed to be a man. You man up and go after what you want in life. You choked, kid. You stood at the line with a chance to tie and shot an airball. Argh!

He couldn't sit in this homemade vexation stew anymore. Push-ups, pull-ups, and sit-ups for the win. Calisthenics to cure the lonely heart. There had been a lot of exercise since the Fourth of July. Unfortunately for Smith, no amount of exercise would fix what ailed him. A specific type of exercise would help temporarily, true, but the activity required a second person, and thanks to this Maria lady, none of the other persons available would suffice.

Surely to God she would come back. There was no way he was the only one who felt the connection. She had to have felt the energy too. Right? She felt the relentless force of nature and would come back to see him again because she would know there was no other way. He gave her the drawing. She knew what was up. What was he worried about? Only five days or so had passed. Not even a full week. She would come back.

Poor fella.

24

Calculating the endless amount of consequences initiated by an event like the fire at Littlethumb's exhibit would be impossible. So many lives were affected in so many different ways. If historians did research, at best they would need to select only a few storylines to document. They would grow old and die before uncovering the true scope of all the lives altered by that fateful evening.

The tragedy became a worldwide story. Numerous guests at the gala were wealthy and powerful citizens of other countries. There were all those poor orphan children in attendance who died. And let's not forget our American elite. We saw many stars burn out that night: Dick Mann, C. C. Constantine, and reporter Alexi Lawson to name a few. What a mess.

If you remember, I mentioned earlier two people escaped the fire alive. One of those was Sawyer Pettimore, the other being his date. I hate to seem indelicate, not my intention here, but the truth is she was little more than a smoking-hot, vacuous cokehead. I'm sure you've met one before. They come in both male and female varieties. I don't remember this one's name. Pleasant girl, though.

When the explosion occurred, Sawyer and his date were celebrating his success in the elevator, two floors below the exhibit. Sawyer stopped the elevator between floors to do some blow and screw.

Coincidentally, during the middle of their pre-coitus warmup the girl asked Sawyer, "What if someone is trying to leave and needs the elevator?"

He responded, "Fuck 'em. They can take the stairs."

By the way, Sawyer was by no means a fulltime cokehead. This was a special occasion. Also, cocaine is bad. Coke's a shitty, shitty drug—Evil! I tell you—and from what I've seen, a relationship with cocaine almost always ends poorly. I hate it, and I hate to include the garbage in this story. Unfortunately, it's a reality.

Anyway...

There was, of course, an investigation into the fire. Sawyer and his date escaped the building in shock and gave slightly varying accounts of what had happened, though in general they told the same story. They heard an explosion. They heard screaming and saw smoke. Sawyer claimed to have tried to move the elevator up to see if they could help, but the elevator would not go up for some reason. Sawyer's date said they stayed where they were, looking up and listening, frozen with fear. When smoke billowed into the elevator shaft, Sawyer took them down and they escaped the building. Neither of them told the whole, true story at the time.

The investigation didn't last long, mostly because there weren't many leads. At least, that's how the case was reported to the public.

Sawyer and the girl were questioned thoroughly and they readily agreed to participate in lie detector tests. Though they both reported hearing an explosion, this information alone did not indicate foul play was involved. The explosion could have been related to the building's gas line somehow.

The only other people at the party who left before the fire were Tommy Toxic, two of his bodyguards, and the bassist in his band. The rest of The Pond Scum and all the female escorts had stayed behind to enjoy the party. The police questioned Tommy but he couldn't offer any assistance, having left before the explosion. The cops never seriously considered investigating the incident for arson because there was zero evidence. Fire investigators had little to work with. Again, that's what was reported to the public.

The behind-the-scenes truth? Every person involved in the investigation understood the possibility an individual or group may have purposefully created the explosion. Yes, one of the guests may have been specifically targeted. The police researched the guests and the list of possible targets was so long there was no way to narrow the field for potential suspects. The investigation continued quietly for a few weeks as various federal agencies joined the effort, but one by one, they all came to the same dead end.

With nothing to go on the investigators concluded that any potential foul play was likely the result of a random sociopath choosing a highly publicized event. If someone had purposely targeted anyone in attendance, there was no way to track them. The authorities had too little evidence to pursue an arson investigation. The case was closed and the fire officially labeled an accident.

After much therapy and with tons of mental justifications in place for his actions, Sawyer Pettimore began to sell artwork left behind by his gifted apprentice. Littlethumb's extended family took him to court for the rights to the art, but due to the nature of Sawyer's previously established financial relationship with the Brookses, the court determined Sawyer had more right to the paintings. Sawyer had assisted in the development of the paintings through his mentorship of Littlethumb and had received a monetary share of every work sold prior to the family's death. Therefore, the judge stated this established Sawyer's partial ownership of the paintings, which became sole ownership when everyone else died.

Sawyer's sales of Littlethumb's paintings and the subsequent hearing that followed were both public scandals. Rumors circulated that Sawyer was somehow connected to the fire, but those rumors were completely unsubstantiated and didn't last long. In the end, most people agreed it would've been crazy for him not to sell the paintings and give some form of positive outcome to that horrible night, though his actions still left a bad taste in more than a few people's mouths. Those people didn't give enough credence to Sawyer's pain.

The fire left Sawyer emotionally scarred. The decadent life he envisioned after the discovery of Littlethumb's talent had somehow seemed ugly after the fire. He moved forward with his art career because the path was inexplicably laid before him. Bills had to be paid, he had to eat, and the tragedy had left him with a fortune in art to sell. What else would he do?

To his credit, Sawyer did a lot of things well. For instance, despite having fought for the rights to the art, he worked out agreements with several of the patriarchs and matriarchs of Littlethumb's extended family. With a little paperwork and business wrangling to keep the transactions aboveboard, he eventually cut them checks which, if used wisely, would establish financial stability for their families for generations to come. He also donated a healthy percentage of all his profits to charity because he knew the Brookses would have done the same. Over time, Sawyer was able to sway the public's opinion of him back in his favor, even becoming a sympathetic figure. Every few years a story could be seen on television or read in an article about how he was still haunted by the fire. He loved the Brookses like family and felt the world had lost something in Littlethumb that might never be seen again.

Owning such a rare collection made him a powerful force in the art world. Coupled with the history of his mentorship over such a rare talent, Sawyer established himself as one of the world's leading art dealers. Along the way he married a saintly woman named Anna who was graceful and loving and easily managed Sawyer's neurotic behavior and insecurities. The Pettimores had one child together, Isabel. They were a happy family.

The plane landed with an unspoken sigh of relief from Sawyer Pettimore. He'd been overseas working for several weeks and had yearned for the sight of Manhattan's skyline again. Despite being one of the largest and most chaotic cities in the world, he felt safe in New York. New York City was his home. Plus, he missed his girls.

Now he was enjoying a cocktail in a service limo on the way home from the airport. The deal overseas had gone well, and though in high spirits, he was brutally jetlagged. A solid excuse for cocktail number two. Sawyer was a bit of a wimp when dealing with jetlag.

The apartment was in Chelsea so his ride from JFK, the last leg of a full day's journey, wasn't terrible. The family had a place out on

Long Island as well. Most of the year the Long Island home was the "family" residence, but Sawyer's work often kept him overnight in the city. In the summers, Anna and Isabel stayed in Chelsea with him during the week and then the family would travel out to Stony Brook on the weekends. They were not living a super extravagant life. Sawyer made a lot of money but Anna ensured that most of their income was saved and her husband remained grounded.

Finally home, Sawyer happily greeted his wife and daughter. Isabel was a ball of energy, elated with the return of her daddy, and particularly excited to show him something.

"Oh please, daddy, can I show you now? It's a drawing of me!"

"All right," he said. "Go get it and I'll take a look."

Quick as she was, by the time Isabel returned with her painting, Sawyer was in conversation with Anna about his trip and had started another drink. When Isabel presented the picture to her father, he declared, "Oh, little Bel, look at how beautiful you are!"

Isabel was delighted but in truth, Sawyer wasn't paying close attention. There was the jetlag, the buzz from the alcohol, and the hunger motivating him about the kitchen to contend with. Not to mention conversation with his wife. Still, he'd done an excellent job appearing interested. He simply didn't look closely at the damn painting.

Until the next day. The next morning Sawyer putzed about the apartment in his pajamas and slippers, coffee cup in hand, thoroughly enjoying being safely tucked away inside a friendly environment with his child and amazing wife. He flipped an egg, ate it, and was about to flop his ass onto the couch for some jetlag rehab when he caught his daughter's painting out of the corner of his eye. He picked up the picture and took a closer look. Sober and more attentive, the quality of the work now stood out to him. So did the tiny thumbprint in the bottom right-hand corner.

His jaw fell open. His coffee poured onto his feet. His heart took five erratic beats in the amount of time normally used for a single thump, causing him to lose his breath. Then Sawyer freaked out.

25

Life had not gone as well for Tommy Toxic as for Sawyer Pettimore since the fateful night of the exhibit fire. Sure he was still rich, relatively speaking, but he was no longer the freewheeling, excess-living cash factory he was in his youth. Tommy lived in the pit celebrities land in when they fall off their mountain. A little money was the only thing that had prevented him from truly hitting rock bottom. Because he was tied into the original promotion of Littlethumb's work, Sawyer ensured Tommy received cuts from the sales of Littlethumb's paintings. I'm certain the loss of Dick Mann played a role in Sawyer's efforts as well.

Residuals were also earned from his early albums, from when he was a hit. Tommy recorded more than a few songs back in the day that were now considered punk rock classics. Unfortunately, at this point in his life he hadn't recorded an album in about ten years.

Actually, that's not quite correct. More accurately, he had not recorded an album anyone knew existed in about ten years. There were lots of records, but they all sucked and he shelved them without release.

Tommy's downward spiral began within five years of the fire. He was devastated by Dick Mann's death. The loss of his own parents hadn't hurt so profoundly. Generally speaking, he'd never hurt that way, period. Sorrow was a completely new and shocking experience. Tommy had no concept of what love was, so he had no way of knowing he loved Richard Feinmann deeply until the man was gone.

When Dick died, Tommy lost the only person who ever told him no. Not good. Recreational drug use turned into abuse, while he continued the quest to transition his image from child star to serious adult artist. Unfortunately, despite his prodigious skill with a guitar, Tommy was a poor songwriter and vocalist. The first album he made after the fire was a strong seller despite universally lukewarm reviews. Fans forgave him the poor quality because they knew Tommy recorded the album as part of his grieving process. A double concept album followed. *An Exodus Through Empty Parts I and II* was an abysmal collection of cock-a-doodle doo-doo. That's shit, I tell ya, just shit. More like an *Exodus Through Awful*.

Don't worry, Tommy and I regularly laugh about how crappy *An Exodus Through Empty* was (Ha! Still is…). Awful or not the album sold well, but not fantastic. Several tracks were leaked early and most people who heard those tunes were turned off. Luckily for Tommy, a lot of fans still bought the concept album with hopes it would turn out well overall. It did not.

Now, what I'm about to tell you next I know through conversation with Tommy, from his own words. Things had already been going poorly for him before Dick died, what with the puberty-induced pimples, crackly voice, and the sudden onslaught of genuine teenage angst. After Dick's death, once Tommy overcame his grief, he needed someone to hate. Littlethumb was the only logical target for Tommy's anger. The little jerk had taken everything from him. He stole Tommy's spotlight and his stupid exhibit was the reason Tommy's dad had died.

By the way, in his grief Tommy always remembered Dick as a father and referred to him as his dad. Back to hating Littlethumb.

Since Tommy had already hated the kid, emotionally charged logic insisted everything bad in Tommy's life was all that little fucker's fault. The conundrum Tommy suffered from was a lack of satisfactory resolution for this hatred. Littlethumb was dead and therefore could no longer be hurt. Tommy's rage was cheated from exacting vengeance and this left him empty.

He didn't feel anything anymore. That's when the drugs got frighteningly bad. He had stumbled through the *Exodus Through Empty* recording sessions and reeled so much from intoxication, he honestly thought the album was an unmitigated success. Though he wasn't happy, of course, because he couldn't feel anything, the "success" of the album encouraged him to continue behaving supremely tormented and artistic. Thus came the epic flop *Searching For My Rage*. A recording so musically challenged people returned the album, including copies purchased in digital format. It was abysmal.

After *Searching For My Rage* bombed Tommy went into hiding. Completely devastated yet again, he spiraled in the first emotion he'd felt for quite some time, though his present devastation closely resembled his previous emptiness. Conflated descriptions of emotional states aside, somewhere in there, he contracted hepatitis-C from the needles.

I'll give Tommy credit for one thing. He had enough self-preservation instinct to scale back his drug habits to a point of sustainability. Or maybe it was the hate. Either way, the hep-C definitely encouraged him to kick the intravenous shit, which helped keep him alive.

In recovery from "full-on junky" status, Tommy tried to remember the things that made him angry when he was younger, before Littlethumb entered his life. The truth was, nothing made him angry back then. He hadn't been angry. He was a little kid. All the punk anger was bullshit fun. The anger didn't arrive until right before Littlethumb showed up. We know the true source of his discontent was puberty and the fear of waning fame. For Tommy, the anger came because of Littlethumb. His displeasure back then had nothing to do with child-stardom fading on its own, no sir.

You get the idea, lots of anger and drugs.

So, Tommy Toxic lived an unhappy middle-class life. At least, middle-class in his mind. Sure, he was on a budget, but I don't think it's fair to call a million dollars a year spending cap "middle class," even today.

As an adult, Tommy had achieved full-on dirtbag status. Recently he'd paid three women to do something filthy as a personal reminder of how awful he was. He didn't hire them because he has a fetish for watching girls use imported baby emu poop as body paint. No, he hired them because he thinks screwing chicks who have emu poop all over them somehow makes him a dark and twisted soul, and that's what he was supposed to be. What he actually was, was a fraud, because no one ever taught him how to be real. Dick Mann tried a little, I suppose, in his own happily twisted way.

Fraud or not, Tommy was working on a new album. This latest effort was as heartless as all the rest. He knew the record was shlock, and the best part was he didn't care. He didn't give a hairy assed shit how bad the songs were, he just kept on recording. I hate to see anyone in pain. At the same time, and Tommy would be the first to tell you, he made a lot of laughably bad songs. Plus, I'm not sure he was technically in pain if he was supposedly so numb to everything.

The last desperate plunge of faded celebrity he'd yet to take, and only because he was still in decent shape financially, was one of those horrible "Where are they now?" television shows, or any of the other assorted "reality" programs that use washed-up celebrities to attract morbidly curious viewers. Instead he kept writing crappy tunes, putting together shitty albums, and sticking them on his shelf. Some-day, that wall of garbage might be considered his opus. We've had a chuckle a time or two about how funny life would be to hit a musical era where those horrible albums were suddenly considered great.

Tommy tinkered with the idea of naming his new album *Hollow Man*. Or maybe *Inexplicably Empty*, making it the fifth installment in his *Big Empty* series, which wasn't a series by design but he kept using the word "empty" in his titles, so eventually, he referred to them as such. The only problem with using *Inexplicably Empty* for the title was Tommy knew why he was empty, so the title did not seem "real." Tommy was nothing if not real as far as he was concerned. Seriously though: What is more real than an angry artist who is fed up with the establishment and convinced the whole world is shit giving a giant middle finger to the entire shebang by intentionally making crappy art? Ain't nothing more real than that, baby. Did I mention Tommy was fantastically delusional?

He was living in Seattle, having moved there because the city was reportedly the gloomiest place in the country. Not surprisingly, he was disappointed. Seattle was often gloomy, that was true, but on the days when the forecast was clear, the city's beautiful weather annoyed the hell out of him. A move to London was considered but he wanted to finish his album first. Tommy felt having a bad album produced in Seattle was cool, and paramount to his legacy. Plus, this chick had moved into the building a month ago. She was such a goody-two-shoes but she had a great body. Before leaving Seattle he was determined to get her into the bedroom to participate in something she would feel terrible about later, and that would take some work. Thus far, she had not been interested in any of the stuff he mentioned. Stupid bitch.

26

I give Sawyer Pettimore credit. When he freaked out, he did so with outward calm. Catatonia, baby.

There were no screams. No running around the house waking everyone and demanding to know where this picture had come from. He stood quietly while his brain melted. Later, he would look back on the moment and wonder if his internal apocalypse was similar to how a nervous breakdown felt.

Luckily for him, Anna was an early riser as well. She came in the room dressed for work, shortly after Sawyer's discovery. With no real need for a paycheck, Anna was a full-time philanthropist. She was intensely passionate in her efforts and held regular office hours consulting for dozens of charitable foundations.

Sawyer was disoriented when Anna entered the room but recovered his ability to speak. After they exchanged morning pleasantries, he asked if she knew the painting's origins. She said no. She didn't know the painting existed until Isabel showed it to Sawyer, which seemed odd. Why hadn't Isabel shared the picture with her? She wondered if Isabel was mad at her for something.

Even while internally suffering a core meltdown, Sawyer managed to reassure his wife. Isabel probably wanted to make sure her portrait was a surprise to him because art was his job. Perhaps she feared Anna might accidentally tell Sawyer and ruin the surprise. This seemed to make Anna feel a better. With a kiss goodbye she headed off to work. On her way out the door, Anna mentioned to Sawyer he felt clammy and needed to stay home from the office today and sleep off his jetlag. She would be back at lunch to check on him.

Sawyer sank into a chair. With a hand on his head, perhaps in an effort to prevent his skull from escaping, he watched as the entire room crumbled away before him. I don't think he suffered a nervous breakdown, but he was definitely having a panic attack.

Shortly after Anna left Maria arrived. The temporarily paralyzed, mind blown version of Sawyer Pettimore had not moved from his chair. Maria was surprised to find him at home and expressed her enthusiasm to see him again. After they exchanged greetings, Sawyer asked if she knew where Isabel got the painting. The question blurted from him with the urgency of a startling revelation, as if he suddenly remembered he was in shock. "Hey Maria, it's great to…holy crap do you know where Isabel got that painting!?"

Maria nodded.

"Where?"

Maria pulled her phone out and sent Sawyer a text message. "Coney Island boardwalk."

"Where?" he asked again. He watched her type then felt his own phone vibrate.

"Three-quarters up the north end, next to a cotton candy stand, back to the beach."

"Thank you, Maria." With that, his legs regained functionality. Sawyer shuffled to the kitchen, placed his breakfast plate in the sink, finished his coffee, poured more coffee, cleaned the plate, chugged more coffee, gasped at the heat of the coffee, then spoke with the broken cadence of a scattershot mind broadcasting through a recently burned mouth. "I've got to go out. Isabel hasn't come out of her room yet, so I guess she's still sleeping. At least, she was sleeping the last time I looked. Feel free to do whatever she wants within reason. I won't be back for several hours."

In his bewilderment, Sawyer forgot his decorum when speaking with a deaf person. Maria smiled politely and nodded, intermittently picking up bits and pieces of what he said, reading his lips in the brief moments he actually faced her. As he scurried out of the room, she marveled at how poorly the man recovered from overseas travel.

Sawyer chickened out on the way to Coney Island. Halfway there, the notion of this man being the real Littlethumb, somehow still alive after all these years, fully registered in his mind. He was unprepared to deal with this reality. Incapable. The onslaught of hypothetical consequences was more than his mind could process, so he convinced himself the scenario wasn't possible.

The artist had to be an imposter, either some audacious dimwit or someone smart enough to construct an elaborate ruse with forged documents and history. Perhaps this was an attempt to seek large financial gain. Either way, this person could be dangerous if confronted. Sawyer wasn't much for physical confrontation, and he had a family to consider. He couldn't risk personal injury, or worse, the possibility of leaving his family without a father and husband.

Still, he was already halfway to Coney Island so he decided to continue. Not to confront the man. He would get a look at him from a distance. I'm not sure what good he thought this would do. Apparently, neither was Sawyer, as he turned around nearly three-quarters of the way to the boardwalk.

Instead of heading home Sawyer headed to his office. From there he called a fraud investigator he was friendly with, last name Fant. Fant worked for an insurance company that specialized in high-dollar possessions such as jewelry and art, protecting them from loss due to thievery or damage. Sawyer asked Fant to investigate a trademark and copyright infringement case for one of his company's clients. Someone could conceivably try to file a claim on these forgeries. Fant said he could only investigate if a claim was filed, but he had an old pal that retired from the police force who could help Sawyer as a private eye.

With a deep breath, several deep breaths in truth, Sawyer reconsidered his next step. *Why don't you let this go?* he asked himself. *Just pretend you didn't see the picture and go on living. It's been fifteen years. Obviously, whoever painted Bel's portrait isn't coming after money or Littlethumb's collection. But what if they did?*

Meh. What difference would it make? Life would go on. *Let it go, man. Go home and hang out with your daughter. You haven't seen her in two weeks.* But he couldn't. How could he? He couldn't.

Something about the painting nagged at Sawyer. He removed the portrait from its envelope for further examination. If he let anything happen to his daughter's current prized possession she would be inconsolable. Isabel would already be upset if she knew he'd secretly taken it from the apartment. He set the painting down in front of him. How in the world had the thumbprint not registered with him the night before? The answer? He was a bad parent.

I was really ignoring her, he thought. Luckily, intrigue prevented a shame spiral. *Stay focused, Sawyer. The painting*.

The painting looked like Littlethumb's work. That's what frightened Sawyer the most. The effort was exceptional for a caricature artist. Remarkably complex. The fear Littlethumb had created the portrait washed over him again. Then he went through his denial process again. Nope. Cheap knockoff. Look at all those mistakes he wouldn't have made. Someone was stealing his signature.

Sawyer picked up the phone to call Mortimer Cross. He chuckled at the name. Seriously? Who the fuck was named Mortimer nowadays? Oh well, Fant recommended him, and if he was anything like Fant he would work perfectly.

For the first time in his life Sawyer called a private investigator. Mortimer Cross answered on the second ring. The man sounded like a gruff old hard case. A bass drum throated, grizzled veteran of countless donut and coffee filled stakeouts. Sawyer imagined him as an overweight, unkempt man. Khakis. Plaid shirts. Food stained ties. A cigar hanging from his mouth.

The art dealer's conundrum wasn't explained to Cross in great detail. Only that he wanted to determine a person's identity and was hoping he could do so if he got a look at the guy, so maybe Cross could start by getting some photos. The detective asked Sawyer a few standard questions, agreed to look into the situation for his normal rate, then told Sawyer he'd get back to him in a few days.

27

Several days later, Sawyer met Mortimer Cross at a coffee shop a few blocks from his office. Mortimer looked like . . . well, a Mortimer, but not at all how Sawyer had envisioned him during their initial phone call. He was tall, probably in his fifties, with cavernous gaps between his bone structure where meat was supposed to be. Yet despite his gaunt physique, Mortimer moved with agility and his height was quite intimidating.

Cross held an arm up with an umbrella in his hand. Sawyer recognized this as his signal and waved to the man who then approached the table. "Mr. Pettimore, I presume?"

"Mr. Cross? Please, call me Sawyer." Sawyer offered a hand for Cross to shake. The tall man ignored Sawyer's hand and began his routine for taking a seat. He removed his raincoat and his bowler, settled his thin briefcase on the table, hung his umbrella by its curved handle on the back of his chair, pulled off his gloves one finger at a time, and took a seat.

"Mr. Pettimore . . ."

"Please, call me Sawyer."

"Mr. Pettimore, I use formal surnames because I am Mortimer Cross. Speaking in such a manner is intimidating, stern, and provides more syllables to utilize for emphasis and tonal intonations. Now, let's move on."

Cross opened the briefcase, blocking his face from Sawyer's view. Sawyer wasn't certain but he felt Cross might be laughing at him from behind the open lid. The briefcase was closed in a swift motion as Cross swished a folder out to the right while shutting the lid at the same time, finishing the movement with the folder centered over the top of the closed briefcase. The movements were uncommonly precise and Sawyer was appropriately intimidated. He gingerly reached for the folder.

Sawyer opened the manila file folder and sifted through photos. As Cross had expected, his client appeared quite confused. "I don't understand? Is he wearing disguises or costumes or something?"

"He appears to be, yes."

"But why?"

"Well, he also appears to be exceptionally clever."

"But, why would he do that? I mean, how could he know someone was taking his picture? Were you standing in front of him?" Sawyer tried to bite his tongue before he finished the question but he was too slow. Cross's only response was a look Sawyer had expected. "Right, of course not. I know. Sorry."

"Can you identify this man from these photos?"

Sawyer ignored the question. "Oh my God, is he doing a card trick in this one?"

"Yes, keep going. There's a series of shots. It's the two of clubs."

"How in the world?" Sawyer's words trailed off as he continued to thumb through the pictures.

"I don't know," Cross replied. "On the first morning I surveilled him, before he arrived I asked the man at the cotton candy stand if the artist was there on a regular basis. He said yes, but he typically wasn't there for another hour or so if I wanted to come back. I thanked him and said I would have to try again another day. The man may have mentioned to our subject someone came by looking for him, but I told the cotton candy man I was interested in having a portrait commissioned and a friend had told me the artist was very talented."

Doubt washed the confusion from Sawyer's face. He couldn't tell if Cross was being serious, or recognized how absurd this excuse might seem coming from him. The detective was impossible to read, until he provided a slight clue. The left corner of Cross's mouth ticked upward so faintly and quickly Sawyer wasn't certain he'd actually seen the movement.

Then Cross said, "Mr. Pettimore, I assume the cotton candy man told our boy someone like me came looking for him. That was the point. Might as well put him on edge. If he is gaming you, my presence will affect his nerves."

"Ah. That makes sense, I guess." All of a sudden Sawyer wondered if he had escalated the situation past an appropriate level of action. Mortimer Cross was scary. What if Sawyer got the artist hurt and nothing was really going on? What if the whole thing was a freaky coincidence? *No. The painting.* Sawyer thought. *The painting, Sawyer.* The style knockoff was obvious, and the signature?

When Sawyer mentally returned to the present Cross was staring at him with an intense level of patience. "I was speaking with you, Mr. Pettimore."

"Yes, sorry."

"As I was saying. If he is up to nothing, someone looking for him will seem odd but not threatening, and he will go about his business. If he's up to something, then he changes his behavior pattern or raises his psychological guard. I won't recognize the former without prior knowledge on the subject. Heightened psychological defense mechanisms, though, I can read those a mile away."

"So that's what this is, right?" Sawyer held a photo of Smith wearing oversized plastic sunglasses, a top hat, and a decent-sized bell clock hanging from a chain around his neck. The clock was exactly three hours and twenty-three minutes ahead of the timestamp on the photo.

"Not exactly," Cross replied. "This, Mr. Pettimore, is curious. Even when his friend the cotton candy man tells him someone like me came looking for him, this behavior is unusual, and requires explanation. Why would he have already been in costume? How would he know I was photographing him?"

"Good questions. And how in the hell would he have known from where? I mean, he's looking right at you in some of these. And the card trick! It's like he was performing for you."

"That wasn't the only one. He performed quite a few sleight-of-hand tricks."

"So odd."

"Odd indeed." Something in the man's tone made Sawyer adjust his gaze from the photos to the old-timey gumshoe. When he did, he realized what Cross might have been implying. "Mr. Cross, I don't know anything about this. I hope you don't think this is some sort of trick."

"I don't. Not now. You just confirmed that for me." I suppose the confirmation came from Sawyer's body language. You have to be a skilled liar to fake whatever the thing is you can see in people sometimes, when you know they're telling the truth.

"Oh. Well, then what do you think?"

"I think he was somehow expecting surveillance, has some form of military or police training, and knew where the most logical position was for someone to observe him. So, he put on a show." Cross stood and began his preparations for departure. Scarf, coat, gloves, check. A well-rehearsed movement smoothly returned the bowler to his head. "I won't tell you your business, Mr. Pettimore, but I will tell you something is amiss with that painter. If you choose to pursue this matter, I think you should let me shake his tree and see if anything . . . falls out."

Confounded, speechless, Sawyer stacked the photos into an orderly pile and held them out for Cross. A persistent tremor to the photos betrayed his nerves.

"Those are yours," Cross said. "You paid for them. Take them home and think about what you want to do next. You have my number." With that, the detective picked up his briefcase, tapped the metal tip of his umbrella against the café floor, turned, and left. Sawyer rose to shake his hand but wasn't fast enough, so he stood there with his hand out, briefly, then let it fall limply to his side as Cross walked away.

28

There were two important facts about Smith the caricature artist that Sawyer Pettimore and Mortimer Cross were unaware of. First, Smith often wore silly costumes and disguises while working on the boardwalk. The disguises helped to attract business and they also put his customers in the right frame of mind. Cosplay is fun.

Second, Smith had his own reasons to be alarmed when his friend, Candyman, warned him about the creepy tall dude. These reasons had nothing to do with Sawyer Pettimore or painting. Make it three facts Sawyer and Cross were unaware of, because third: Smith actually called the cotton candy guy "Candyman," and did not know the man's real name.

Under normal circumstances Smith would have relocated his caricature operation, but he couldn't this time. There was still hope the deaf chick would show up looking for him. Smith was a bit of a romantic. Notice, I did not call him a hopeless romantic…

News of the tall man's inquiry had mildly alarmed Smith. He put the word out a possible offensive was set against him. The other members of his organization needed to know, for their own safety, though the inquiry was probably nothing of concern with the man having been so bold. Anyone looking to find Smith's men had to know exposing their search would immediately send his fellows into hiding, where they were impossible to find.

When someone knocked on his door the following Tuesday morning, Smith was mildly alarmed again. Startled might be the better word. The reaction was an unusual sensation for him.

His first thought wasn't, *Who could that be?* But rather, *Damn kid, you got the jumps.* Followed by, *That girl has you fucked up bad. Yes, she does. Yes, she does.* He checked the monitor for the front door security camera and found a close-up shot of a large black shape. Odd. The person knocked again and moved around enough so Smith could tell the shape was a hat. *Hmph, dude is tall.*

On the third knock Smith made his way to the door and quietly unbolted its numerous interior locks. While maintaining his leverage, in case the guest became pushy, he opened the door a precise width. *Yes,* he said politely in his mind. The word did not actually come out, which he quickly realized, so he cleared his throat and tried again. "Yes?"

"Hello, sir. I hope you can help me. My name is Joseph Williams. Here's my card." Cross held out a business card representing his alias. He had several. Joseph Williams was a certified public accountant. The phone number on the card was untraceable, but the number would be routed to Cross's mobile phone if dialed.

Squeezing his hand through the door Smith took the card, studied it briefly, nodded his head in approval, and looked back at Cross with a smile. Smith was wearing a fake handlebar mustache and rose-tinted sunglasses. His hair was frosted white with temporary dye. Aging hippy was his costume for the day. After Candyman told him about the tall fellow looking for him, he had decided to wear a disguise every day, at least for the time being.

Cross waited for a tick, then continued speaking when he realized Smith wasn't going to say anything. "Oh, yes. So, I was wondering if you might be able to tell me if the man who painted this portrait lives here." Cross held a photo of Isabel's painting up. "I've been trying to locate him."

"Why?"

"To hire him for my daughter's birthday party."

"How nice." The fake 'stache he was wearing lifted as he smiled and took a big, wide-eyed glance at the painting. "No, sorry."

Cross tilted his head in response as if to say, *Sorry for what?*

"I don't recognize the picture," Smith continued, discretely padding the mustache down as he spoke, using one of those openhanded stroking movements that mustache guys love to do.

"Are you sure?"

"Yes." Smith nodded his head in agreement with his word.

"Oh. I apologize for bothering you then. I was told an artist lived here."

Now, Smith knew whoever this man was, the man understood Smith was lying. Smith also knew the man knew that Smith knew that he knew Smith was lying. Right? Yes. They both knew they were each feeding the other one a bunch of crap. This guy knew damn well Smith would know his local people wouldn't have told some creepy motherfucker like this where he lived, though Smith was impressed at how quickly the guy had found his home. He hadn't felt anyone following him. This dude was good.

"My roommate is an artist," Smith said. "He lives here."

"Hence the description 'roommate.'"

"Exactly."

"If this were one of your roommate's paintings, do you think he would know anything about this signature down here at the bottom?" Cross held the photo closer to the door, pointing at the thumbprint.

"I suppose he would know the signature was his."

"Indeed."

Smith smiled again at Cross and shook his head in agreement. Neither man spoke for a few beats. They each sized up the other man, trying not to look like they were doing so, knowing damn well discretion was a waste of time because each man knew the other man was damn well sizing him up. But decorum ruled. There is an etiquette to these situations if you're a gentleman. Only a brute declares aloud he is deciding how to break you.

"Well," Cross continued, "if you could mention to your roommate I stopped by. If this painting is his work, you have my card."

"I do." Smith shut the door before the man turned to leave. He raced over to the monitor to see what the man did next, but when he got there Cross was already gone. *Williams, my ass*, Smith thought.

This dude was a pro, that's for sure. Knew exactly what he was doing. He knew damn well he could have had this conversation with Smith down on the boardwalk. Hell, "finding" him on the boardwalk would have been way more plausible. No, he wanted Smith to understand he knew where Smith lived, and to know how easily he'd found his home. The man was trying to rattle him.

Smith did not rattle. Not over shit like this. Over the nanny he fell apart, true, but shit like this was his deal. Smith saw through William's obvious charade, but he was slightly confused. Or whoever the guy was. He couldn't keep calling him Williams in his head when he knew the name was bullshit. Uncle Joe. Yes. He would refer to him as Uncle Joe.

Anyway, the curious thing about Uncle Joe was the painting. The possibility this was all somehow connected to Smith's other job was genuine, but how? Where's the connection? Obviously Smith had recognized the painting as his own, and he knew damn well who he painted it for. The little girl. The nanny.

The nanny. Blood moved at the thought of Maria. He looked down at his crotch. *Not now.*

Back to the puzzle of Uncle Joe. The possibility this was all some part of an elaborate plot to expose him and his compatriots could not be ignored, but he wasn't feeling that in his gut, despite Uncle Joe appearing to be a legitimate force to reckon with. No, Smith's gut told him their meeting was truly about the painting. But to what end? Why hire a private investigator, or whatever the hell Uncle Joe was, for that? And what was with the thumbprint? He'd never signed a painting that way before.

Smith guessed the situation had some connection with his past. Correct or not, he needed to report back to his people about his conversation with Uncle Joe. His cheeks tightened into a smile, this time sincerely. Uncle Joe, Uncle Joe, you rascal you.

Despite the circumstances, our caricature artist was feeling pretty damn lucky. Whatever the hell was going on, he boiled the whole mess down to one amazing possibility: There was a chance he might see Maria again.

29

The following day Cross reported back to Sawyer Pettimore. Meeting the artist face to face confirmed his suspicions. The man was either a completely paranoid sociopath or involved in some form of intrigue. Cross' guess was the latter. No simple caricature artist would keep his home under surveillance in such a manner, and Cross had never met a paranoid sociopath who behaved as cool as this guy did. He was definitely hiding something.

"Mr. Pettimore, do you understand I know who you are?" Cross sat across from Sawyer in the art dealer's office.

"What do you mean?"

"I mean exactly what I asked you. I'll rephrase. Do you understand I am well aware of the most publicized piece of your past?"

"Oh." Sawyer shuffled some papers on his desk, took a deep breath, and let the papers rest as he gathered himself. When he looked up, Mortimer Cross was studying him intently. "Honestly, sometimes I'm able to block out my past. Like I wasn't there. It all happened to someone else, or was a dream or something."

"Do you believe this man could actually be Littlethumb Brooks?"

The question punched Sawyer's fragile psyche in the stomach. Cross watched Sawyer twitch nervously, cowering from the question. Or maybe the answer.

"Can't be," Sawyer finally replied. "I hired you to prove to myself the guy isn't him, not the other way around."

"What really happened that night, Mr. Pettimore?" Cross didn't wait for an answer. If Sawyer bothered to offer one, the response wouldn't be useful. "According to history, everyone inside the building died except for you and your date. How could this man possibly have been that boy?" The conversational tone was friendly, not a third degree, lamp in your face grilling. Cross was only gathering information, but Sawyer responded as if he was being interrogated.

"I don't know. How could I know? I suppose it's impossible."

"If it's impossible, then why did you hire me, Mr. Pettimore?"

The look on Sawyer's face was a perfect mix of curious and incredulous. "Because the guy is using Littlethumb's brand, which I own. He's committing fraud. Trademark infringement. I told you this from the beginning."

"Of course." Cross read his body language perfectly. Nail struck on head. Somehow, Sawyer thought there was a chance the kid was alive. Perhaps the real question wasn't did Sawyer believe the boy was alive, but was he *afraid* the boy was alive? If he was afraid, then why?

"Do you mind if I make a short drink?" asked Cross.

"No, of course not."

"Would you like one?"

"Why not?"

Cross made his way to a liquor cabinet built into the wall of Sawyer's office, buying himself a moment to think. "I'm having scotch. Does that suit you?"

"Sure. Thanks."

"Neat?"

"Two rocks."

"Particular, Mr. Pettimore. I prefer a person who is particular with their libations." Cross made his way back to Sawyer's desk and handed him a drink.

"Thank you." The glass never hit the desk. Straight to the lips.

"May I ask you a sensitive question, Mr. Pettimore?" Cross spoke as he sat down, resting the glass of scotch on his knee with his right hand.

"May I reserve the right not to answer?"

"Of course. You're paying me."

Sawyer held his hands out, welcoming the question.

"Why are you so disturbed by this painting?" Cross nodded toward the envelope containing Isabel's painting on Sawyer's desk. "I'm sorry, no. That's not quite right. Why does the thought of the boy still being alive bother you so much? Wouldn't that be a wonderful thing?"

Sawyer squirmed a little in his chair.

"Please, Mr. Pettimore, I'm not trying to make you uncomfortable."

Sawyer wasn't so sure. He was fairly certain this man enjoyed making people uncomfortable. "I'm not sure, but I'm getting there. I'm working it out up here." He pointed to his head. "I think, maybe because that night was so horribly tragic. The Brookses were my friends. I cared about them and several others who died in the fire. Do you know what that's like?"

"I've been on the front lines of war," Cross said calmly.

"Okay. Good. I mean, that sucks you were at war, but at least I know you understand." Sawyer took another gulp of scotch. "That night was such a huge part of my life for so many years. Recovering from the loss. Having the whole thing blown back up again when I started selling the paintings. It took a long time for me to leave the pain behind. I don't want to go through the madness again. If Littlethumb were alive and living out on Coney Island… Do you have any idea what would happen if he's discovered?"

"Understood, but then, why pursue investigating this man's identity? Why not let it go?"

"I suppose I need to know he's not Littlethumb. Remove the uncertainty." Sawyer nodded in agreement with himself and drained his scotch as final confirmation. He decided on another. Why not? "I'm having one more. Want one?"

"No, thank you." Barely a sip was missing from Cross's first drink. "You do realize odds are infinitely in favor of this boardwalk artist simply having stolen the boy's signature?"

"Yes, I do." Sawyer timed his response so the word "do" coincided precisely with the last little dab of alcohol he let loose from the bottle, topping off his drink.

"Then what's the real issue, Mr. Pettimore? Why did you hire me?"

"The painting," Sawyer finally admitted. "It looks like his work. If the picture was a simple, stupid caricature, then obviously some schlub thought stealing Littlethumb's signature was cute. Or maybe an homage. Or maybe there's a slight chance the guy doesn't know about Littlethumb and thought a thumbprint signature looked cool. Would be tough to believe but is possible if he's young enough and hasn't studied. But it's not a simple caricature. The work is complex, and looks like Littlethumb's. That's what has me so fucked up about the whole thing, Mr. Cross. I've been trying to convince myself I'm being paranoid, pointing out flaws in the work, but that's the truth." Sawyer points to the envelope on his desk housing Isabel's portrait. "The portrait of my daughter inside that envelope looks like a Littlethumb and that scares me, because if he were alive my life would flip upside down."

"Are you willing to have your life flipped upside down to determine this man isn't Littlethumb Brooks?" Cross turned in his chair and looked at Sawyer with one eyebrow raised.

"Ha! Good question." He set down his glass and rubbed his face with both hands. "I don't know, I don't know. This is all so fucked. I mean, the guy can't be Littlethumb. So if he's not him, he's a fraud. A fraud whose ambition so far has been to make ten dollars a pop doing portraits on the Coney Island boardwalk. But, it's so random Isabel came home with that fucking painting. And the pictures you took of the guy. How crazy are those? Jesus. I mean, if this is some guy out to scam me or make a fortune by assuming Littlethumb's identity, how in the hell could he have possibly known Isabel was my daughter? Or that she would wind up sitting across from him on the boardwalk? It's unbelievable."

"That part is, yes," Cross agreed. "I have no idea how he could have planned the painting of your daughter. We may have to accept their meeting as pure coincidence. But here's what I do know. The man is no simple boardwalk artist. If you took away the surveillance cameras discreetly surrounding his apartment, my conversation with him, his presence alone, showed me this."

"Then what do you think is going on?"

"My initial guess? He's a grifter, and this is a scam. To what end, I'm not certain. The most obvious answer is he's somehow coming after the Littlethumb fortune. However, I'm not sure that's his game. He could be trying to get at you personally, Mr. Pettimore. Is there anyone you can think of who might want to hurt you or your family?" Cross said the last part as casually as possible. Over the years he'd discovered the idea alone did the work. There was no need to overdramatize the question. The results were always the same, fear and an extended paycheck, although this job offered more than a steady, albeit temporary income. He'd happened into the middle of a genuine mystery.

"No." Sawyer was taken aback at the thought, as Cross had intended.

"Good." Cross stood, swished down his scotch and returned the glass to the liquor cabinet. No need to let good scotch go to waste. "Let's hope that's the case. In the meantime, if you are interested in retaining my services, I have two suggestions. First, let me have a friend of mine compare the thumbprint on your daughter's painting to one from a piece in your collection. That could solve our mystery quickly. Though with so many of the real Littlethumb paintings available for study, it's possible this man could've had his fingerprints manipulated to match the boy's. Or, if he were Littlethumb still alive, he could've had his fingerprints changed to hide his identity. The analysis won't offer a complete answer to our question, but is usable data and worth looking into, one way or the other." He gathered his things to leave.

"Okay. I'll e-mail you magnified photos. Why didn't we do that to begin with?" Sawyer's question wasn't asked with any aggressive attitude, merely curiosity.

"Well, Mr. Pettimore, because you didn't tell me who you thought I was investigating. You asked me for pictures and I gave them to you. When you decided to pursue the situation, you still chose not to give me any further information, so I went to have a talk with him."

"Okay, okay. I get it."

"Also, my friend charges for favors like this. The cost will be reflected on your invoice." Cross almost smiled.

"Ha, okay. No problem. And what's the second suggestion?"

"I think you should go talk to him," Cross said nonchalantly.

"I'm sorry, what?"

"Go down to the boardwalk and talk to him. See if he recognizes you." He turned and headed for the door. To this day I'm still not certain if Mortimer Cross simply enjoyed messing with people's heads or if he had some instinctual control mechanism that insisted he keep people on edge.

"Are you kidding me?"

Cross stopped with his hand on the doorknob, pulling the door open and turning to face Sawyer at the same time. "No, I'm not," he said. "I can go with you and keep an eye on the situation from a distance. If this man is out to get you, facing him on his ground is a bold move, which may provide us an advantage. If this is all some crazy coincidence, and the fact he is clearly not so simple as he seems has nothing to do with you or your family, then what's the harm? He won't know who you are and nothing will happen. Either way, if I observe the meeting I may find clues in his behavior."

"What if he attacks me?"

"I wouldn't worry about that, Mr. Pettimore. You will be in broad daylight in a crowded area and I will be there in case anything goes wrong." With that, Mortimer Cross exited the room and shut the door behind him, smiling as he headed down the hallway to the elevator. He had Sawyer Pettimore right where he wanted him, sitting with his checkbook open. Don't get the wrong impression. Cross was no scam artist. This was a legitimate puzzle and he was compelled to put the pieces together, but he had to eat. If he was going to unravel this mystery then someone had to pay the tab. In the end, he wasn't certain the answers would have anything to do with Sawyer Pettimore, but if he was going to uncover the truth Cross had to keep his client on the hook.

30

Sawyer Pettimore never made the trip to Coney Island. When Cross reported that results from the examination of the thumbprint on Isabel's painting were inconclusive, Sawyer decided meeting the artist was pointless. What exactly would meeting him solve? How would he have any idea if the man were Littlethumb? Fifteen years had passed. Instead, Sawyer requested a cease-and-desist order, filed a lawsuit for trademark infringement and false representation, and had a summons issued to the caricature artist.

While Sawyer Pettimore and Mortimer Cross went about their business, Smith continued with his own. He discussed meeting Uncle Joe with his comrades. Though they found the timing curious, they all agreed the man's inquiry most likely had nothing to do with their current operation. If he were as well trained as Smith suspected him to be, the possibility remained he was a well trained non-threat. They concurred with Smith's initial assessment. Odds were much more likely Uncle Joe's inquiry was truly based on curiosity for the artwork Smith had sent home with the little girl. To what end Smith had no idea, but neither he nor his comrades were overly alarmed, though Smith did not mention the unusual use of his thumbprint as a signature on the portrait. In hindsight he wasn't certain why he kept that fact to himself.

The group did not pursue the greater discussion of whether Smith should continue operating as a boardwalk artist or not. The matter had already been discussed on numerous occasions and the result was always the same. Smith would not stop painting. Period. He had sacrificed plenty for the team. He wasn't giving up his love of painting people, and since his family ran the organization this was the way things would be.

Several days after his meeting with Uncle Joe, a cease-and-desist letter was delivered to Smith's apartment. The letter demanded he stop using his thumbprint as the signature for his artwork. Apparently, his thumbprint so closely resembled the licensed trademark of another artist, using it was worthy of legal action. The funny thing was, as previously mentioned, Smith wasn't in the habit of using his thumbprint as a signature for his paintings, at least not that he was aware of. He was surprised to see the one he placed on the little girl's portrait and equally as surprised when he realized he was finishing every painting of Maria the same way.

Speaking of Maria, the deaf beauty was all Smith fully remembered from that day. He could barely visualize the child. When he tried he saw Maria's face on the little girl's body, which was fairly unnerving, so when he remembered the encounter he focused solely on the woman. The beautiful woman he was painting once again, her beckoning form laying naked in a field full of daffodils. Keep in mind, Smith spent a considerable amount of time alone.

Smith would have been pleased to know Maria thought about him as well, though slightly disappointed to know those thoughts weren't inspired by his drawing of her. Okay, the picture was cute and he was too. Maria readily admitted this to herself. But seriously? No, not seriously. Any notions of flirtation or a love affair with a caricature artist from Coney Island was easily discarded as she moved on with her life. That is until her boss asked her about Isabel's painting.

Maria was intrigued, especially with how the painting upset Sawyer. Somehow, Sawyer's reaction made the painter even more attractive. The artist's identity was a curiosity, along with why her boss wanted to know where to find him. She casually asked Sawyer why he wanted to meet the guy. The excuse was to hire him for Isabel's upcoming birthday party but Maria knew this wasn't true. I think I've mentioned to you before that Sawyer Pettimore was not a good liar. Still isn't.

Anyway, Maria assumed Sawyer was interested in representing the artist's work. Isabel's painting was obviously special, but if Sawyer was trying to represent the guy, why didn't he say so? Why keep that a secret? She couldn't let the thought go. What was going on between Sawyer and the artist?

Barely nine years old when the Littlethumb exhibit tragedy occurred, Maria didn't know anything about the fire or Sawyer's tragic past, so she never considered researching her boss's history. Suspicion wasn't natural in her and she had no reason to think there was anything to find. Nevertheless, her boss's behavior was curious, and made for an easy excuse to see the handsome painter one more time.

Imagine Smith's pleasant surprise when he looked up from his easel to see the beautiful Maria standing in front of him again. He was paralyzed. Only his eyebrows and eyelids functioned and they spoke for the rest of him. They let her know he was clearly surprised and enthusiastic to see her again.

Maria handed him a note. He offered her a seat. While he unfolded the piece of paper, Maria sat down across from him.

The note read: *Who are you?* Using sign language, Smith asked Maria if she could sign.

"Of course," she replied, as pleasantly surprised by his ability to sign as Smith was that she had come looking for him. "How, no, why do you know sign language? Were you raised in a deaf-mute home?"

"Not that I'm aware of," he signed. "I thought it would be a useful skill. I taught myself about ten years ago."

"You would have been a teenager."

"I had a lot of time on my hands."

Maria smiled at him. *So odd,* she thought. "Who are you?" she signed. "Why would my boss want to find you? Did he come see you?"

"No, I think he sent someone else."

"Who are you?" She repeated the question, wearing a smile so sweet it made Smith's teeth ache.

Smith was afraid to tell Maria the truth for fear he might scare her away. But he didn't want to lie. This woman's presence sent him over the edge of a romantic cliff, complete with visions of hand-holding, beach strolls, and babies. Yep, he saw their lives together flash before his eyes and then he told her the truth. "I don't know," he signed. She furrowed her brow and his desire back-flipped off the high-dive. *Adorable,* he thought. *My god.*

"What do you mean?"

"I don't know who I am. I know this may sound crazy, but I had my past blocked from my memory by hypnosis."

"Why would you do that?"

"Because it hurt."

"Everybody hurts. It's part of life."

"I know. The hypnosis wasn't an easy decision." He paused for a moment. An internal debate showed on his face. Finally he continued. "I had amnesia when I was young. When my memories eventually returned, I let them. I dealt with the past and then I decided to make those memories go away again. I had already moved on with my life."

"I still don't understand. How can you live without your memory?"

"I move forward. My amnesia began when I was ten or eleven. I remember everything after, including when I chose the hypnosis. Whatever I've had blocked is still inside me, but I can't see it."

"That is such a strange thing to do." Maria shook her head to solidify her confusion. "I'm sorry. I don't mean to offend."

"It's okay. I know how weird it must seem." The artist lost himself in Maria's eyes. He thought about how badly he wanted to take her home and show her his paintings. Then he admitted to himself his true desire for taking her home and bowed his head with an embarrassed grin. Boys will be boys, ladies, even when they are grown men.

"What?" A mildly suspicious look crossed her face.

"I'm sorry," he said. "I...nothing."

Maria smiled and shook her head a little, attempting to rattle out her confusion. *Who is this guy?* she thought, for about the hundredth time. "So what will you do?"

"I don't know. I don't really know what's going on. The guy showed up and asked me about the painting I made for the little girl. I don't know what the big deal is."

"Me neither. I've tried to read my boss's lips to catch some information, but he hasn't brought the painting up again at home." Maria was careful not to use the family's last name. Though her intuition told her this man was not harmful, she knew there was some chance he was dangerous. Perhaps that's why Sawyer had freaked out.

"Well, I'm sure the whole thing will play itself out. Your boss sent me a cease-and-desist order, as well as a summons. I think I'm being sued."

"Really?"

"Yes."

"What are you going to do?"

"I was hoping I could take you to dinner."

Smith was not surprised when Maria politely declined his offer. She explained to him that for all she knew he could still be dangerous. Smith assured her, wielding what he considered his sexiest grin, that he was most certainly dangerous. But, he promised she and her charge's family had nothing to worry about.

"Perhaps," she signed. "If that's the case, I suppose I'll find out, and maybe we'll see each other again someday."

Smith explained to Maria he already saw her every day because he couldn't stop thinking about her. Then he took a paintbrush from his easel and whacked the handle against his knee, turning the brush into a bouquet of flowers. He handed the bouquet to Maria with a puppy's hope in his eyes. Maria blushed as perfectly as a human being could blush. Then she left, flowers in hand, looking back at him several times as she walked away.

31

Sawyer Pettimore's attorneys requested a pretrial hearing to which Smith was summoned. Sawyer didn't want to wait until an actual court date to discover this caricature artist's identity. This madness needed to end as soon as possible. Weeks had passed since he noticed the thumbprint on his daughter's painting and his nerves were shot. His brain had yet to completely re-solidify from its meltdown. The ol' gray matter was currently in a gelatinous state, functioning at below optimum levels and very jiggly.

Sawyer hoped to uncover the information he needed at the hearing and move on. Said hope was fairly unenthusiastic however, wilted by his fear this ordeal might drag on indefinitely. He was not surprised when the day arrived and Smith did not show up for the hearing. Not surprised, but still disappointed that a man who was clearly *not* Littlethumb Brooks raised from the dead had not arrived on time so the whole mess could finally be laid to rest. Sawyer's attorney requested for Smith to be arrested immediately and held in contempt of court for ignoring the summons.

Judge Harold "Gavel Smasher" Lograve was by all accounts a fair and reasonable judge. He was also a charismatically theatrical one, hence the name. More on that later. First, before any theatrics were necessary Judge Lograve explained having Smith arrested wasn't quite that simple or quick. There was paperwork involved. Thus, instead of having Smith arrested, Sawyer's attorney, at the prodding of Mortimer Cross, asked for a recess. The judge granted the recess and Cross sent two strong-arms out to pick up Smith.

As unsurprised as Sawyer was at the artist's absence from the hearing, Smith was equally as unsurprised when he looked up from his painting station to see two well-dressed goons standing in front of him. "Are you Smith?" Nice Suit Number One asked him.

Smith nodded his head, then made both men aware of his respect for their clothing without speaking. Both men acknowledged the compliment by adjusting buttons at the cuffs of their blazers with pride. Smith picked up a canvas sitting next to him. Painted on the canvas were the following words: "You fellas want a portrait? Only ten bucks each." Both dudes declined, of course, and Nice Suit Number One told Smith to gather his things and come with them. Smith shrugged his shoulders at the quick dismissal of his offer and obeyed.

I'm not certain why Smith decided to ignore the summons. I'm convinced he wasn't certain either. He wasn't going anywhere and the people who wanted him in court already knew where to find him, so not attending the hearing was a bit of a moot point. The decision may have had something to do with Maria. Women like when a man who breaks the rules? Who knows? One thing was certain, the commute into Manhattan was much quicker by thug-mobile than bus, so that was convenient.

Smith was mildly impressed. If the snoop who showed up at his house, the lawsuit, and the summons weren't enough evidence of his unknown adversary's potential power, two handsome A-list hitmen showing up to collect him barely an hour after his scheduled court appearance was definitely an indication.

While the hearing was in recess, word got out that Sawyer Pettimore was involved in a legal proceeding. One of the court clerks who dealt with the daily dockets noticed his name. She was in her fifties, had been a huge fan of C. C. Constantine, and had gotten emotionally swept up in the drama surrounding the deaths of Constantine and so many other famous people fifteen years earlier. When she saw Sawyer Pettimore's name the clerk immediately messaged one of her friends. The friend encouraged her to contact one of those trash magazines or television shows to sell the information.

"Ooh, definitely call a show. They will offer more money. Try that show, *The Vine*."

As you might imagine, *The Vine* (short for *The Grapevine*) was one of those god-awful celebrity scoop shows. They stuck their cameras straight in the face of famous people and harassed the shit out of them when the celebrities were trying to go about their daily lives. I think they were eventually sued off the air. Whatever. I don't participate in the process by paying any attention to the garbage, but I don't have a problem with the celebrities being annoyed. If you want to be famous, well, I suppose being harassed by paparazzi is part of the price you pay in this country, and you get what you pay for.

The thing was, Sawyer Pettimore wasn't famous. Not pop-culture-trash-newsworthy famous. Not at that point. His fame from the Littlethumb case had long since dissipated. The Vine was not interested in any news involving an art guy named Sawyer Pettimore. Some people on the Internet were interested however. Plenty of websites were devoted to discussions on art. These websites were frequented by at least several people every day. Yes, I am making fun of the popularity of modern art, but all sarcasm aside, forest fires start with a spark.

When Smith arrived the courtroom's gallery seating was full. The crowd had started slowly. Sawyer, the judge, and the attorneys noticed the first few onlookers arrive without giving them much thought. Sawyer was a little curious, but a few random observers weren't unusual to the people in the room who were part of the court process on a regular basis.

As the crowd had continued to grow, Sawyer sat in awe, dumfounded as to how it could be happening. He sent a questioning look at Mortimer Cross who remained his typical unaffected self. By the time the room had filled completely, Sawyer was officially mortified.

The sequence of events was fairly simple. Once a single legitimate media outlet discovered the little piece of gossip and determined the info newsworthy, other outlets followed. Literally followed. If I had a nickel for every time a reporter said, "Hey, where's he (or she) going?" that day, I would have a bunch of nickels and I would exchange those nickels for pennies. I've always liked pennies.

The two hired goons ushered Smith into the courtroom without any fanfare. There wasn't a bold throwing open of doors or any other form

of dramatic entrance. First of all, the courtroom doors were left open until the judge called the hearing back to order. Second, everyone in the room chatted and moved around as they pleased, coming and going from the bathrooms, having cigarette breaks, and visiting the vending machines while they waited for the hearing to resume.

No one noticed Smith's entrance. He was led to a seat next to his publically appointed counsel, who had been waiting patiently, passing the time with a salacious phone call to his lover, Keith. Smith was fairly certain he overheard the word "strumpet" as he sat down. He nodded an approving hello to his lawyer, who ended the phone call with mild embarrassment.

Judge Lograve called the room to order and the doors to the court were closed. As everyone in the room refocused their attention, they strained their backs and craned their necks to get a look at the man who now sat at the defendant's table. Sawyer Pettimore also attempted to get a look at the man he was suing, without looking like he was trying to get a look at the man, of course. It was an awkwardly discreet effort that eventually failed. Sawyer could not have been more frustrated by the way this whole mess had begun.

The judge ordered Smith to rise and be sworn in. The bailiff asked Smith if he swore and or affirmed to tell the truth, the whole truth, and nothing but the yadda, yadda, yadda. Smith confirmed his intentions to do exactly as asked with a pronounced, affirmative nod of his head. The judge had looked away momentarily. When he did not hear the expected "I do" after a few seconds, instead hearing a few discreetly repressed but undeniable chuckles, he looked at Smith and the bailiff with a puzzled expression.

"Mr. Smith," Judge Lograve said.

Smith responded by saying "Yes" with his eyes and a smile on his face.

"Would you mind confirming your oath to this court to provide an honest testimony?"

Smith looked at the bailiff, who turned to the judge.

"He nodded his head yes, sir," the bailiff said.

"Out loud please, Mr. Smith," Lograve said.

Smith opened his mouth to speak but nothing came out. He cleared his throat, coughed a few times, then whispered the words, "I do."

With a tinge of frustration in his voice Judge Lograve said, "Mr. Smith, loud enough for the entire court to hear you. I suggest you get it right this time."

Smith wasn't fucking with the judge or the rest of the court, nor was he trying to be funny. The number of people in the gallery intimidated the quiet artist. He hadn't known what to expect from the proceedings but a room full of reporters and other unknown observers had not crossed his mind. In an attempt to ensure he got it right this time, Smith looked at the bailiff and yelled, "I do!"

The shout surprised everyone in the room, but before anyone could make a sound, the Judge rapped his gavel hard. Lograve was called the Gavel Smasher because he had a penchant for letting his gavel do the talking for him. Especially when frustrated. He could maintain the iciest of calm, unemotional expressions on his face while pounding his wooden mallet of justice with unadulterated fury.

"Good." Lograve spoke calmly, quite pleased with his gavel having preemptively curbed a hubbub in the gallery. "Mr. Smith, take a seat at the witness stand please." Smith obeyed and the judge continued. "Mr. Smith, before we begin I would like to impress upon you how much I hope the rest of these proceedings move along more smoothly than they've begun."

"Apologies, your honor. I don't speak often. It can be difficult."

"Do you have some form of impediment or disability the court should be aware of and take into consideration?"

"No sir. Nothing wrong."

"Just the quiet type?"

"Yes sir."

"Any particular reason why?"

This question caught Smith off guard and he immediately decided he liked this judge. He cleared his throat again. "I don't care for the sound of my voice."

I can't remember if the judge appeared more irritated or interested at this point, but he said, "Is that supposed to be some sort of metaphor?"

"No sir."

Judge Lograve looked at Smith and gave a wave of his hand, imploring him to continue. "It's the tone. I've never cared for it."

"I'm sorry," Lograve responded. "You're telling me, under oath, you don't care for the sound, the tone, of your own speaking voice?"

"Yes sir."

"So you barely speak?"

"Yes sir. I'm told even as a child."

There were snickers in the courtroom. Judge Lograve did not wield his gavel this time but instead shot the gallery a stern, disapproving glance. "Told?" he said.

"Yes sir."

Judge Lograve was about to demand Smith expound upon his comment once again when Sawyer's attorney spoke up. "Your honor?"

"Yes, yes, of course," Lograve said without looking at the lawyer. "I'm sure whatever that meant will come out as these proceedings move forward."

"Most likely," Smith replied.

One loud "Ha!" erupted from the gallery, inciting the rest of the room. Everyone who wasn't a lawyer or named Sawyer Pettimore laughed uproariously. Except Mortimer Cross, who was instead enamored with the difference in Smith's voice from their previous meeting. Cross had not considered the possibility Smith was using a fake accent when they spoke. The modulation was remarkable.

Lograve slammed his gavel down on its block so hard the hair on the top of his head jumped. A blow so powerful Mortimer Cross was shaken from of his musings, while everyone else in the room was shocked into silence. The judge smoothed his hair back down and said, "Counsel, your witness."

32

"Please state your name again for the record." Sawyer's attorney stood with his fingertips resting on the table in front of him. The attorney's name was Michael Meredith.

"Smith."

"Your full name please," Meredith said. "Is Smith your full name?"

"Yes."

"Given?"

"No."

"Legally changed?"

"Yes."

"Interesting," Meredith said. "We may need to revisit this later." Smith intently stared back at him, which made him slightly uncomfortable. The courtroom wasn't Meredith's forte. Most of his work for Sawyer concerned contract review and writing. "Mr. Smith, would you like to explain why you chose to ignore your summons to attend this hearing today?"

"No thank you," Smith said politely.

Meredith was obviously caught off guard by this response. Rather than pursue the subject further he made sure everyone was watching as he checked the question off his legal pad with fraudulent confidence. "Mr. Smith, do you understand why you're here today?"

Smith shook his head and said, "Do you?" He couldn't help himself. The room laughed. Judge Lograve raised his gavel in fair warning. Everyone hushed, immediately.

"Mr. Smith, I suggest you simply answer the questions," Lograve said. "I won't accept your continually inciting my courtroom." The judge would have been much more agitated if not for Smith's tone. Smith's question had seemed earnest and hopeful, not smart-assed.

"Sir," Smith said with an affirmative, apologetic nod.

"Proceed, counselor," Lograve said.

Meredith stepped out from behind the table and walked toward Smith with Isabel's picture in hand. He held the painting for Smith to see. "Do you recognize this painting, Mr. Smith?"

"Yes."

"Did you create it?"

"Yes."

"Do you recognize the thumbprint here at the bottom?"

"Of course."

"Is it yours?"

"Yes."

Meredith returned to the plaintiff table and set the portrait down. Along the way he smiled and gave Sawyer a thumbs-up, excited by how well he was doing. Sawyer politely shook his head in acknowledgment of Meredith's strong work thus far.

"Mr. Smith," Meredith began again, "returning to my previous question. The reason you're here today is to determine whether or not you have been illegally using a registered trademark owned by my client. As confirmed by your own admission, you made the thumbprint mark that resembles my client's trademark. Due to the nature of your work, this is not only theft but also false representation."

"Okay," Smith replied. He turned to Judge Lograve and smiled, holding his hands out with palms up as if to say, "This guy, this guy over here," like a Hollywood accepted Italian dude stereotype.

For whatever reason, Judge Lograve took as much a shining to this Smith character as Smith had taken to the judge. Most people liked Smith, honestly. Judge Lograve's taking to him shouldn't come as much of a surprise. "Let's keep the proceedings moving, counselor. We've all been here a while as it is."

"Of course, your honor," Meredith said. "Mr. Smith, my client owns an extensive collection of work by a deceased artist who signed the bulk of his paintings with a thumbprint similar to the mark you made. As I mentioned previously, Mr. Pettimore also owns said thumbprint logo as a trademark."

"Okay," Smith said again, this time in anticipation, trying to help the lawyer get to the point before the judge fussed at him again.

"Aww, fuck it. Who are you?" As I mentioned, Meredith was not much of a trial lawyer.

"Counselor!"

"Sorry, your honor." Meredith turned back to Smith. "Look, you know why you're here. Do you honestly expect us to believe you had no idea you were stealing the signature of Littlethumb Brooks for your paintings?"

"Yes."

"This is a big coincidence?"

"Yes."

"One you can prove you're telling the truth about?"

"Yes."

"How?"

"I have no idea who I am."

The courtroom erupted in shock-and-awe chatter. The judge pounded the room back into submission with thunder from his gavel, eventually snapping the handle in half on the sounding block. He retrieved another gavel from somewhere under his robe, twirling the head in small circles to let the room know there was more where that came from. Once the crowd was subdued, the judge instructed Smith to explain himself.

"I don't have any memory earlier than around ten years ago," Smith said. "I suffered some form of trauma as a child. At first, I had amnesia. Then nightmares. Then my memories returned. Then I had them hidden through hypnosis."

"Hidden?" Judge Lograve and Counselor Meredith asked at the same time.

"Yes," Smith answered. "Locked away through hypnosis."

"Counselor, if I may. . ."

"Of course, your honor." Meredith knew where the judge was going so he returned to the plaintiff's table, taking a seat next to his client. He could not have guessed the emotions happening behind Sawyer's face but he did notice the pitcher of water at the table was now empty. So was the glass Sawyer clutched, yet he still put the tumbler to his lips and attempted to take a drink.

"So you mean to tell me you chose to have your childhood erased?" the judge asked.

"Yes, your honor."

"And you would be willing to submit to a lie detector test to verify your statement?"

"Of course."

"How in the world could you live like that? Don't you wonder who you are?"

"I'm a painter," Smith replied. "What else do I need to know?" Once again the crowd roared with laughter. Lograve went to work with his gavel, this time standing as he reared back for the first strike before smashing the wooden mallet down over and over. This gavel's head flew off, narrowly missing the bailiff's head as it flew past. The judge pulled another gavel from his robe as he sat back down. He waggled the end of the handle menacingly at Smith with a smile on his face.

Smith smiled back. He was pleasantly confused by the judge, though he understood what the man expected. Despite his efforts to speak as few words as possible, Smith liked this dude, so he gave him what he wanted. "Your honor, my uncle raised me. I was fifteen years old when my memories returned. They were horrifying. Deeply saddening. When I told my uncle I wanted them to go away again, he found a hypnotist who was willing to make them disappear. Somewhere in there my name was legally changed. I know Smith isn't my given name, and I don't remember my own, though I can remember making the decision to have my memories repressed. I understand it's difficult to believe someone could live this way but I do."

"Mr. Smith, what if you wanted them back someday?" Judge Lograve shook his head, considering his own questions. "And for that matter, your legal guardian let you do this when you were still a minor? Was he even your legal guardian? How would you know?"

"Technically I don't."

"Did you ever stop to think this man might not be your real uncle? You could be a kidnap victim or something. The man could be a criminal."

Smith snickered at the last comment.

"What was that?"

"My apologies, your honor, it's just the thought of my uncle as a criminal."

"But you get my point?"

"Yes sir." Smith looked at Sawyer Pettimore and back at the judge. "Your honor, as far as I can remember I don't know that man. Not now, if ever. I mean no harm. I'm not trying to steal trademarks, impersonate anyone, or make money illegally. Honestly, I don't remember putting my thumbprint on the painting. I was surprised when I saw the mark. All I see when I think of that day is his daughter's nanny. She was beautiful."

Smith spoke that last line with such crystal clear love-struck awe that women in the gallery cooed. Some men too. Lograve raised an eyebrow and they quieted themselves.

"Never mind all that," Lograve said, returning his focus to Smith. No longer worried about the case at hand, he was instead confounded by the life story of the eccentric young man in the witness box. "What about your memory? What if you wanted your memory back?"

"Oh, there's a trigger phrase to release my memories back into my conscious mind."

"Well why didn't you say so to begin with?" The judge showed more than a hint of exasperation.

"I . . ." Smith began, then stopped, unable to offer a good reason other than he hadn't thought to yet. "It wouldn't matter," he said instead. "Only the hypnotist and my uncle knew the phrase, and the hypnotist is dead."

"What about your uncle?" Lograve asked.

"Yeah, where the fuck's he at?" the bailiff agreed. Apparently, the bailiff had endured enough suspense for one day and needed resolution to this situation. Judge Lograve turned to the bailiff who, when he realized he had spoken his thoughts aloud, sheepishly returned to his business of staring at his shoes while the gallery laughed.

This time the judge spared his gavel, bringing the house back in order by raising his hands in the air and lowering them back down with a chuckle of his own. The man put on a good show when dispensing justice. "Your uncle?" Lograve repeated.

"I have no idea where he is," Smith replied. "He travels a lot."

"Your honor, if I may," Meredith said as he rose to his feet. "I'm not sure I understand how this is relevant to my client's suit against this man. It's his current actions which have . . ."

"Shh," Lograve shushed, cutting off Meredith. He raised a hand at the same time and pinched two fingers together as a visual aid. Meredith got the hint, shut his mouth and returned to his seat, casually checking his belt, his tie, and his hair. "Mr. Smith," Lograve continued, "do you understand why your past might be relevant to my ruling in this case?"

"I believe I do, but I'm not sure how to help."

An old woman's voice came from somewhere in the gallery. "Your honor, pardon my interruption but I believe I may be of some assistance."

"Who said that?" Judge Lograve asked. "Standup and explain yourself. And keep in mind, if this is some sort of joke I will hold you in contempt and fine you. Hell, at this point I will probably have you thrown in jail."

"Yes, yes, of course. I promise, your honor, this isn't a joke." The old lady rose slowly from her seat, mixing in several grunts, groans, ehs, hmphs, and other old-person noises. Once she had finally made her way up to a standing position she smiled warmly at the judge and the rest of the people. Then she disrobed. First she removed her hat, next her shawl, and then her face. The old lady was Uncle Daring Bird.

33

This time, Judge Lograve tossed his gavel over his shoulder, put his hands behind his head, leaned back in his chair, propped his feet up on his bench and allowed the madness to ensue and simmer down on its own. All the while Daring Bird stood there in an old lady's dress, basking in the chaos he'd created. Finally, the crowd returned to a nominal level of order and Lograve reclaimed a physical position of authority on his throne. He finished off quieting the room with a finger to his lips directed at several specific chatterboxes. Lograve returned his focus to Daring Bird and gave one last little head shake of disbelief before speaking again.

"Sir," Lograve said. "Who are you?"

"I'm Samoset Jones, the boy's uncle," Daring Bird replied, motioning to Smith.

"If I may be so bold as to ask, is the women's clothing a lifestyle choice?"

"Of course not!" Daring Bird said with gusto. Then he remembered to show the judge his respect. "Uh, your honor."

"Then why are you wearing a costume in my courtroom? Do you want to be fined?"

"Oh, I'm not wearing a costume, sir." Daring Bird ignored the second question.

"You're not?"

"No sir. I'm wearing a disguise."

"Oh for Christ's sake," Lograve replied. "Then why are you wearing a disguise in my courtroom?"

"I thought it would be exciting?" That's not a typo. Daring Bird stated the reply like a question, holding his palms out and shrugging his shoulders. Between you and me, Daring Bird had gone a little cuckoo after surviving the fire.

"You wanted your entrance to my court to be exciting," Lograve said with mild disbelief, practically mumbling the words to himself.

"Well, I traveled a long way, your honor, and I haven't seen my nephew in quite some time." Reasonable or not, Daring Bird's answer was one hundred percent honest.

Judge Lograve sighed and rested his head in his hands for a moment, finishing off the show of frustration by removing his glasses and rubbing his temples. Everyone hung on his movements, halfway expecting him to start banging his gavel despite the already quiet room. Instead, he eventually looked at Daring Bird with a thumb pointed toward Smith and said, "Please tell me you're the same uncle who knows how to get his memory back."

Daring Bird was indeed said uncle, which he heartily confirmed to Judge Lograve. His response was either, "Your honor is goddamn right I am," or, "Fuck yeah!" with a thumbs-up. I can't remember.

On second thought, his affirmation may have been, "Does a one-eyed mother love her baby twice as much?" Slightly confusing but still got the point across.

Daring Bird explained to Judge Lograve he could prove this was not some big scam. "That's right, your honor. Right now my nephew is wearing a key to a lockbox around his neck that will help prove his identity." The crowd gasped. "And he knows me!" Daring Bird pointed to Sawyer Pettimore who sat frozen in shock, his mouth stuck open since the moment he had recognized Daring Bird. The crowd gasped again. Sawyer Pettimore fainted.

Lograve allowed Daring Bird and Smith to borrow his chambers for a brief reunion, though not without a little sarcasm while giving his instructions. The gist was they would not be left alone and were not to misbehave in the judge's chambers. The bailiff joined them and the stenographer was also instructed to record their interaction for the court's records, in case the lawsuit ever went to trial. Once they had all received their instructions, Lograve sent for an EMT to check on Sawyer Pettimore. When he fainted, Sawyer's head had struck the table with an uncomfortably loud thud.

"Why didn't you tell me you were coming?" Smith and his uncle were in the Judge's chambers together, almost alone.

"I really wanted my entrance to be exciting," Daring Bird replied. "I thought the surprise might be fun."

"It was!" Smith patted his uncle on the shoulders and clapped his own hands together. Daring Bird removed the rest of his disguise. "Why did you come?" Smith asked.

"When you told me what was happening, I figured I should come help. I didn't want you arguing with me so I didn't tell you I was coming."

Smith studied his uncle for a moment. Over three years had passed since the last time they were in the same room together. Daring Bird looked like he had been hitting the gym. "Uncle, you look a little ripped."

"Yeah. Been fairly bored lately. Lots of push-ups and dips." There were several plush chairs in the Judge's chambers for guests. Daring Bird motioned for his nephew to have a seat.

Smith obliged, chuckling at his uncle's definition of boring. He knew well what Daring Bird had been up to lately. "Boring" was not an accurate description. "So what's the deal? Why are you really here?"

Daring Bird sat down across from Smith, giving him a familiar smack on the knee before he leaned back into the chair. "I'm sure you've figured out by now this isn't some random thing happening."

"Yeah…was starting to look that way."

"The man who's suing you, Pettimore."

"Yeah?"

Several times, Daring Bird opened his mouth to speak then stopped himself. Finally he said, "You're a man now. The time has come for you to be whole again."

Understanding set in on Smith's face. "I see." He sat quietly for a moment, allowing those words to hang in the air while the recognition truly settled into him. "Why did you let me do it?" he finally asked.

"You were a teenage boy when you chose this. The pain was yours to manage so I let you choose your own path. You weren't hurting anyone else with your decision."

"So who is that guy?"

"Someone from your…from our past. You will know in a minute."

"I guess so." Smith understood what was coming and was trying to maintain his stoic demeanor. "Are you sure this is a good idea?"

Despite asking the question, he knew what was necessary. He also knew what he was about to endure would suck big time balls, at least at first.

"Fate is unavoidable. There's no surprise to me this day has come or that the gods have delivered Pettimore back into your life." There was no irony or sarcasm in Daring Bird's voice.

"How could this happen?" Smith's tone wasn't maudlin. He was literally weighing the odds in his mind. "It's unbelievable."

"Says a man who intentionally erased his own memory."

"Right! This whole deal was unbelievable enough without the guy's kid showing up to have her picture made. What are the freaking odds of that?"

"You have seen the forces that bring people together and pull them apart." Daring Bird sounded confused by Smith's confusion. "They are alive within us."

"What the hell are you talking about?"

"Oh, right, we erased that part too." Daring Bird gave a light-hearted shrug. "Listen, this will hurt."

"What part? What do you mean this…"

Before Smith could finish his sentence, Daring Bird silenced him with a finger held in the air. Then he said, "Once, when he was a boy, Littlethumb sneezed and the whole world froze."

34

While Daring Bird and Smith were in the judge's chambers, Judge Lograve had the sheriff's department send a deputy to retrieve the lockbox that matched the key around Smith's neck. The lockbox was in a post office on the Upper East Side near where the Brooks family had lived so many years earlier. The hearing had started at nine in the morning. The news story grew legs during the first recess while Smith was being retrieved from Coney Island. By this point, the day had reached mid-afternoon.

Word got out among art aficionados that Sawyer Pettimore was involved in some sort of court hearing. The multiple bombshells dropped during the proceedings had been instantly reported by every mobile phone in the room, either having been sent to another person (and so on, and so on…) or posted directly to the worldwide webernets. Once someone in the gallery had wondered aloud, "Wait, so, are we thinking there's a chance Littlethumb Brooks somehow lived and the guy with no memory is him?" the story became a true sensation.

Tommy Toxic sat on his couch picking at his guitar and watching the stock market channel. He lived off investments at the time, so he often watched the market all day as if he understood what any of the graphs, statistics, and other tracking graphics meant. In the middle of a segment about a large descending red arrow, some nerd came on with a live report about a hearing in which Sawyer Pettimore was involved, and how the value of some of the most sought-after art in the world could plummet if it turned out the artist was still alive.

Tommy immediately picked up a phone and called Sawyer Pettimore. He found a channel running the story live and watched as a cameraman who had worked his way into the courtroom filmed Sawyer Pettimore's reactions. Sawyer had been revived after having fainted.

That's freaking hilarious, Tommy thought. *What a pussy.*

Sawyer finally answered his phone after multiple calls.

"Hello." Sawyer was confused by the call, why he answered his phone, and the general state of affairs in the world around him. To his credit, after being roused by the EMT he maintained a reasonable level of manic outward calm.

"Is it true?" Tommy asked. "Is it really him?"

"Who is this? I don't recognize this number."

"Who does it sound like, dickbag?"

"Tommy? Is that you?"

"Who else would I be?"

"I didn't recognize the number."

"It's my junkie phone. I only use it for my drug dealers and pimps."

"Nice, Tommy. That's such a nice thing to know…for you to say."

"Or for you to be, ha-ha." Obviously, Sawyer couldn't see the smile on his face, but Tommy was certain Sawyer could hear it. Tommy was incorrect. Sawyer was so out of sorts he would scarcely remember the conversation had occurred at all.

"Listen, Tommy, it's been awhile. It's great to hear from you, but I'm kind of tied up right now."

"No shit you are. I'm watching you on TV. Look straight up and wave." Tommy was surprised when Sawyer actually did. "Now smile for the cameras, Uncle Saw."

Sawyer smiled awkwardly. The reporter on Tommy's television described with confusion the scene being relayed from the courtroom. Who could be on the other end of the phone call with Sawyer Pettimore?

"Listen Tommy, I need to go."

"Well do you think that guy's him or not?" Tommy spoke hastily before Sawyer could hang up.

"I . . . I don't know." Sawyer's voice was shaky. "I need to hang up now." This time Sawyer didn't wait for Tommy to accept the conversation was over.

"Fine, but call me back. Call me back." Tommy watched Sawyer Pettimore hang up the phone from several thousand miles away. Tommy was excited. This was exciting. If that little fucking bitch was still alive . . .

Inside the judge's chambers, Smith was becoming Littlethumb again. As you might imagine the flood of memories was a lot to absorb and easily moved him to tears. He wept inconsolably as he relived the horrible night he lost his family. He studied Daring Bird with sad understanding, realizing the scars on Daring Bird's face were from the night his uncle had saved his life. Slowly but surely Littlethumb's tears were completely emptied. Daring Bird encouraged him to get the day over with. They reentered the courtroom together, shortly after the sheriff's deputy returned with the lockbox.

The box was opened and the documentation of Littlethumb's ownership of his *Mona Lisa* was revealed. A handwritten note was folded up inside the box. The note contained the words Daring Bird had used to release Littlethumb's memories. Daring Bird explained that in case he died suddenly, he had placed the note there for Littlethumb to find so his memories weren't lost forever.

Of course, once Littlethumb was himself again, his love for Sawyer Pettimore returned. Upon re-entering the courtroom, rather than immediately returning to the witness stand, Littlethumb asked the bailiff to escort him to Sawyer's side. No words were necessary. Littlethumb hugged Sawyer and Sawyer wasted no effort fighting back tears of his own.

Littlethumb eventually made his way back to the witness box. He explained to the judge he was indeed Littlethumb Brooks and that he must have subconsciously placed the thumbprint on the painting. Without going into detail, Littlethumb insisted he could describe what happened the night of the fire and would be willing to do so in a deposition once he had more time to sort through the fifteen years' worth of memories that had flooded back into his mind.

Judge Lograve suspended the case and the hearing. There was still much to discover and validate from the day's proceedings. This man's ability to describe the night in question, though helpful, would not be enough. The court would have to find out if there were medical records or any other form of identifying documentation still available to verify Smith's true identity. Of course, none of this would play out in court if Sawyer Pettimore decided to drop his lawsuit.

Once adjourned, Littlethumb noticed Sawyer's family had made their way to his side. Maria was there too, and she looked over at Littlethumb.

"Hi," Littlethumb signed discreetly to her.

"Hi," Maria replied.

"Crazy day, huh?" Littlethumb signed, wearing an awkward smile.

"That's one way to put it," Maria's facial expression said back to him.

Daring Bird noticed the conversation between his nephew and Maria as he made his way to Littlethumb. "Hey, kid," he said. "Let's get you out of here."

"Okay," Littlethumb said. At the same time he signed, "I want to see you again," to Maria.

"Okay," she replied.

"Now listen," Daring Bird said. "This will be crazy. There'll be mics in your face coming at you from every direction. What do you want to do? You want to answer some questions or 'no comment' our way out of this mess?"

"No comment," Littlethumb responded.

"Listen, kid, I've got to know what you want to do. Do you want to talk to the reporters or not?" Daring Bird smiled at Littlethumb.

Littlethumb smiled back but his was a tired smile. The emotional chemical dump brought on by the return of his memories had exhausted him. He looked over to see if he still had Maria's attention. She was looking at him so he waved goodbye and signed, "I'll call you," to which she tilted her head and smiled, uncertain if he had intentionally made a deaf joke. Littlethumb looked up at the honorable Judge Lograve, still seated on his throne enjoying the madness in his court. "Is there a back door to this place?"

35

In case you were wondering, I'm not going to share with you all the gruesome details of that dreadful evening. I will tell you the explosion killed both of Littlethumb's parents before the ensuing fire. His brother and sister as well. The blast knocked Littlethumb unconscious, while the young lady he escorted through the crowd had her head severed by an airborne cymbal from The Pond Scum's drum set.

The explosion also knocked out Daring Bird, blistering his face with shrapnel. When he woke the room was in chaos. Bodies were strewn everywhere. People were on fire. The ones who weren't completely knocked unconscious by the explosion writhed about in flames or fell out from smoke inhalation or both. He was disoriented. His ears rang loudly, damaged by the explosion. He could hear himself breathing like an echo inside his head, but the screams and chaos of the room were muffled.

Daring Bird ripped one of his own shirtsleeves off at the shoulder, tied the sleeve around his head to cover his mouth and nose, and then crawled in search of his family. With a heavy heart he discovered the dead bodies of Elizabeth and Walter. He briefly cradled Elisabeth's head against his own body before remembering the children. Heather and Freddy were found nearby. They were gone as well. His anguish was devastating. He almost laid down right there to die with them, but he couldn't. There was still the little one. Where was he?

A picture of the room the moment before the explosion flashed in Daring Bird's mind. He saw Littlethumb leading the little girl back towards Walter and Elisabeth. He crawled several feet in the direction his instincts sent him, patting the ground around him as he moved, reaching as far in every direction as he could in the hopes of finding Littlethumb. He found the little girl's lifeless body first. Then he discovered his nephew, still breathing.

Daring Bird carried a pistol that evening. He'd been armed continuously for several weeks, as protection against retaliation from the Electric Medicine Men's enemies. Instinctively, he knocked one of Littlethumb's teeth out with the handle of the gun and left the tooth behind. Then he tore his other shirtsleeve off and tied it over Littlethumb's mouth and nose. Daring Bird scooped Littlethumb into his arms and searched for an escape, but the elevator would not rise and the door to the stairwell would not open.

The shaman staggered around the room looking for the window with the fire escape. Other people continued to struggle around him. A few called for help as they stumbled about. Most coughed and crawled on the ground before they passed out from asphyxiation. Smoke from the paintings had quickly filled the room with a deadly rainbow-colored fog. The poisonous cloud burned Daring Bird's eyes badly as he made his way, feeling for windows. When he found one he smashed a hole in the glass to see if the fire escape was outside. The room was so smoke-filled that busting a hole through the glass was the only way he could see out. The fresh air allowed him a deep breath before continuing his search, but of course, the oxygen rich breeze also fueled the fire.

After breaking several windows, Daring Bird finally discovered the fire escape in a corner of the room furthest from the stage. The window to the fire escape was caged and locked. Daring Bird felt around for the window's lock, wedged his gun's barrel directly against the latch, shielded his face and fired. He opened the cage and placed Littlethumb safely onto the landing.

Daring Bird turned back toward the room. "Over here!" he attempted to shout, but when he tried to scream all that came out was blood, coughed onto the shirtsleeve tied around his face. The cloud of smoke was so dense it was impossible to see if any other people were still standing. Daring Bird took one futile step forward, a last desperate want to help the others, then turned, crawled through the window and carried Littlethumb to safety, not only from the fire but from the tragedy of his life.

Convinced his dealings with the Electric Medicine Men had caused the catastrophe, Daring Bird fled with Littlethumb to escape his enemies. There was a good chance they would still be after him. Accordingly, Daring Bird thought it best if the world believed Littlethumb died with the rest of his family. As for his own whereabouts, there was no record of Daring Brid attending the party. No one in New York knew whom he was save for his relatives and they were used to him disappearing.

Daring Bird stole away with Littlethumb to an E2M safe house in Quebec. He took everything he could fit into the chop-shop minivan he'd been driving since his move out to the Bronx, including Jojo

Monkey. The van was untraceable, with a license plate registered in the police system to a cop who did not exist. If the plates were run by another cop, they would see the vehicle was owned by a fellow officer and move along without further investigation. Or so the theory was. Is there anything that can't be done nowadays with a laptop computer and some caffeine?

The keys to his apartment were donated to a vagrant on the street with instructions to go take whatever he wanted and encouragement for the man to use this opportunity to turn his life around. Surprisingly enough, I can tell you the man actually did. He went from third place in the pecking order of his homeless dude crew who lived under a bridge together but now had an apartment to first place. Briefly. Then down to second when they lost the apartment and went back to the bridge. But he was no longer third! No sir. He would never be third again.

Anyway, one of the members of the Electric Medicine Men was Canadian and had family land northeast of Ottawa, pretty much in the middle of nowhere. The trip took a few days. Once they arrived, Daring Bird and Littlethumb did not leave the woods for several years except to buy supplies. While he raised Littlethumb, Daring Bird continued to be the eyes and ears of the E2M as he had in New York. However, with C. C. Constantine's financial support no longer available the group limited its activities and eventually went on hiatus.

While Daring Bird homeschooled Littlethumb he also groomed the boy to be the brains behind the machine, with hope the Electric Medicine Men could eventually get back to work. The gaps in Littlethumb's memory were filled in as much as necessary, though Daring Bird reserved the right to limit retelling the tragedy of his family's death to, "your family died in a horrible fire."

He also encouraged Littlethumb to paint, albeit without explaining the significance of his talent. That information was too intertwined with the fire and Daring Bird didn't want to discuss that subject any more than absolutely necessary. Instead, Littlethumb was provided with materials and told painting was a hobby before he lost his memory. No big whoop.

When the time felt right, Daring Bird told Littlethumb about the Electric Medicine Men and their work. After Littlethumb's nightmares began, Daring Bird finally told him the whole truth about his artistic talent and the night of the fire. Littlethumb knew something was missing from the story but his uncle insisted he was no longer withholding anything about Littlethumb's past.

The first clear memories that returned to Littlethumb were of his excursion into the spirit world. At first he thought the memories were weird dreams as the mental images seeped through cracks in the barriers to his subconscious. Eventually, as with any cracked dam under pressure, the mental floodgates crashed open and bombarded him with his past. Littlethumb understood the "dreams" were actually recollections from his childhood. He also realized the Occurrence was the missing piece of his uncle's story, which now made perfect sense. Daring Bird hadn't known.

Everything came back to him. The Occurrence, his paintings, his family, how happy he'd been. He was devastated.

Littlethumb lived with his tragic memories for a while. I don't want you to think he ran from them immediately. He suffered them, but eventually decided erasing his memories would serve dual purposes. The procedure would ease his pain for a time while also assisting in a grander scheme he and Daring Bird hatched to get the Electric Medicine Men back together.

When Littlethumb was old enough he would take control as the organization's central nervous system, allowing Daring Bird to get back out in the field. As I mentioned to you previously, Daring Bird went a little extra nuts when his sister and her family died. He loved his nephew and considered it a blessing the boy survived, that he was able to raise him, but Daring Bird grew stir-crazy hiding out in the Canadian wilderness.

Littlethumb did as well. He was ready to be a part of the world again, in his own way. He wouldn't be a "normal" part of the world. That was for sure. Normal was basically out the window the day he sneezed and the world froze. Which, by the way, he finally told his uncle about. Daring Bird was enthralled by Littlethumb's tale. Of course he was. He was also a little jealous, which he openly shared with his nephew. Littlethumb was simply relieved to finally share his big secret with another person.

In spite of Daring Bird's jealousy for Littlethumb's journey, which he labeled, "perhaps the most profound vision quest ever taken," he still agreed to Littlethumb's plan when the boy decided he wanted his memory erased. Littlethumb was tired of seeing the explosion engulf his family every night when he tried to sleep. He wasn't running away forever, he just needed some rest.

Daring Bird and Littlethumb developed the "Smith" alias together. Once Littlethumb was ready to be on his own, Daring Bird wreaked havoc on the world's bad guys again while Littlethumb directed the E2M's efforts from the command center he installed on Coney Island. Littlethumb could have set up shop anywhere he wanted in the world. Daring Bird had a strong intuition Littlethumb's subconscious mind was keeping him close to home, and to the reality of his true identity. They may have locked Littlethumb's memories away in the recesses of his gray matter, but those memories would not be denied their effect on Littlethumb's essence. You can run but you can't hide. We're all the sum of our experiences. Who shall I be, if I am not me, other than who I am? Something like that.

36

Daring Bird gave the day in court a proper ending when he yelled "Huzzah!" and threw down several ninja smoke bombs, creating a diversion while he and Littlethumb escaped the throng of reporters in the room and exited through the court's back door.

"Well, no one noticed that," Littlethumb said, to which Daring Bird gleefully laughed and laughed.

The next few days were spent sorting through fifteen years' worth of memories. Littlethumb grieved the loss of his family all over again. Most of his time was spent in bed asleep while his monkeys watched over him. Occasionally one of the monkeys jumped down and slapped him in the face to wake him, making sure he was still alive. On the third day, he got out of bed and got back to living.

Daring Bird sat in front of the command center drinking coffee and reading something intently. Spectacles rested below the equator of Daring Bird's nose. This was a new feature. Wearing glasses made his uncle appear a lot more scholarly and a tiny bit less insane.

"Well, well," Daring Bird said without looking up. "How do you do?"

"I think I do well," Littlethumb replied. "I like the glasses."

"Piss off."

Littlethumb passed through the room and into the kitchen, then returned with a mug of hot tea in his hand a few minutes later. "Whatcha up to?" he asked without speaking, motioning with his head at the monitor his uncle studied.

"Saving the world, one shipment of caviar at a time," Daring Bird said. "Would you believe someone started gobbling up all of the Beluga?"

"Of course I would," Littlethumb said dryly.

"Well, I've tracked a truck with about a hundred pounds of stolen beluga caviar, among other lesser contraband, and I'm watching the satellite relay of our brothers and sisters about to steal that truck." Daring Bird removed his glasses with a sweeping motion Littlethumb was certain had been rehearsed, then leaned back in his chair and propped his feet up. "It's more fun than watching football."

"Who we giving the fish eggs to?"

"I was thinking maybe the monkeys." Daring Bird and Littlethumb both laughed when the monkeys entered the room at the perfect time. The monkeys, despite not knowing why, immediately joined in the laughter. As the hees, haws, and disconcerting monkey screech-laughing settled, Daring Bird continued. "Truthfully, I think we send the shit to the White House with a big fuck-you to the president for wasting time and money on imperialistic efforts overseas instead of focusing on fixing the problems we have here at home. But then those assholes would get to eat a hundred pounds of fine caviar."

"Yeah. I don't think they care if we care more about fixing our country than controlling the world. They know what's going on."

"I got it. We send them one fish egg with a big F-you note and a video of the monkeys eating the beluga. We'll dress the monkeys up like politicians."

"Too esoteric for a politician to understand the insult."

"I got it. We'll film homeless people eating it. Can't make a more obvious statement that."

"And homeless people need food. It's perfect." Littlethumb took a seat at one of the computer stations.

"So, you all squared away?"

"I think so. I . . ." Littlethumb trailed off on his own, waving away with his hand whatever he might have said next.

"The nanny came by here looking for you," Daring Bird said, breaking the silence.

"She did?" Littlethumb perked up immediately.

"No."

"Dick."

"You got it bad, don't you, boy?" Daring Bird flashed a hangman's smile.

"Maybe," Littlethumb admitted. Then he was caught off guard by an onslaught of horrible emotions. His face contorted and he began to weep.

"Good lord, what the fuck?" Daring Bird spit coffee from his mouth.

"I don't know!" Littlethumb blurted. "I can't control it. It's awful."

"Get out of here, would you?" Daring Bird chuckled, but not without empathy. "I don't want to see that shit."

Littlethumb was already leaving the room. He held his arm out behind him, saluting his uncle with his middle finger on the way.

"That a boy," Daring Bird said to himself. The sentiment was confirmed with a loving smirk and head nod of agreement.

After Daring Bird and Littlethumb's dramatic exit from the court-room, but before the smoke had completely cleared, Mortimer Cross made his way to Sawyer Pettimore's side and told Sawyer to let him get his family out of there. The dazed man readily agreed. Cross moved Pettimore through the crowd, instructing Anna, Isabel, and Maria to grab on and follow behind him.

The detective repeated the phrase "No comment" to no avail as he watched the reporters turn into human-sized locusts. They swarmed and jabbed their mics at Pettimore, who was too weak to fight back on his own. Cross took his defense up a notch. "No comment" was now accompanied by open-handed slaps, palm-handed face-shoves, two-fingered eye gouges, and at least one headbutt as he forced a path through the reporters. The headbutt required the dainty removal and safe return of his bowler.

Much like Littlethumb, Sawyer went through several days of emotional turbulence after the trial. To escape the mob of reporters camped out in front of the apartment in Chelsea the family headed for Long Island. In shock from the entire situation, Sawyer never stopped to wonder why Mortimer Cross acted as his chief of staff, organizing and spearheading all the family's movements. The Pettimores were safely tucked away in their house on Long Island for a few days before Anna finally asked her husband why Mr. Cross was staying in the guest bedroom. Sawyer said he wasn't certain and agreed the detective's continued presence seemed a little odd.

"Baby, I know you're frazzled right now, but do you think you could ask him?" Anna requested.

When asked, Cross explained to Sawyer his intent to unravel the mystery behind the night of the fire. "Mr. Pettimore," he said, "we still don't know for certain this man is who he says he is. If he is not who he claims to be, your family could be in danger, and the reason could go all the way back to the fire. If he is who he says he is, well . . ."

"It's him," Sawyer said before Cross could finish.

"How do you know?"

"I just do. Somehow I knew from the moment I saw Isabel's paint-ing, but I avoided the truth as long as possible."

"That's very human of you, very understandable." Cross feared he was losing his footing in the situation.

"Thank you, Mr. Cross."

"You're welcome. And please, call me Mortimer. I believe we have come that far, to say the least." Cross attempted a welcoming smile. It did not work.

"Mr. Cross. Mortimer." Sawyer corrected himself with a smile and a nod. "I appreciate your services, everything you've done, especially getting us out of the courtroom the other day, but I think it's okay for you to leave now."

"Of course, Mr. Pettimore." Despite his awkward attempt at a smile, Cross wasn't bad at taking on a fatherly tone when he spoke. "If I may, sir, surely you would understand my own curiosity about some of the unanswered questions involving my work for you?"

"Of course."

"I was wondering . . ." Cross paused in a show of gathering his thoughts. "Do you think an occasion for all of us to sit down together, perhaps over dinner, may be possible? I know you and…should I call him Smith, or what was his last name?"

"Brooks."

"Yes, Brooks," Cross confirmed. "Mr. Brooks. I know you two will have much to catch up on. And of course, you will have to deal with ownership of his work, and whether or not he's entitled to any of the fortune you have made from selling his paintings."

Sawyer looked curiously at Cross. "Actually, I don't care anything about that right now."

"Good, good. Of course not." Cross did not want to insult Sawyer, he was just looking for the right angle.

Though mentally rattled, Sawyer was no dummy. It dawned on him what Cross was doing but he was too emotionally drained to be offended or suspicious. "Mr. Cross, I'm sorry. I'm a little slow on the uptake right now. Of course you still have questions. I suppose you wouldn't be a private investigator if you didn't."

"Probably not."

"But you don't have to lead me around by my nose though. No need for scare tactics."

Cross pursed his lips in response, adding a slight, apologetic nod of his head. Sawyer recognized the effort and silently accepted the apology. Then he said, "You know, he may not be interested in seeing me."

"I rather doubt that."

"Yeah. Me too."

37

Cross and Sawyer decided to have Maria, if she agreed, invite Littlethumb for a casual evening at Sawyer's home. Cross noticed and relayed to Sawyer the brief exchange between Littlethumb and Maria in the courtroom.

"I believe he's smitten with your nanny," Cross said.

"Oh really?" Sawyer responded in a playfully sarcastic tone. "What gives you that idea?" Everyone in court had heard Littlethumb's comments about the beautiful nanny.

Cross held the pointer finger of his left hand up next to his head. "Not only his description of meeting her and your daughter. Before he left the courtroom, Mr. Brooks signed to Maria he would call her later."

"You know sign language?" Sawyer was half playfully and half earnestly surprised. "How does everyone know sign language all of a sudden?"

"I don't know sign language. I read lips. It's a useful tool for a detective. I was able to read his lips because people who can speak have a tendency to mouth the words they're signing."

"Oh, of course," Sawyer said. "Makes perfect sense."

Maria happily agreed to the assignment. Though she was caught off guard when asked of her interest in delivering the invitation, she appreciated Sawyer's honesty about his reasons for asking her. Mostly, the clear attraction between her and Littlethumb. With unexpected bashfulness she admitted she was indeed attracted to the painter, and was curious to learn more about him. But did Sawyer think Littlethumb was trustworthy? His life seemed very strange.

"If he's still the same boy I knew," Sawyer replied, "he might be the safest, most loving, most trustworthy person on this planet." This was a hefty endorsement. Being a typical male, Sawyer didn't realize the effect his words had on Maria's heart.

Littlethumb was pleasantly surprised when he saw Maria's face on the front door's surveillance monitor. Not only surprised, but also spontaneously sweaty, nervous, and awkward. Maybe a little hungry too. She held what appeared to be a cake.

He scrambled out of a chair, almost falling when she rang the doorbell a second time. In effort to recover his balance he knocked a pile of files off the corner of a desk. In effort to recover the files he stepped into a short wastebasket. In effort to remain calm, he stood with the wastebasket attached to his foot as he checked himself in a mirror, desperately licking his palms and smearing hair away from his face.

Holy cow, I look like shit, he thought.

Maria felt the vibrations of a commotion coming from the house. When Littlethumb opened the door, she wore an inquisitive expression that quickly transitioned to a warm smile. She could not see his right foot still stuck in the metal trashcan and hidden behind the door.

Littlethumb cocked his head in wonderment, infatuation oozing from his pores, and Maria held the cake out for him. The top was covered in white icing with the words "Invitation Cake" written in chocolate icing. A note card stuck out from the cake. Littlethumb pulled the card out of the cake and removed the icing from the envelope with his finger. He promptly stuck the finger in his mouth to clean off the icing, then opened the note.

The note read: "I baked you a cake to invite you to dinner." He took the cake and set it on a table by the door, inviting Maria inside.

"No," she signed. "I can't stay."

"Bummer. Guess I'll have to take you up on dinner then."

"Yes, you will."

"I have to admit, I'm kind of surprised you're here. How did you find me?"

"The tall man working for Mr. Pettimore."

"Oh. Yeah, that makes sense." Littlethumb was slightly disappointed.

"Before you make up your mind, you should know I'm here for Mr. Pettimore. He asked me to deliver the invitation."

"Oh." Littlethumb wasn't exactly sure how to sign disappointment but he figured she would see the pain on his face.

"But I sincerely hope you will come."

"Will you be there?" *Argh? Really dude?* he thought. *She just said she hoped you would come. Why would she care if she wasn't going to be there?*

At precisely the correct time all four of his monkeys decided to see what was happening at the door. The two smallest, Sir Alister

Pickney and Stevie Two-Sharks, jumped up onto his left shoulder while their older brother Zeus jumped onto his right shoulder. Jojo landed gently atop his head. Littlethumb smiled awkwardly.

Maria giggled and signed, "Yes, I will be there."

"Then I will be too." At that, Stevie Two-Sharks smacked Littlethumb in the face and laughed his monkey ass off. Littlethumb playfully shooed the little guys away, never taking his eyes off Maria. "Are you sure you don't want to come inside for a minute?"

"Yes. You look like you have your hands full, but I will see you on Thursday."

"Okay. Oh, by the way, we haven't officially met yet. I'm Littlethumb." He stuck his hand out for a shake and, as he did so, was suddenly embarrassed. He realized his name felt a little juvenile so he pulled his hand back and signed, "But you can call me LT if you like," then stuck the hand out again.

When Maria took his hand the Universe sent a very clear message: Let go now or get those damn clothes off. She gently pulled away and said goodbye.

Our hero staggered back into his apartment. *Well, that was super smooth*, he thought. *You're a regular old Don Juan Casanova there, ain't-cha, kid?* He sighed and replayed the meeting in his mind, with hope that upon review he might not seem as awkward. Unfortunately, during his mental playback he couldn't remember what Maria looked like.

Have you ever been so infatuated with someone you can't remember their face? When you're with the person you're head over heels to such an extreme that when they're gone, your memory of the interaction is so hazy from all the butterflies you were feeling in your head that you can't remember stuff, sometimes even what the other person looks like. Let me tell you, brain butterflies are much more debilitating than stomach butterflies. You feel so elated and confused. Well that's what happened to Littlethumb. Thus, when his memory failed he headed for the studio to stare at her portraits, hoping that would help sort out the mess she'd made of his head.

When Daring Bird returned he found Littlethumb in his studio tinkering on the piano. All of his portraits of Maria were uncovered and on display. The cake sat on top of the piano with a large corner section missing. Daring Bird walked to the center of the room and took in the paintings. "She is beautiful, isn't she?"

Littlethumb did not respond, though a key struck on the piano several times like the "ding ding ding ding ding . . ." noise on a game show when a contestant answers correctly. Daring Bird walked over and broke off a chunk of cake, tossing it in his mouth. He hummed with approval.

"Hmmmmm, hm. Good cake. Moist." Daring Bird weaved in and out of the paintings on display as he spoke. "I like that word. Moist. A lot of people don't, you know, and I understand why. It's one of those words. But I like it."

Littlethumb chuckled quietly and shook his head, momentarily breaking from his befuddled, not-quite-melancholy state. Daring Bird caught the reaction from the corner of his eye and whirled on his nephew, crossing back over to the piano with a jaunty step.

"I gotta have more. Yes I do, yes I do. This cake is good!" I don't know what fake accent Daring Bird was going for but whatever he was doing, the creaky pitch was off-putting. Still, his attempt to lighten the heavy air in the room was successful.

Littlethumb shuddered. "Never do that again," he said with a fake grimace.

Daring Bird teetered, as if he were considering the request, then said, "So what's the invitation for?"

"Dinner."

"Man oh man. That's my boy. Barely knows who he is and broads are showing up at the front door with cakes and dinner dates." Daring Bird took another chunk of cake. "Good cake, too."

"Yes, you made note of that."

"So what's the problem, kid?"

"It's not dinner with her. It's dinner with Sawyer."

"Pettimore. Well, that makes sense." On that note, Daring Bird walked over and took a closer look at one of the portraits of Maria, then changed the subject. "Good to see you haven't lost your touch."

"Thanks."

"So, again, what's the problem? Why are you in here torturing yourself?"

"I'm not torturing myself," Littlethumb explained. "I...I couldn't remember what she looked like."

"Ah. I've been there. If that's what she does to you, you gotta go get her."

"What about our work? I could put her in danger."

"So could waking up in the morning. Look, kid, you got smacked in the face with a ton of shit to cope with all over again. I know what you're thinking, and feeling. For fifteen years I've been dealing with the possibility my bullshit killed your mom. And everyone else. I understand."

Littlethumb noticed the tiniest trace of tears in the corner of Daring Bird's eye. Daring Bird never wavered, however. If he was stirred emotionally, his voice did not betray him.

"In the grand scheme of things," he continued, "we don't control jack shit. You know this. Life is worth very little except for a few amazing things like music and art. What you can do with a paint-brush. Laughter. Brief moments of intense sadness so we know exactly how wonderful laughter is. And love. You're the most loving creature I believe I've ever met. You remind me of my father." Daring Bird's words weren't impassioned so much as instructional. He spoke with a warm-hearted professor's tone. "In summary, the point of my little speech here is threefold: Without all the shitty parts of life we wouldn't recognize the great ones. We can't control shit, like when it's someone's time to die, despite all of the illusions of control we create to protect our own sanity. And three, love trumps everything."

"Should I be taking notes?"

"Hopefully you learned something," Daring Bird said, then he playfully smacked at the back of Littlethumb's head.

"You need to go to the dinner with me. I want you to."

"I've got no business with Pettimore."

"Yes, you do. Whatever your distaste for him is, I need you to for-give him."

"Good luck with that."

38

Despite his disdain for Sawyer Pettimore, Daring Bird agreed to attend the dinner party with Littlethumb. He never explained his contempt. I'm not sure he could have. The feeling came from his gut, which made it unfortunately difficult to let go of.

Still, he behaved like a perfect gentleman, at least for a gentleman who was slightly insane. For the most part the dinner went well. The presence of Mortimer Cross initially had Littlethumb and Daring Bird a little on edge, until they learned his purpose for attending. Cross beseeched Littlethumb and Sawyer Pettimore to finance an investigation into the night of the fire. Neither man was interested. On the other hand, though he said nothing at the dinner table, Daring Bird was intrigued.

The group shared considerable discussion and laughter about Cross's surveillance of Smith. Cross and Sawyer discussed their befuddlement with Littlethumb's disguises. Everyone fell into hysterics at the revelation the costumes were coincidental and purely something Littlethumb enjoyed doing. Littlethumb and Cross each recounted their version of their initial face to face exchange, inciting another round of laughter.

They talked about what Littlethumb and Daring Bird had done for the last fifteen years. The story Littlethumb and Daring Bird told was mostly true, though they omitted large portions involving any dealings with the Electric Medicine Men. The gist of the tale was they had gone into mourning for a necessary period of time, afterwards choosing to live a quiet existence out on Coney Island where they'd been ever since. The two men kept the summary brief but readily shared their founding of onedollarprayers.com and their charitable work.

The presentation was smooth, one they prepared many years ago and relayed now as reflex action. Mortimer Cross did not inquire as to why they felt the need to have their home under such high-tech surveillance. He hoped he might learn the answer eventually, but his instinct was not to question Littlethumb and Daring Bird in front of everyone else.

Littlethumb and Daring Bird weren't the only ones at the dinner table with a secret. Of course not. Everyone has secrets. In this instance, I mean a secret specific to others at the table.

Isabel having been shipped off to her grandparents for the evening held more significance than accommodating an "adults only" conversational atmosphere. Inside Isabel's closet, covered in sheets, was the portrait of Daring Bird painted by Littlethumb so many years earlier. The portrait Sawyer Pettimore had specifically agreed to destroy. Yet another source of guilt for Sawyer. During his period of mourning after the fire, he'd wondered more than once if he had somehow caused this cosmic injustice by not fulfilling his promise to the shaman. Still, the idea of destroying the picture had not grown anymore palatable once everyone was dead.

So the portrait survived, eventually hung in Isabel's room where it remained her entire life, serving double-duty as the spiritual protector of a young lady's dreams and a somber reminder to Sawyer of his lies, petty desires, and mistakes. He hoped entrusting his daughter to the watchful eye of a man with such a noble spirit was a fitting homage to Daring Bird, perhaps offsetting the fact he hadn't destroyed the portrait as promised. Of course, whether his plan worked or not, his choice was made long before Isabel was born. He could never bring himself to damage such a beautiful work.

Anna suggested Sawyer tell Daring Bird the truth, but Sawyer eventually won her over to the idea of waiting to see how things went at dinner. Anna had finally agreed their first reunion in fifteen years might not be the best time for Sawyer to admit he betrayed his promise to Daring Bird. This meant the painting had to be hidden to avoid accidental discovery, and Isabel had to be removed from the dinner equation. Though Daring Bird had aged considerably and earned many new scars, on several occasions since the day in court, Isabel had noted how much the weird old-lady man at daddy's court thing had looked like the monkey-pirate man in her painting.

As they finished the main course, Sawyer uncomfortably broached the business of Littlethumb's work. He was nervous and his anxiety showed. Littlethumb quickly put him at ease.

"I don't want any of the money," he said. "I'm fine. All of my paintings you own are still yours."

Sawyer wasn't concerned about the money or the rights to the paintings. He excused himself from the table and asked Littlethumb to join him on the patio. Once safely outside on the back deck,

Sawyer broke down. The tears started slowly at first but quickly escalated into a full-fledged sob. He explained to Littlethumb the guilty burden he'd carried with him for so many years, and how he escaped the fire out of cowardice.

"I don't understand," Littlethumb said. "You've had all this time and you didn't do anything but feel guilty?" The question wasn't intended to make Sawyer feel worse. Littlethumb was earnestly confounded by the idea.

"What could I have done?" Sawyer replied. "I've tried to live right, to do right. But there's nothing I could ever do to make up for that night. I took advantage of you and your family, and then I ran when you were in danger." Sawyer put his face in his hands in shame and fell to his knees. The scene was a little melodramatic, and definitely out of character for Sawyer, but his emotions were authentic. After all, he had repressed this stuff as much as possible for a long time. He went to hug his former student's legs but Littlethumb intercepted him before he could, pulling him up by the armpits.

"Okay, this is a little weird. Come on. Up you go. Up." He helped Sawyer to a standing position. "Wipe that shit off your face, will you?" Littlethumb produced a handkerchief, seemingly out of thin air.

Sawyer took the hanky and wiped the tears from his cheeks, then the snot from his nose. "Jesus, what a wuss I am."

"A little bit, yeah." Littlethumb agreed with a smile. He placed his right hand on Sawyer's shoulder. "Sawyer, my family loved you, but I guarantee my parents weren't blind to your ambition. They were too smart, and it was only natural for you to get swept up in everything."

Sawyer didn't say anything, instead he simply nodded his head in agreement.

"I think you've suffered long enough. On behalf of my entire family, I forgive you. No, I absolve you. There is no reason to forgive you because you didn't do us any harm. Now, get in here. You need a hug." Littlethumb embraced his long-lost teacher, who returned the embrace with enthusiasm.

"Thank you," Sawyer said when they finally parted. "Funny, I was your teacher and I feel like the kid here."

"It happens," Littlethumb replied.

Sawyer took one last swipe at his face, this last scrub intended to wipe off the melancholy, then held the handkerchief up for Littlethumb to take back. "You always keep one of these up your sleeve?"

"Most days, yes. Never know when it might come in handy." Rather than take the handkerchief, Littlethumb pushed Sawyer's hand back towards his body. "You keep that one though, I've got more."

"Oh, right." Sawyer wadded the snot rag up and stuffed it into a pocket.

"Say, now that we have that all squared away, what can you tell me about Maria?"

Maria was of Spanish heritage. Her last name was Holguín, and her surname was likely the only unattractive thing about her, though the name meant "to be happy." Being a Spanish word, the *i* has an accent and is pronounced in a manner I don't prefer. The hard *g* sound right before the *u* and *i*, to my ears, is aural sandpaper.

Anyhow, Littlethumb really only wanted Sawyer to tell him if Maria had a man or not, and if she had been asking about Littlethumb at all. Otherwise, he wanted to peel away at the mystery of the woman on his own. The thought of learning her was exhilarating.

The subject change from debilitating grief and regret to Littlethumb's infatuation with Maria put Sawyer further at ease, and he laughed warmly at his former apprentice's romantic stupor. "You've got it bad, don't you," he said, in almost the exact same manner as Daring Bird had before. "That's beautiful. She's a lovely young woman."

The two men returned to the dinner table with a renewed sense of élan, joining everyone else for dessert. Sawyer's puffy eyes and cheeks were not lost on the others, but no one mentioned them. Anna would wait until later to ask Sawyer what happened.

As the evening wound down they adjourned to the living room for coffee. The conversation splintered as Littlethumb focused more and more attention on Maria. Eventually, he mentioned stepping out onto the patio again and asked her if she might like some fresh air.

Once outside, Littlethumb asked Maria if she would like to see a trick. She agreed, as long as the trick wasn't mean. Littlethumb smiled and made a notecard appear from behind her ear. A message was written in crayon on the card: "VIP invitation for Maria: 1 private carousel ride, animal-pole seat of your choice." The invitation expired in two weeks.

With a mischievous smile, Maria signed that she would make sure to save the invitation in her coupon book.

"May I hold your hand?" Littlethumb asked. Maria agreed. Holding hands made using sign language tricky, so Littlethumb led her to the deck's railing where they stood quietly together, staring at the moon.

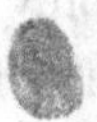

Back inside the conversation had become a little awkward. As you know, Daring Bird was no fan of Pettimore and had not wanted to come to the gathering to begin with. Although well behaved at dinner, he'd grown weary from the effort. Now he sat in the living room quietly emitting a gruff persona and making everyone else uncomfortable. As he watched Pettimore and Anna make conversation with the old fella, he almost forgot he was in the same room with them and that they could see him studying them with a scowl on his face.

Eventually, Anna excused herself to the kitchen to put the food away. Without Anna in the room to encourage the awkward conversation, the men fell silent. Mortimer Cross and Daring Bird were totally comfortable with uncomfortable silence. Their host was not. After a few minutes, Sawyer excused himself to see if Anna needed any help.

"Finally," Daring Bird blurted. Then he looked at Cross and said, "I think you and I need to talk about that night."

Back on the deck, Littlethumb shifted his gaze from the moon and turned Maria towards him. "Would you think I was creepy if I told you I wanted to know everything about you?"

"A little." Maria batted her eyelashes hard enough to break any man's will. "But I would also find it very flattering."

"I want to know everything there is to know about you, Maria. From the first time I saw you on the boardwalk."

"That's very flattering."

"Do you believe in providence?"

"I think so. I'm not one hundred percent, but I usually lean in that direction."

"Good. I don't want to scare you but I think that's what this is." He was about to continue when Maria took his hands and kissed him delicately. Their lips remained barely connected for what felt like an eternity. The insufficiency of their embrace was tantalizing. Littlethumb wanted to grab her and pull her in tight, smashing their faces together more passionately, but he resisted the urge, instead taking the moment slowly and basking in Maria's gentle radiance.

When their lips finally fell apart, Littlethumb gazed into Maria's green eyes with a love-struck moron's smile. Then, instantaneously, he began to sob uncontrollably. Again.

His blubbering was a pretty odd sight for Maria. One minute he was smiling, then tears suddenly ran down his face, which made the smile seem scary and insane. "Damn it!" he said loudly. Maria did not need to hear or know how to read lips to recognize what he'd said.

"What is it? What's wrong?"

"Nothing," he signed. "You've got to be fucking kidding me," he said aloud, turning around on his heels and staring up at the sky as his arms flopped up and down. He looked back at Maria. "This is embarrassing. Please forgive me, but I'm gonna get out of here."

"Can't you tell me what's wrong?"

"I promise, I would if I knew. It's uncontrollable. It comes out of nowhere and I can't stop. It started after I got my memory back."

"Oh. I suppose that's understandable."

"Yeah, but it sure does suck." Littlethumb wiped a rather large and embarrassing "crying-fit" snot bubble from his nose with the sleeve of his shirt. "This could go on for an hour or so. I should leave."

"Okay." Maria radiated empathy. "Will I see you again soon?"

"As soon as possible, please." he signed, then he turned and got the hell out of there.

Littlethumb shot through the house, making eye contact with his uncle while pointing to his own, emotionally contorted face. Daring Bird understood immediately. "I believe that's my cue," he said. Cross was obviously curious about Littlethumb's sudden flight but Daring Bird didn't give him a chance to raise any questions. "Something to do with the amnesia. Nothing really. Please, give our regards to the Pettimores."

"Yes of course." Cross rose as he spoke.

Daring Bird stepped forward to shake Cross's hand. "I look forward to hearing from you."

Cross returned the handshake with an affirmative forward tilt of his head, then watched as Daring Bird followed after his nephew.

39

Littlethumb's rebirth inspired many unforeseen consequences, not the least of which was a renewal in the life of Tommy Toxic. Once Tommy confirmed with Sawyer the man in question was indeed his nemesis, the fires of his hatred for Littlethumb burned brightly again. He slept better, ate better, started exercising, stopped getting fucked up, and most importantly, wrote music that wasn't terrible. In fact, most was quite good.

It took weeks of effort to scale back his substance abuse. Getting clean was no easy task, but the opportunity for revenge was not to be overlooked. Plus, he was fueled by malice. Tommy returned to a reasonable level of fitness and before he realized what was happening, went to work on a concept album.

The return of his vigor also saw Tommy's advances toward the sweet little thing down the hall rewarded. Well, vigor and date-rapey drugs. What a wonderful combination, though in the end he didn't need to drug her. The young woman suddenly found herself susceptible to Tommy's devilish charms. She led him willingly to the bedroom. Of course, being the son of a bitch he was he still roofied her, just for fun. Unfortunately for Tommy, but luckily for the young woman, she wouldn't remember a lot of the stuff they did, so she wouldn't regret their evening together quite as much as he hoped. But Tommy knew. He knew what he tricked her into. His actions were despicable, which pleased him to no end.

With his physical health restored, his talent operating in full form, and his depravity confirmed without question, the time had come to leave Seattle. Thus, Tommy Toxic headed for Los Angeles to reinvent himself for public consumption.

While Tommy put his life back on its demented track, Mortimer Cross investigated the mystery of the fire. There were several factors behind Daring Bird's decision to hire Cross. Daring Bird was intrigued by him in general. A man with his apparent capabilities might be useful to the Electric Medicine Men, as Cross seemed potentially inclined toward enjoying their line of work. Daring Bird also appreciated Cross's compulsion to unravel the mystery. Clearly the man liked to see things through to their end.

If Cross was able to discover the fire's cause, he would prove himself a worthy investigator and Daring Bird would invite him into the E2M. Oh, and of course, if Cross discovered the explosion had been created intentionally there was the hope he would also discover the perpetrators. Then Daring Bird would get to kill them. Daring Bird had never taken another human's life but he was fairly certain he would if given the opportunity to avenge the deaths of so many.

Confirmation of Littlethumb's identity occurred during this time as well. In the end, they were able to prove his lineage through blood sampling and DNA testing. Littlethumb's missing tooth, which

Daring Bird impulsively left behind the night of the fire, wound up serving no purpose. I'm not certain whether or not the tooth was recovered at the time of the original investigation. At some point during the process of verifying Littlethumb's identity Daring Bird wondered aloud whether or not it had, which forced him to explain the entire thing to Littlethumb. The empty socket in Littlethumb's mouth became a perpetual source of teasing between him and his uncle for the rest of their lives, and the phrase "Good thing I didn't need that tooth" took on a life of its own for them and their people.

Once news spread the mysterious Littlethumb Brooks was alive, the world was intrigued with learning more about the man into whom the boy had grown. Where had he been? How had he escaped the fire? Why did he hide? Was he a bachelor?

Everyone involved was bombarded with requests for interviews. Out of respect, Sawyer refused to accept any interviews until Littlethumb chose to break his own silence. Mortimer Cross and Daring Bird retreated back into the shadows, hard at work on their missions, and Tommy Toxic sure as hell wasn't going to waste his time talking about that geek. Besides, he was too busy working on new music that would blow the heads off the entire goddamn music industry. His new album was gonna be so killer. Fuckin' musical homicide.

Most importantly, Littlethumb's courtship of Maria persisted despite his sporadic, surprise bouts of spastic crying. Maria's comfort eased the pain that caused the outbursts. What had started as infatuation quickly spiraled into an unbridled, feverish, insatiably passionate love affair. The hyper-awareness of their every moment together felt like taking baby steps as they checked off all the boxes of a fairytale romance, but they took those baby steps so quickly the lovers felt like they were traveling through an emotional time warp together.

The affair began with another surprise visit from Maria, who wanted to see how Littlethumb was doing and redeem her free carousel ride. Homemade chicken soup was brought for lunch. Before they ate, Littlethumb formally introduced Maria to Jojo Monkey and the other three knuckleheads. Stevie Two-Sharks appeared to have a serious crush on her. The other three simply made passing attempts at casual affairs.

After lunch, Littlethumb showed Maria his paintings. He was nervous to share them, especially the portraits of her, but his anxiety was easily relieved. Maria was absolutely enthralled. So much so, they made love for the first time right then, right there on his studio floor. So much for baby steps.

I won't lie, the sexy time wasn't perfect right out of the gates, but they had fun. They were in a room full of paint and blank canvas. Use your imagination. They did.

Speaking of which, and this may seem awful to you, but please don't be offended because it's an innocent truth. Littlethumb had been curious as to whether or not Maria would make noises when they made love, and if so, what those noises might sound like. If you've been around someone who lived their entire life without hearing, there's a good chance you're familiar with the noises deaf people sometimes emit which are different sounds than one might be used to.

What can I say? Littlethumb's curiosity wasn't a hang-up or anything, but if I'm telling an honest tale I must admit the thought crossed his mind. He was curious what Maria might sound like in the sack.

As it turned out, he should have been more concerned with the goofy facial expressions he would make, because Maria sounded like a damn songbird. I kid you not. She literally made noises resembling the joyful chirps of a Western Meadowlark mixed with the satisfied kitten purrs of a Burmese Rumbler. Until she got on top. Then she sounded like a Siberian tigress.

The overwhelming intoxication of love in its purest form turned Littlethumb into a desperate, lusty, adoring, Maria junkie. A fool whose only hope for a cure to his illness was learning everything there was to know about this amazing woman. Maria, equally lovestruck, would share with him the most intimate details of her life, her heart, and her soul. You only get a quick summary.

Maria's parents were first-generation Spanish immigrants. When their daughter was born deaf they relocated to the United States, with hopes she would have better educational opportunities tailored to her specific needs. Once Maria was of age her parents returned to Spain. They'd grown weary of the U.S. and were nostalgic for their home. Maria chose to stay. New York was the only home she'd ever known.

She completed a nursing program for people with "different" abilities. The program earned these folks their nursing certifications and also helped the graduates find employment where their supposed disabilities weren't liabilities. Maria happened across the Pettimore's ad for a full-time nanny and thought the job sounded better than working in a nursing home or hospital. With the Pettimores' progressive mindset, Maria's disability was a unique notch in her favor during the interviews. The job was hers.

Maria's favorite color was red. Her favorite food was pizza. Her favorite musician was "who gives a shit" because she couldn't hear. (Even though she was only teasing him with her response, Littlethumb felt bad about the question.) She liked watching graceful sports, making bird-houses, wearing loose-fitting skirts and cooking with copious amounts of unsalted butter. She was extremely intelligent. She was a Virgo.

The Pettimores granted Maria a week off and Littlethumb took her up to the safe house in Canada. There, he swore her to secrecy and told her about his and Daring Bird's dealings with the Electric Medicine Men. The decision to confide in her was his only option. She had to know of the potential dangers before deciding whether or not to stay involved with him, but he was too late for that. She was already in love. No turning back now.

With that settled, Littlethumb also told Maria about the Occurrence. Several days were spent recounting his adventure, paintbrush in hand, as Maria played the naked muse. She marveled at his perception of her, but insisted the nudes were destroyed. Despite his reluctance to do so, Maria made Littlethumb an offer he couldn't refuse. In the evenings, they would place the paintings in the fireplace to watch them burn while they made love.

Their week alone in the woods consummated the couple's spiritual marriage to one another. By the time they returned to Coney Island,

Littlethumb's sudden bouts of uncontrollable sobbing were no more. Though his last one had appeared mid-coitus, which made for a highly dubious grand finale. In the end, Maria's tenderness and his head-over-heels-in-love status for her cured him. Littlethumb no longer felt continuously haunted by the loss of his family, and though he remained deeply saddened at times when he thought of them, Maria's presence eased that pain. Eventually, he learned to think fondly of them without fear of spiraling into uncontrollable despair.

Once Littlethumb's crying fits were gone, Daring Bird decided to take off and get back into the action. His nephew didn't need him clogging up the works if the young couple was to be engaged in a proper love affair. Having a crusty old uncle for a roommate wasn't exactly a sexy attribute for the young artist in love.

There was one last piece of business, however. The requests for interviews continued. Up until this point, Daring Bird understood Littlethumb's hesitancy to participate. The last thing most people would want is to be seen babbling like a fool on television. Now that Littlethumb's fits had stopped, Daring Bird told him the time had come to tell the world who he was. Littlethumb was apprehensive, which was understandable but unacceptable. I believe Daring Bird's exact words, paraphrased here of course, were, "You have a gift, son. Share it with the world and enjoy yourself. Don't be afraid."

As Daring Bird left the room he paused and shook his head in frustration. I'm not sure who he was arguing with up there in his middle-aged melon, but when he finally spoke again he said, "Just go live your damn life and take what's coming to you."

40

Littlethumb agreed to an interview with a television personality named Doug Sullivan. *The Doug Sullivan Show* was a nationally syndicated talk show, aired live in the mornings and geared toward housewives. Doug's show was chosen for three reasons. First, Littlethumb liked to wake up early and attack the day. Second, they offered him the most money, which he could donate to charity. And third, Littlethumb had always liked the name Doug.

The appearance transported Littlethumb into a new stratosphere of celebrity. His story and handsome features stole the heart of the American housewife, and you know what that meant. The value of his art plummeted. Don't worry, it comes back.

Perhaps the most important outcome of the interview, Littlethumb realized he was comfortable speaking in public. Though he still preferred a highly economical use of words, the success of his *The Doug Sullivan Show* appearance convinced Littlethumb he could manage a few more guest spots. So, he accepted several of the largest financial offers and continued to tell his story.

The tale was always the same, from the deposition he provided during the hearing through multiple television and radio interviews. While he omitted the Occurrence and his work with the E2M, Littlethumb told the truth about everything else involving his disappearance. The gist was: Daring Bird saved his life on the night of the fire, the explosion gave Littlethumb amnesia, his uncle raised him in secrecy, the hypnosis thing, yada yada, yada yada.

Where was his uncle now? Off doing mission work in South America. What about the rest of his family? Why did his uncle let them continue to think he was dead? Why did they hide? The hiding began as a temporary situation, to protect everyone, as Daring Bird thought someone may have tried to kill Littlethumb on purpose. Why? They didn't know, but he was convinced the explosion was a bomb. Why didn't he go to the police? Well, if you haven't seen the footage from the hearing, Daring Bird is a little crazy. The audience would laugh, Littlethumb would bat his eyelashes, and donations would be collected for onedollarprayers.com.

One savvy interviewer asked Littlethumb how he was able to maintain his daily meditations with all of the traveling he'd been doing, not to mention his blossoming romance with Maria. Littlethumb politely explained he could log into the website remotely, then invited his host back to the hotel for the afternoon's session. The television network made an impromptu scheduling change and the host participated in the meditation on live TV. The ratings exploded and onedollarprayers.com's computer server almost collapsed under the weight of the Internet traffic.

The success of Littlethumb's public appearances, coupled with his newfound comfort for life in the public eye, led to a new phase in his life as an artist. With money earned from the talk show circuit he opened an art studio on Coney Island. Employing a bit of an unusual design twist, Littlethumb made the space a theater in the round. The room had four rows of stadium seating that went in a full circle, save for two entrance hallways. One entrance was for guests, the other for Littlethumb and Maria. The studio also had a standing room only, balcony-level observation deck. When construction was finished the doors were opened to the public. Guests were invited to watch daily painting sessions with the tiny caveat they made a donation to onedollarprayers.com in the amount of at least…you guessed it…one dollar.

While not without trepidation and tears, Maria resigned from her position with the Pettimores. Maria was deeply attached to Isabel but her heart belonged to Littlethumb. She left Manhattan and moved out to Coney Island. The young lovers were married by the cotton candy guy, who happened to be an Internet approved, certificate holding ordained minister. The ceremony was very sweet.

Maria joined Littlethumb in his daily meditations, managed the art studio, and acted as host to the studio guests. She also DJ'd Littlethumb's painting sessions. Sometimes Littlethumb provided her a set list. On other occasions, Maria would completely surprise him with music selections of her own. He joked about how much "that woman" must love him to agree to be his DJ, being deaf and all. How she was the deafest DJ on the block. How she gave the term def DJ new meaning. There were more puns and punchlines, but no need to review them here as they were all just as bad.

In truth, the DJ idea was Maria's. She said she could feel the music's vibrations in her body when he worked, and the sensation turned her on. Sometimes they would dance around the room together with paintbrush in hand, stabbing and swiping at the canvas as they spun past.

They interacted with the audience throughout the show, and Littlethumb often gave his finished works to onlookers, specifically those whose auras piqued his curiosity. Sometimes he would finish a work in one day. Sometimes he could do several in a day. Sometimes, one piece would take several days, or weeks, or on the rare occasion, months. Though I'm sure the studio's environment affected his work, quality art remained the central focus. That was the key. Everything else about his little show was not to detract from the art he was tasked with creating.

The show was such a hit they brought Sawyer in on their production. With his connections they booked Littlethumb to perform in larger venues. He painted for audiences in theaters and arenas around the world. All of the profit went to charity save for the relatively meager costs of Littlethumb's and Maria's relatively meager existence on Coney Island, and the portion used to help fund the efforts of the Electric Medicine Men, which was in effect a form of charitable giving as well, though that money was completely off the books, of course. This all happened at light speed, but when it did, Maria and Littlethumb were so head-over-heels for one another their meteoric rise to stardom felt insignificant in comparison.

41

When Tommy arrived in Los Angeles he quietly re-infiltrated the music scene. He played the open mics in bars, coffee shops, and these new underground freak shows called art gasms, also known as A-gasms and AGMs. The art gasms were "happenings" organized by a bunch of young punks and wannabe artists of all varieties who found safe places to hang out and get wasted. While getting wasted they would paint, play music, sing, dance, and do what people do when they're getting wasted in the name of freedom and art.

Art gasm was a new name for an old tradition, but the term *gasm* was hot. Everyone was gasm-atic, or gasmed up, or about to gasm right through their pants. However you rocked the new slang, if you confidently ended your sentence with the word, "baby," people dug your style. "Ima 'bout to gasm my eyeballs out, baby." Something like that.

Tommy specifically targeted places where he could play in front of the younger generation. He knew he had to reach the kids first. Most of them didn't know much about Tommy Toxic.

Speaking of which, he publically changed his name to Tommy Tox-in. He wanted to create separation between "Tommy" the child and "Tommy" the adult. When people asked him why he made the slight change, he responded, "Because I'm alive." Then he would explain the difference between toxin and toxic.

When he'd realized his new material was shaping into a concept album, Tommy decided to keep most of his new work a secret. He played his old stuff in public, often reworking the songs a bit to suit what were mostly solo acoustic sessions. The kids were even digging a few of his shitty post-puberty tunes. This was a whole new generation of weirdos.

Once the buzz was out among the youngsters, Tommy popped up in the Hollywood bar scene. The rebirth of his charisma and confidence saw Tommy wield his guitar with a heavy dick. His contemporaries would snicker when they heard he was taking the stage, expecting him to make a joke of himself. Instead, they heard the dulcet moanings of a soulful punk balladeer who intermittently blew their minds with iconoclastic guitar play.

Every once in a while Tommy played one of his new songs to plug the "secret" album he was working on. The first was "Frenemy Mine, or My Frenemy Is My Nemesis and I Am His Enemy," which would be the opening track and lead single. Then he leaked part of "You Fucking Douche," an aria about the first meeting between the album's protagonist and villain, where the protagonist describes how he can tell what a goody-goody jerk the villain is. The bridge from "Where's Your Family Now" was played as an interlude between older tunes. Tommy never finished these new songs when he played them live, which made recording a full bootlegged copy to circulate impossible and drove his fans crazy.

Tommy's resurgence turned out to be a complete rebirth, a true American comeback story, and he was once again selling something to the American audience they had never before witnessed. We're talking about a filthy, wretched punk rocker taking a song like "Rape Manifesto," slowing the time signature down, and singing a cappella so you could clearly understand the horrific lyrics. Then, while slowly cutting himself with a razor blade, Tommy politely and charmingly explained the story behind the song, describing his rage and how much he hated himself for being what he was. People ate his bullshit up with giant, swooning spoons. I mean, he had grown into a handsome dude, but still, to this day I'm amazed he was able to get away with such nonsense.

"He's so dark and wistful and sexy," people would say. No, you dumb shits, he was fucking insane. And calculating. And evil.

Admittedly, extremely talented as well. But mostly insane, calculating, and evil.

Then there was Mortimer Cross. Once Daring Bird agreed to pick up the tab, Cross dove into his investigation of the tragedy that killed Littlethumb's family. He quickly discovered why, for the most part, things had been swept under the rug.

Cross had friendly informants in most branches of federal law enforcement and within the upper ranks of the New York City police force. Most of these relationships dated back to his military service, before his time as a police officer. Only a few phone calls were necessary to gather most of the case files from the investigations into the fire. There were files from Homeland Security, the CIA, the FBI, and of course the local police, not to mention foreign agencies investigating their own losses.

The list of potential targets at the exhibit was long. There were activists, heads of state, other assorted dignitaries, and a lot of wealthy scumbags who ran around with Dick Mann. The federal investigators surprisingly chose not to waste their resources trying to discover which guest might have been the central target.

The one angle they did investigate was whether or not there was any reason to believe the fire was a general act of terrorism. But when numerous terrorist organizations claimed responsibility for the bombing, there was no point in figuring out which one had caused the explosion, if it had been any of them at all. Usually, when multiple terrorist groups try to take responsibility for something like this, none of them is the actual perpetrator.

The situation was quickly and quietly relinquished to the metro police. The police did a little more work than the feds. They investigated the scene, sifting through the ashes for clues in the initial days after the fire. Though the official cause of the accident had been reported to the public as a gas leak ignited by old, faulty electrical wiring, some evidence suggested a bomb had been set.

The blast radius and pattern of the projectile debris led the police to believe the explosion originated on or near the stage area. They could not pinpoint an exact spot, but definitely felt the blast came from that general vicinity. However, according to the building plans the area contained no gas lines. This made them think the explosion may have been a bomb.

Cross scoured through photos from that evening, trying to get a vantage point of the stage. Before the explosion, hundreds of pictures taken at the exhibit were launched into cyberspace, both from the phones of guests and the Wi-Fi ready cameras of professional photographers on the scene. Cross found dozens of photos that included at least a small portion of the stage and attempted to piece them together.

The old gumshoe exhaustively researched the guest list to determine if anyone in attendance was marked for death before the night of the exhibit, and if so, who had wanted them dead. His search was an endless maze of rabbit holes. The police were prudent in choosing not to chase the rabbit considering all their active cases to solve. Mortimer Cross, however, had nothing but time and zeal.

He read the depositions given by the survivors of the party. The original two were from Sawyer and his date, of course, and the more recent account provided by Daring Bird. Cross read them many times, hoping with each pass that some previously overlooked clue would suddenly jump off the page, but there was nothing. Nada. Zilch. Zip. Scadoosh. The search went nowhere. Except, there was one thing that bothered him.

The one thing. Daring Bird recounted the detail in his memory of the evening. The door to the emergency stairwell would not open. A detail easy to overlook or explain away. The door's frame could have expanded or warped from the heat of the fire, causing the door to jam, but that didn't feel right to Cross. Still, chasing this tiny possible-clue was such a reach in discovery, the idea felt like wishful thinking. He convinced himself he was creating an angle that wasn't there. Until…

One night when he was a little blurry-eyed from scotch and sitting in a mental stew, pondering the case while sorting through forensic photos yet again, he noticed something for the first time. He found a photo of a ground shot of burned debris. Sticking out among the debris was what looked like an ax handle. The photo was of the stairwell interior. He shuffled through more photos and found one of the doors to the stairwell after the fire. There, fused to the stairwell side of the door, was an ax head. The handle had burned off and fallen to the ground.

But why wouldn't an alarm have gone off? he thought. *The building was too old, that's why.* The ax box wasn't hooked up to an alarm system.

Someone used the ax to bar the door. This meant one of two things. The killer was an unknown assassin who would never be discovered, or the only person anyone knew of to have left the party through that door.

42

The recording sessions for Tommy's new album reached a gasmatic point. The time had arrived to bring Littlethumb back into his life. He'd finished production on the track "My Bloody Anima" and was feeling vastly self-aware. Oddly feminine as well, but he was getting plenty of ass so he didn't put much thought into that.

Tommy found out Littlethumb would be in Los Angeles for a live painting performance at the Hollywood Bowl, got in touch with Sawyer, and coerced Littlethumb's number from him. On second thought, coerced is probably too strong. He asked Sawyer for the number, who felt awkward not providing it, so he did. After all, Tommy was basically family. He's the second cousin you don't want around, but family nonetheless.

Tommy called Littlethumb and insisted they have lunch or dinner or something when Littlethumb was in Los Angeles. Tommy apologized for not contacting him sooner. He felt terrible about his tardiness, but had been so busy and insulated working on his album he'd only recently found out Littlethumb was still alive. And now married! That sure was fast. He had to meet the lucky lady. Just had to.

Though he tried not to oversell his enthusiasm, Tommy couldn't help himself. He went on and on about catching up with one another. Littlethumb found Tommy's request a little odd. When he was a kid, Tommy was just an older boy whom he met a few times and was a little frightened of. Most, if not all of the complicated dynamics of their relationship, lived in Tommy's mind. Littlethumb never put much thought into their acquaintance as a child, other than he found Tommy's presence unnerving, and painting all of the darkness within Tommy had made him sad. Still, being the person he was, Littlethumb could not say no. Brunch was scheduled at a little place in Silver Lake.

Mortimer Cross was damn near manic, sucking down way too much coffee and nicotine than he should have been, eschewing sleep for obsessive ramblings and floor pacing. Countless hours were spent piecing together the last fifteen years of Tommy's life to no avail, but he could not shake the feeling. Something in his old soldier's gut swore to him that Tommy started the fire. After searching for clues in Tommy's personal life and finding nothing, Cross delved into the punk's music.

Cross analyzed song lyrics for clues. He listened to the records backward for hidden messages. He studied the math of the written music, cross-referencing the numerical patterns with other alphabets and code languages in search of hidden meaning.

Eventually Cross came to two conclusions: He, Mortimer Cross, was potentially off his own rocker, and Tommy Toxic's music contained many subtle references to having actually killed people in real life. Not to mention the not-so-subtle hidden track Cross discovered on the album *I'm a Killer Who Kills*, one of the immediately-shelved albums from Tommy's self-produced catalog of music. The hidden song was titled, "Seriously, I Killed Like 263 People," and was nothing but a disjointed guitar solo played over the sounds of raging fires, explosions, and human screams.

Cross believed this was more than art imitating life. The song was Tommy's confession to the world. Tommy was a murderer and Cross was convinced that Tommy was currently up to something. He monitored Tommy's movements, including what appeared to be a friendship blossoming between Tommy, Littlethumb, and Maria. Something was going on but he didn't have enough proof. Any admission of guilt he felt was present in Tommy's music could easily be written off as artistic license.

No, Cross couldn't move in yet, and he didn't want to alert Daring Bird until he had tangible proof he was correct. If he had to, Cross would interrogate Tommy. Interrogation wouldn't be pleasant, but if Tommy was innocent the truth would come out. That was better than being dead, and Cross was fairly certain when he told Daring Bird what Tommy had done, Tommy would die. No, he needed more proof first. If only he could get his hands on this new, secret album Tommy was working on, perhaps it might tell the tale.

Spring was in full bloom in New York City. Springtime, in my opinion, is the best time of year in New York, perhaps second only to the beautifully decorated winter wonderland the city becomes during the year-end holidays. Yes, the vista of Central Park gently covered in a fresh blanket of snow, colored by the reflection of holiday lights, is hard to beat. For my money, the season of rebirth tops even that.

In spring, not only do the plants and animals come out of hiding, the people do as well, *and* they start to come out of their clothes. Suddenly there are bare shoulders and legs everywhere, not to mention smiling faces no longer hidden by scarves, floppy hats, or their own frowns brought on by winter gloom. While winter is a time for bedding down cozily next to your favorite warm body, spring is for lighthearted lovers romping in fields of daffodils. Or, in this case, the Lower East Side of Manhattan.

Littlethumb, Maria, and Tommy sat around an outside table at a little coffeehouse down in Alphabet City. None of them frequented the area, so they thought an afternoon walk-and-stop would be a fun excursion on a Saturday. The three of them were having a blast watching the streets buzz with humans enjoying a beautiful day. The conversation turned to making fun of how serious coffee had become when Maria suddenly got excited about something else and signed energetically to Littlethumb. Tommy watched as Littlethumb sheepishly argued with Maria.

"No, no," Littlethumb signed. "I don't know. Because I don't want to."

"What? What is it?" Tommy asked.

"Oh, all right," Littlethumb looked to Maria. "Now I have to tell him," he signed with a chuckle. "Look at the commotion you caused." Littlethumb looked back at Tommy and said, "She wants me to tell you about this project I've been working on."

"Well c'mon then," Tommy said. "No fuckin' secrets here." *Except mine*, he thought. "Fess up."

You may be wondering what the hell is going on here. Well, their first reunion back in Los Angeles was surprisingly fun. Nowhere near as awkward as Littlethumb had feared. Of course, this wasn't without some design. In his mission to restore his fame, Tommy had turned into an irrepressibly charismatic conversationalist.

If Littlethumb thought he was surprised by the outcome, the initial reunion had provided Tommy with yet another surprise twist to the story of his life as well. He was totally smitten with Maria. From the moment Littlethumb introduced them Tommy wanted her. The easiest way to be in her company was to befriend the little dickbag, so Tommy pursued the friendship, making a continued effort to find ways to interact with Littlethumb and Maria. He booked gigs in the same towns where Littlethumb performed, pretending the run-ins were mere coincidence. He friended Maria and Littlethumb all over the Internet, persistently instigating web-based interaction, having "liked" so many posts the mere thought of social media made him want to vomit. Eventually, he purchased a brownstone in the East Village and told his friends he would split time between Los Angeles and New York, with schemes of infiltrating the New York underground music scene as he had in Los Angeles.

As Tommy's plan to infiltrate the life of his nemesis succeeded, an unfortunate problem arose when, against his will, Tommy realized he truly enjoyed Littlethumb's company. This kinship made him hate Littlethumb more than ever, and these conflicting emotions perplexed Tommy. This internal strife gave him a substantial case of writer's block for his big project, which kept him more on edge than his usual, I hate everyone, I hate me, fuck the world, fuck you, fuck me, where's my goddamn coffee, self.

Meanwhile, despite his disapproval for much of the lyrical content of Tommy's music, Littlethumb discovered he had a lot of respect for Tommy as an artist. He not only stopped feeling unnerved by Tommy, he also grew to genuinely enjoy Tommy's company. Perhaps this transition was inspired by the desire for greater understanding of someone so different from him. Or, perhaps it was their commonality. The fact that Tommy had also suffered great tragedy, losing his parents and Dick Mann as Littlethumb had lost his family. Maybe a bit of both? Who knows? Either way, Littlethumb grew to love Tommy as a true friend.

So there they were, basking in springtime. The three friends enjoyed iced coffees out on the sidewalk. Pretentious iced coffees would be all the rage that summer and this particular joint had jumped in early as a trendsetter. Littlethumb's drink was aptly named the Minty Kitten.

The Minty Kitten was Indonesian Kopi Luwak coffee with pomegranate-infused coconut milk, lime, and fresh mint poured over seven cubes of kitten-head shaped ice made from artesian water. Don't worry, the coffee house only used Kopi Luwak beans harvested from the shit of wild civets. They proudly displayed a sign in the establishment stating no coffee served there contributed to the unethical treatment of animals. Whatever helped them sleep at night while all the babies were dying…

Anyway, Littlethumb took a drink of his Minty Kitten and informed Tommy of something no one in the world knew but Maria and Uncle Daring Bird. "She wants me to tell you about this piano piece I've been working on. It's nothing. Not a big deal."

Maria playfully slapped Littlethumb on his arm and clearly indicated with her body the deal was indeed, most assuredly, big.

"I didn't know you played," Tommy said.

"Well, I don't. Not really. I've never been taught or anything. I started tinkering with a tune when I was a kid. I could hear the notes in my head, but I didn't know how to play, so finding the right keys on the piano took a long time. I've been working on this one composition most of my life. Sort of. I don't know. It's basically like the story of my life up until now. Things got a little weird there for awhile with the amnesia and the hypnotherapy, but the piece came together and made sense once I got my memory back."

"Interesting," Tommy said calmly, but internally the doomsday clock in his brain began its final countdown. *You little motherfucker*, he thought. *Music is mine. You want to fucking be the greatest painter in the world, who gives a shit, but you don't fuck with music.*

Maria and Littlethumb both watched Tommy. His face froze and the right side of his mouth was twitchy. Tommy shook his head and snapped out of the maniacal internal dialogue to which he had briefly succumbed. Returning to the conversation, Tommy said, "So, go on."

"Oh, well, I kind of came to a place, a logical conclusion to the piece the other day, at least for the time being."

"Nice, congrats."

"Thanks. So anyway, I played for Maria, and she thinks I should perform for the public. Or at least, she thinks the piece is good enough, so I was . . ."

Tommy cut Littlethumb off. "I'm sorry," he said, "you played for Maria?"

"Oh, yeah. I know. It's crazy, but she says she can feel the vibrations from the piano strings. She dances in perfect time with the music. It's amazing. Smoking hot too." Littlethumb wistfully shook his head and looked at Maria with a grin, and she knew damn well what he said. She blushed.

"I can only imagine," Tommy mumbled vacantly. "Sorry. I interrupted you…"

"Well, I was thinking about doing a one-night-only recital for charity."

And that was the straw that broke the camel's back.

Kaboom! The sound of the atomic bomb exploding in Tommy's head. Not only was this little bastard everything Tommy wasn't, not only was he plowing the woman of Tommy's dreams, but now this goddamned nancy-boy, goody-two-shoes, look-at-me-aren't-I-just-the-greatest-most-loving–kindest-person-to-ever-be-born mother-fucker was going to steal music from him? *You may have stolen the spotlight from me when we were kids, buddy boy, but there is no way in hell you're taking the one thing I've got,* Tommy thought. *Music is the one thing that makes me special, you piece of shit, and you can't have it.*

Suddenly, Tommy had an epiphany. He knew exactly how he would finish his album. Or at least a close approximation. "Holy shit, I think I know how I'm going to finish the album."

"So that's what that was." Littlethumb motioned to his own face, mimicking Tommy's frozen facial expression from a few moments earlier. He and Maria had watched Tommy's silent meltdown with curiosity. "When are you going to tell us more about this mysterious new album, anyway?"

"When the time is right," Tommy said with a playful smirk.

"Hey, pal. You said no secrets."

"No secrets except mine. You were stealing my thunder, and I'm a hypocrite. But don't worry, my friend. You will be the first to know, and you will know in due time. Yes, sir." Tommy gave an affirmative nod of the head. "And, as a matter of fact, I think I know when the time should be. I think we should do the show together. You can premier your piece, and afterward, I will play my new album."

Littlethumb sat back in his chair as Maria looked at him with en-couragement. "Interesting," he said.

"It's more than interesting,"Tommy agreed. "It's brilliant. Think of all the money we can raise! Plus, I mean, it's like, karma or some shit. I've been stuck for months, and you literally just gave me the ending to my story. That has to mean something, right?"

"Hmph," was Littlethumb's only response. He sat quietly for a few minutes then voiced his most earnest reservation. He had a few, but this was the most pressing. "I don't know, I'm not sure I'm good enough to play in front of people."

Tommy had a quick answer, as if he had spent the silence thinking of rebuttals for whatever Littlethumb might say next. "Think of it like this. If either one of us sucks, hopefully, it will get overshadowed by the other one kicking ass."

"But what if we both suck?" Littlethumb said with a smile, to which Tommy confidently answered with a facial expression of fleeting, sarcastic concern. They all laughed.

"Let me think about it," Littlethumb said after the laughter died down. "Please don't take offense, but I'm not sure I'm ready. The idea scares me a bit, to be honest."

"No problem," Tommy replied. Then he gave a frighteningly toothy, huckster's smile and said, "Take all the time you need and let me know by next Friday."

That night while getting ready for sleep, Littlethumb brought the subject back up with Maria for her counsel. "Interesting idea Tommy had," he signed, before pulling one of his legs out of his pants.

"Yes," she agreed. "It was."

"You know, besides being nervous in general, I'm not sure how I feel about playing a show with him. I love him but his music is filthy."

"Ha. Indeed it is," Maria signed, "to say the least."

"What do you think?"

"I think you should do whatever you feel is right. Doing that always works for you."

"Well, it did seem like doing a show together would mean a lot to Tommy."

At this, Maria crossed the room and gently kissed her husband's lips. The man always put others first. She stepped back and signed, "You are a great man, Littlethumb Brooks."

"I don't know what I would do without you," he replied. "You are my life."

"And you are mine."

43

The day of the show arrived. Only a few hours remained before an epic concert in Philadelphia would begin. Littlethumb and Tommy chose Philadelphia as the location for the performance as a thank-you to its citizenry for their remarkable work combatting homelessness. As a reward, all of the profits from the concert would be distributed equally to city residents who currently earned a below-average income and who also signed up to do one hour of community service for the city's parks department. Another one of Maria's ideas. Besides the obvious benefit of thousands of people putting in an hour's worth of work, registration for the community service was used to track the contact information for people to receive their money.

While the people of Philadelphia anxiously awaited the unprecedented event of the year, Mortimer Cross laid in Tommy Toxic's apartment, desperately trying to survive a heart attack. I don't think it's feasible to claim the discovery Cross made had nothing to do with the heart attack. It must have. Of course, so did the chain-smoking and scotch.

Two days earlier Cross finally managed to get his hands on songs from Tommy's new album. The album was rumored to finally be completed and ready for release. Cross was convinced the record meant something but didn't have enough of the album's material to know what that something was. Then, lucky coincidence removed Tommy from the city for the concert in Philly. Knowing he was gone allowed Cross to break into Tommy's apartment and snoop around.

Once inside, Cross wasn't so much shocked at his discovery as wildly validated. Alas, his was an "I knew it!" moment followed by intense pain. Now he struggled on the floor. The heart attack had dropped him to his knees and then a nice big stabbing shot of pain had tossed him forward, face-down onto the hardwood. Cross focused on his breathing and willed his heart back into action at a normal pace. He was a stern man. The effort worked.

Cross rolled over on his back and fished for his mobile phone. As if on cue, the phone vibrated in his pants pocket with an incoming call. He pulled his hand free, gingerly raising the phone, and saw the initials DBJ on the caller ID.

That's convenient, he thought. "Where are you?" Cross answered with a gasp.

"Listen," Daring Bird said. "I've had a vision. I need to tell you."

"Wait, just wait, damn it." Cross took two deep breaths to collect himself and maintain the steady heart rate he was struggling to control. "I was about to call you. I found something. You might find this difficult to believe, but I'm convinced Tommy Toxic created the explosion. I think he planted a bomb on the stage and barred the stairwell door when he left. I know I may sound crazy but…"

"I don't think it's crazy," Daring Bird said. "My vision was you holding a key, offering it to me."

"Outstanding."

"Providence."

"We'll see. Your nephew is in grave danger."

"The concert?"

"Yes. We've got to stop it. Wait. Where are you?"

"I'm on Coney."

"Coney? Perfect. That's perfect. When did you . . ."

"Last night, to watch the monkeys. The kids are leaving for a week after the show."

"We have to get to the concert. I'll pick you up and explain on the way." Cross hung up the phone. He attempted to get to his feet with a quick move before his body reminded him he had suffered a heart attack. "Well, shit," he said, then he rolled back over onto his stomach and started crawling towards the front door.

Maria and Littlethumb made love in his dressing room. Though his performance wasn't perfect by any means, his recital had been well received. He sheepishly begged the audience's forgiveness for mistakes a few times early on, but as the concert progressed he became more comfortable and playful, making silly faces or sticking his tongue out at the crowd when mistakes occurred. Once the concert was over, Littlethumb breathed a huge sigh of relief as the crowd cheered him off the stage. He retreated to the safety of Maria's arms in his dressing room. Maria, so inspired by the vibrations of the movement dedicated to her entrance into his life, had welcomed Littlethumb into the room with a lusty twinkle in her eye. The fluffy shag carpets requested for the dressing room, due to Littlethumb and Maria's preference for bare feet, wound up serving a much grander purpose.

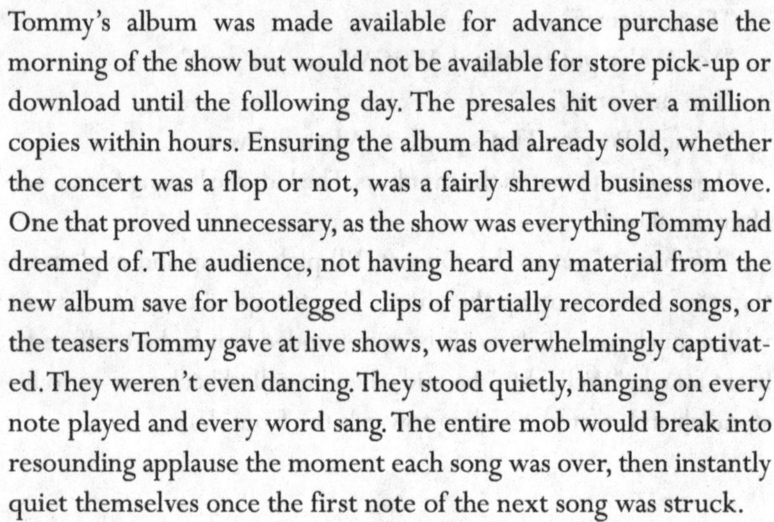

Tommy's album was made available for advance purchase the morning of the show but would not be available for store pick-up or download until the following day. The presales hit over a million copies within hours. Ensuring the album had already sold, whether the concert was a flop or not, was a fairly shrewd business move. One that proved unnecessary, as the show was everything Tommy had dreamed of. The audience, not having heard any material from the new album save for bootlegged clips of partially recorded songs, or the teasers Tommy gave at live shows, was overwhelmingly captivated. They weren't even dancing. They stood quietly, hanging on every note played and every word sang. The entire mob would break into resounding applause the moment each song was over, then instantly quiet themselves once the first note of the next song was struck.

Mortimer Cross and Daring Bird flew down I-95 South. Daring Bird dialed Littlethumb and Maria's mobile phones over and over.

"Damn it, why won't they fucking answer?" Daring Bird said, ending one attempted call and starting another.

"The venue may have insufficient mobile service inside," Cross responded.

"It was a rhetorical question. Can't this bucket go faster?"

"I am going one hundred and three miles an hour."

"And you're doing a great job. Go faster."

The concert was almost over. Tommy finished "No One Worth Hating But You" and "I'll Show You Fucking Demons," having played the two songs without a break in between. At center stage, basking in the adulation of the enormous crowd, Tommy stood in a quintessential rock and roll front-man pose. He wiped the sweat from his brow, then took a razor and added a fresh cut to his forehead while the crowd cheered. "Thank you, thank you," he said, huffing and puffing like he'd just played full-court basketball. "As you know, I've been working on this album for a while. I'm glad you dig it!" His fans erupted with affirmation. Diggeth they did, good sir. Diggeth, indeed. "So, a few months back, I was struggling with how to end this fucking madness, but I broke through, and I gotta say, the discovery was at least partially, you know, a tiny bit, I will admit, in thanks to my good friends Littlethumb and Maria Brooks." He paused to let the crowd cheer their names. "Oh, who am I kidding, they totally fucking inspired me!"

Roars.

"So, as you all know, the album was made available for advance purchase this morning when the world clock hit 6:06:06 am. You'll be able to download your copy as soon as the show is over. The hard copies will be available on disc within the next week. I do apologize for the delay, but I promise I have a good reason. There's one song yet to be recorded." Tommy paused and briefly indulged the murmur of confusion from the audience before continuing. "You see, I wanted to do something special for you guys. So, I haven't recorded the final track of the album yet, because we're going to record the song together, right here, right now!"

The crowd went nuts.

"Fuck yeah!" Tommy shouted. "This song will never be remastered or fucking chopped up in a production lab. The recorded version for the album will forever be the one you and I are going to make right here and now! Can you dig that, Philadelphia?"

Yes they could. The audience was already licking his boots. Diggeth, they shall.

"Now, that's not my only surprise for you. To commemorate this amazing moment, my friend Littlethumb is going to come out and do a live painting for you! Ladies and gentlemen, please puts yo' hands together again, for Littlethumb-uh, uh-Ba-rooks-uh, yeah!"

Littlethumb hopped out from the side of the stage and waved to the audience as they cheered. He bowed and walked over to his painting station. The canvas was four feet by four feet and rested on an easel facing the audience, which kept Littlethumb's back to the audience as he painted. One of the giant video monitors supplying the crowd with close-up shots of the band was used to show Littlethumb at work.

"All right," Tommy said. "Here's how this is going to work. I'm going to play my ass off and you're going to raise hell with me. When I point, you're going to sing the words to the title of the song as the chorus, are you with me?" The crowd responded with a deafening shout. They were totally with him. "Fucking-A right," Tommy shouted. "Okay, the name of this song is 'When You Die, I Killed You.' So when I point, you scream 'When You Die, I Killed You' like the fucking animals you are! Now let's fucking rock!"

Cross wove in and out of the Philadelphia traffic, almost to the arena.

"Goddammit, why won't they answer the fucking phone?" Daring Bird lamented for the one hundred and third time.

"Did you attempt sending them a text message?" Cross spoke calmly, jerking the steering wheel hard to the right.

"What? No. Why?"

"Maria's deaf."

"So she couldn't see her phone ringing, or have the vibrate on?" At Cross' suggestion, Daring Bird furiously worked his thumbs in the composition of a text message.

"For all we know, they may have text-only mobile phone plans for the hearing impaired." Cross jerked the steering wheel hard left.

"You gotta shut up, man," Daring Bird said, still typing. "You're killing me."

Maria had finished putting her clothes back on and was headed to the stage to watch the finale when she felt her pocket vibrate. She pulled her phone from the pocket and saw the text messages sent by Daring Bird. The phone dropped to the floor as she ran out of the dressing room.

The mind blowing finale was supposed to unfold during the fourth and final chorus, but once the music started, Tommy had trouble containing himself. He played his way through the opening verse and refrain just fine. At the start of the second verse his hands shook so badly from the adrenaline he stopped playing his guitar, though he managed to continue singing while his band played. By the end of the song's third verse he could restrain himself no longer.

The crowd was gleefully chanting the chorus when Tommy pulled the gun he had tucked into the back of his pants out from underneath his shirt and held it in the air. A few moments passed before everyone soaked in the fact that Tommy had a pistol. When they finally realized what he was holding, the crowd didn't devolve into panic, nor did the band stop playing. They all assumed the gun was part of the show.

Cross and Daring Bird squealed into the concert hall's loading dock. As Cross headed straight for the back of the building he spoke to Daring Bird with a grimace. "When we stop, get out and go."

"Yeah."

"Don't wait for me. I'll follow."

"Wasn't planning on it."

"Good. I can't run."

"Why?"

"I'm pretty sure I had a heart attack back in Tommy's apartment."

"That's impressive." Daring Bird looked at Cross and noticed the man had gone pale. "Um, you don't look so good right now either."

"I think I'm having another one." Cross exhaled painfully through gritted teeth, then his head fell forward onto the steering wheel. Without anyone in control of Cross's body, his right foot grew heavy, leveling the accelerator to the floor as the car headed straight for the wall of the loading dock.

Daring Bird scrambled to attach his seatbelt and said, "Oh, fuck me."

Tommy Toxic dragged the microphone across the stage in one hand while he pointed the gun at the back of Littlethumb's head with the other. He was butchering the last verse of his song, too exhilarated to competently sing the words, instead growling the lyrics as he closed in on Littlethumb. The crowd continued to cheer, assuming Tommy's antics were part of the show. The band continued to play, not knowing what else to do.

But, as Tommy continued his achingly slow march across the stage, eventually, the members of his band began to look around at one another with questioning faces. This had not been part of their rehearsals.

Daring Bird attached the seatbelt a split second before impact. Both front airbags blew when the car crashed. Badly stunned, but conscious, he reached for Cross's neck as he shook the cobwebs from his own head. Within seconds he verified Cross had a pulse, unlatched his seatbelt, and exited the vehicle, stumble-running as fast as he could for the stage.

Littlethumb was in his zone, painting furiously in time with the music, off in the other place he traveled to when he worked. The world around him didn't completely exist when he was truly engaged with a painting. A feeling similar to having your head under water. Everything happening outside his mind was muted, muffled. Still, from the corner of his eye he saw someone run out from the wing and onto the stage.

Maria intercepted Tommy several feet from Littlethumb, before Tommy could splatter Littlethumb's brains all over his painting. She grabbed for the arm that carried the gun. Littlethumb turned to see her struggling with Tommy. In his confusion, registering the gun in Tommy's hand took a moment. Tommy held the pistol up in the air away from Maria, who pulled at Tommy's elbow with one hand and pushed him away from Littlethumb with the other.

Littlethumb dropped his paintbrush and stepped toward the scuffle. Tommy saw him and jerked hard, away from Maria, stumbling back a bit and freeing his arm from her grasp. Maria stumbled forward toward him, tripping. As she fell, Tommy instinctually moved his arms to catch her or block her fall onto him. Whichever he intended, he did neither. Instead, when she collided with him, Tommy accidentally pulled the gun's trigger, sending a bullet into her side and up through the top of her left rib cage.

Littlethumb saw the exit wound open on the back of his wife, up near her shoulder blade. He opened his mouth to scream but nothing came out. His heart stopped momentarily and he lost all breath as he watched Maria fall to the stage. Despite the lack of air in his lungs, he managed to charge Tommy, diving on him from several feet away.

Tommy and Littlethumb scuffled on the ground as the band, the crowd, the production staff, even the show's security detail, all watched in complete shock, unable to scream or react. Eventually, Littlethumb wound up on top of Tommy, sitting on his waist. He pinned Tommy's gun hand to the ground by the elbow as he pummeled Tommy's face with his free hand. After a particularly stunning blow, Littlethumb wrestled the gun from Tommy and began to beat him with the gun's handle.

Daring Bird ran onto the stage, quickly took stock of the situation and bolted for Littlethumb, who had decided to stop beating Tommy with the pistol and had turned the gun around to shoot Tommy in the face. Before Littlethumb could pull the trigger Daring Bird lunged and tackled him aside. The gun went loose and Daring Bird dove on top of it.

Littlethumb was sprawled out on his back. He rolled onto his knees, facing Tommy, but before he could remount Tommy to continue his beating he saw Maria lying on the stage and snapped back into reality from the violent place his mind had gone. He scrambled over and examined her. She was alive but her breathing was shallow. Littlethumb propped up her head and screamed for help, uncertain if he was really screaming. The world seemed hazy, or muffled. Like his head was under water. Like he was painting.

Littlethumb looked down at Maria and wailed with baleful agony. Her eyes were open, and she managed a smile, but the corner of her mouth ended with a stream of blood. He wiped the hair back from her forehead and mouthed the words, "Don't go. I love you. Please don't go."

Maria pulled her hands up near her face and signed, "I love you," back to him. She coughed up more blood, then with her dying breath, signed the words, "the baby."

44

I know this may not be what you wanted. I promise you it's not what I wanted. But we aren't quite done yet. Maybe, just maybe . . .

Let's play this out. I suppose the tale has taken me long enough.

Maria was pregnant when she died, almost six months to term. No one knew but her and Littlethumb. When they discovered Maria was expecting, the couple agreed to see how long they could keep her pregnancy a secret. Springing the news on everyone last minute would be fun. Littlethumb proposed setting up a live broadcast directly from the delivery room. He was only joking, of course. Poking fun at fame. Maria had caught him off guard, as usual, with a coy smile and mischievous twitch of her nose.

"We'll see," she had signed.

Somehow, their baby girl survived long enough for the ambulance to deliver Maria's body to the hospital. The baby was cut out and incubated, and Littlethumb named her Hope. He was clinging to his sanity and had no qualms admitting he named the child Hope because he felt very little remained for his own life. She was his only reason to live.

Littlethumb gave the baby to Sawyer, Anna, and Isabel Pettimore for safe-keeping. He was too frightened by the nature of his existence to raise her. Or be near her, for that matter. The people he loved seemed destined for tragedy when he was around. She would be safer with the Pettimores.

For Sawyer, parenting Littlethumb's daughter was an opportunity for redemption. The guilt of his cowardice had burdened him for so many years, the time had come for Sawyer to be set free. He would raise Hope as his own child for as long as Littlethumb asked.

Tommy Toxic was arrested, convicted, and sent to prison. Littlethumb had beaten Tommy badly, to the point his face was permanently disfigured. Once Tommy could finally speak again, he admitted to the bombing of the art exhibition so many years earlier. He pled guilty to all the charges brought against him and requested the judge sentence him to death. The judge refused, citing not only that the State of New York did not carry the death penalty but that if it had, the judge would not deliver the sentence because he felt a death penalty conviction would somehow be giving Tommy the ending he wanted for the tragedy he had created. Instead, Tommy was sentenced to multiple life terms in prison without the possibility of parole.

Tommy's final album was never released. Having produced the album himself, Tommy had hired a small record label to handle distribution. The label cancelled the release after Sawyer Pettimore's attorneys made sure they understood the family of Maria Brooks would sue them every which way from Sunday if they ever tried to sell the record, with or without the final song. The label did not have the resources to combat someone with the wealth and power of Sawyer Pettimore. All of the people who had pre-purchased copies of the album were reimbursed.

Surprisingly, no bootlegs of the entire show survived. Several recordings surfaced shortly after, but their sound quality was extremely poor and they quickly faded into obscurity. The continued existence of any true copies of the album *32*, as well as the meaning behind the album's title, are now the source of perpetual urban legend debates among pop-culture and music nerds.

Mortimer Cross survived the multiple heart attacks he had the day of the concert. Daring Bird was impressed by Cross's uncovering of Tommy's plot and recruited him into the Electric Medicine Men. Cross readily accepted the invitation.

As for Littlethumb? Daring Bird took him back to Coney Island and watched over him for a while. The grieving was rough going at first. Daring Bird had to fight Littlethumb several times. On one particular instance, Littlethumb tried to burn his paintings of Maria. Daring Bird stopped him after the first few were set on fire, but not without a square punch to the jaw that knocked Littlethumb unconscious. Littlethumb woke up to smelling salts, with Daring Bird crouched over top of him.

"Now don't you try that shit again," Daring Bird said, wagging his finger in Littlethumb's face. "Those paintings are too important. They're part of her legacy."

Daring Bird was correct. Still, Littlethumb couldn't look at them, so he turned the *Marias* over to Sawyer Pettimore to do with as he pleased. Sawyer sold one of the paintings from his holdings company to himself, then sent the painting and the millions of dollars he paid for the work to Maria's parents. I don't understand all the mechanics behind the paper trail, but somehow or another the transaction was all legal and tax-free for Maria's folks.

In honor of Maria, Sawyer put the rest of the paintings on a worldwide exhibit tour. Any proceeds received from the exhibits were donated to schools for the deaf. Sawyer hired Mortimer Cross as well, who split time between work for the Electric Medicine Men and commanding the *Marias'* security detail when the artwork needed to be safely moved from one exhibit location to the next.

Once Littlethumb returned to a nominal level of calm, he shut down his studio on Coney Island and headed back to the E2M's safe house in the Canadian wilderness. Resigned to a life sentence of never-ending sadness, and considering the fact almost everyone he cared about eventually died tragically when he was around, he figured it was best to find a safe place to hide. So, he took the monkeys and the command center gear and set up permanent shop out in the middle of Canadian nowhere.

No one went looking for him and they wouldn't have found him if they did. Most of the locals in the nearest town had no idea who Littlethumb was, and the few who did seemed fine to leave him alone and keep their nice, quiet town free of reporters and hubbub. He continued onedollarprayers.com, but his daily meditations stopped. A recorded loop of previous meditations was substituted on the website. He couldn't go into his mind like that anymore. All he saw in there was Maria.

The painting and piano playing stopped as well. Both diversions brought him such joy he couldn't allow himself to use them to indulge his grief. He wanted to die. The only aspects of his life that kept Littlethumb going were taking care of those damned monkeys and thoughts of his daughter.

Despite his pain, Littlethumb was grateful Daring Bird stopped him from killing Tommy. Murder would have been a stain on his soul he could not clean off, and once his rage subsided, he was desperately relieved to have not killed another human being. It is one thing to take another life when the responsibility has been thrust upon you through no fault of your own, and still a hard enough thing at that. It's quite another when you willfully *create* death to satisfy some ridiculous human emotion.

After many months in isolation, Littlethumb visited Tommy in prison. His decision to do so was pure compulsion. He felt like he was supposed to. Tommy had been assigned to a federal penitentiary in upstate New York, a couple hours drive from Littlethumb's hideout. He drove down every few weeks, got a cheap hotel room, and sat with Tommy during visitation for a few days. They talked about life. They talked about what Tommy had done. They talked about death.

Tommy's disfigured face hurt Littlethumb, regardless of the misery Tommy had caused. You may debate whether or not Tommy deserved worse than the beating he had taken, if you like. For Littlethumb, what Tommy deserved didn't matter. What mattered was his own atonement. Seeing what he'd done to Tommy was penance.

Over the course of many visits, Tommy told Littlethumb everything. He admitted to killing his own parents, though he did not kill them intentionally. His father had instructed Tommy to poke the needle in and depress the plunger, for him and Tommy's mother, because he was too weak to do so himself.

Tommy and Littlethumb had a long, slightly morbid laugh when Tommy lamented the death of Dick Mann, who was supposed to have left the art show with Tommy. "I loved Dick," Tommy said. The somber moment was broken when Littlethumb snickered, which Tommy picked up on and, realizing what he said, began to snicker as well. The snickers turned into irrational guffaws as the two men laughed away everything the world had ever done to hurt them.

For the most part, Tommy discussed the events of his life with such emotional vacancy, it was as if they'd happened to and been caused by someone else, though he was never speaking in third person. His was a surreal detachment only the truly insane can maintain. The fact he decided to trigger the bomb at the art gallery after his performance was a failure, that was simply a logical progression from having decided to put a bomb in the bass drum in the first place, just in case he decided to blow everyone up. "The secret was, the bomb was going to blow everyone up anyway. *Especially* if my show had gone well. I hated you."

Littlethumb understood much of Tommy's identity had been outside his control since childhood, and he pitied Tommy for his lot in this life. On one visit, in a rare moment of clarity, Tommy apologized to Littlethumb for everything he'd done. As soon as the apology escaped his breath, Tommy reverted back into his shell of insanity, lamenting to Littlethumb his disappointment over how their concert had turned out. "You were going to die, but we were all going to live forever," Tommy said. "It was supposed to be the greatest piece of mixed media conceptual performance art of all time."

"I think it still was, Tom," Littlethumb said, which made Tommy smile.

"Yes. I think it was, too."

Eventually, Littlethumb picked up his paintbrush. When he first started back, his paintings kept turning into representations of his dead family. His grandpa Kicking Rocks watched a baseball game. His parents and siblings waved to the camera from atop the Eiffel Tower. All five of them sat on a sailboat off the coast of Greece together, basking in the midday sun.

In the paintings, his family members were ghosts, visiting these spots and many others as the real world swirled around them. Littlethumb chose to believe he was somehow catching a glimpse into their afterlives. Perhaps they really were traveling the world, enjoying themselves, seeing the sights they were never able to before Tommy had stolen their breath. Perhaps they were still out there for Littlethumb to meet again someday.

You see, despite the Occurrence, Littlethumb had no idea whether or not he would ever be with any of his dead loved ones again. True, he bore witness to something the rest of us never do. His journey showed him death wasn't necessarily the end of existence, but that was about all he knew. Though he had traveled to the spirit world, seen ghosts, spent a considerable amount of time conversing with his dead grandfather, *and* seen the forces of good and evil at work within man and woman, none of this meant he would be reunited with the people he loved in some wondrous, gold-encrusted afterlife.

There were endless possibilities for what might happen when he died. He considered taking his own life but decided if there was any hope of being with Maria again, committing suicide to hasten his journey would not work. It felt like cheating. Nope. If there was any hope of seeing Maria again, he would have to suffer through the rest of this shit with a smile on his face. Plus, there was Hope to think about. Someday, maybe, there was a chance he could safely be a father to her.

As he continued to heal, Littlethumb discovered a particularly disheartening aspect of his new reality, one he feared might never change. He couldn't bring himself to paint Maria. A part of him was terrified of what he might see, like the possibility she was having a good time in the spirit world without him. What if Maria had moved on and met some other dude in the afterlife who was making her happy? Littlethumb was equally terrified by the possibility he might paint her in some form of peril and have no ability to help her. As ridiculous as they might seem, these thoughts plagued his mind.

And time rolled on. Littlethumb painted, took care of his monkeys, managed the Electric Medicine Men's escapades, and operated onedollarprayers.com. He put a line of "Where Is Littlethumb?" T-shirts for sale on the Internet and they got hot for a while. All of the proceeds were donated to charity, of course.

He continued his visits with Tommy. He even tinkered at the piano again. A tune he could no longer ignore had invaded his head. Littlethumb was still alive, he would live, but every time he sneezed he tried to keep his eyes open, a desperate hope the world might freeze again. Maybe, just maybe, Maria would be there in the spirit world waiting for him, and they would get to spend a little more time together.

The End

EPILOGUE

So that's my story, which pretty much brings us to right now. I'll leave you with this good news before I say goodbye for the time being. For me personally, it's hard to believe it is mere coincidence that what I'm about to tell you occurred when I was finally done writing all of this down.

Several nights ago I was asleep and had a dream I was able to remember. I looked into the spirit world. In the dream, I could tell I wasn't physically in the spirit world. The view was like looking through a microscope while moving the slide around.

Suddenly, there she was. Maria sat on a bench at a bus stop. She looked at ease, completely serene and beautiful. A bus arrived and blocked my view. I became frantic, desperately calling out to her. I was so relieved when the bus pulled away I began to cry. She was still there but she didn't seem to have heard me scream. I reminded myself she was deaf and lamented my stupidity. She was so close, but I couldn't reach her. It was agonizing.

Then she looked at me.

"There you are," she signed.

"Yes! Yes, I'm here!"

"I knew you could see me." She smiled so warmly I staggered.

"I miss you," I signed.

"I know," she replied. "But don't worry. I will wait right here for you. I promise. I love you, and I will wait right here."

Then I woke up.

Truant Delighted Memphis is a writer. He was born and raised in Texas. An orphan, he wandered away from home on foot and never went back. He is married to Daffodil Fields. They have two children: Daniel Trate (adopted) and a baby girl named Peaceful Dreaming Memphis (Sweet Pea, for short). This is his first published work. He hopes you like it and encourages you to be kind, learn kung fu, and laugh your ass off as much as possible. Now get the fuck outta here.